Praise for *The Codger and the Sparrow*

"Semegran deftly blends humor with heart in a road trip romp that crosses generational divides. A coming-of-age for one, a coming-to-terms for the other, Semegran's characters are deeply drawn in a way that envelops readers from the start of their journey to its unexpected end. *The Codger and the Sparrow* is a fun, fresh meditation on friendship, loss, and new beginnings."

— James Wade, Spur Award–winning author
of *All Things Left Wild* and *River, Sing Out*

"Scott Semegran's characters capture the essential human contradiction: that deep flaws and bad decisions exist right alongside our beautiful capacity for kindness and compassion. With equal parts heart and humor, *The Codger and the Sparrow* is an ode to the strange, messy, and transformative power of friendship."

— Stacey Swann, author of *Olympus, Texas*

"*The Codger and the Sparrow* is a wide-open heart of a novel, filled with empathy and populated by flawed but loveable characters. A tender, funny ode to families—the ones we've lost, the ones we imagine, and the ones that come along when we least expect it."

— C. Matthew Smith, author of *Twentymile*

"*The Codger and the Sparrow* marks a leap forward in Scott Semegran's already impressive narrative artistry. Semegran brings to mind Hemingway's dictum that we are stronger in our broken places, as he brings us inside two very different characters—an aging, irascible widower and an artistically gifted orphan—and shows them coming together in a compelling story of grief and renewal."

— Thomas H. McNeely, award-winning author of
Pictures of the Shark and _Ghost Horse_

"*The Codger and the Sparrow* captures many of the joys of the stories it tells—road trips and friendships, chasing curiosities and relationships, the surprises of ourselves and the wonders of the larger world only discovered on the other side of awkward silences and things gone wrong, the beauty of life when fully embraced. It made me want to go on a road trip, to call up an old friend or make one anew, to take a sketchbook with me out into the world and draw the places that have made me who I am."

— Aaron Burch, author of _Year of the Buffalo_

THE CODGER AND THE SPARROW

FOR TOM —

Scott Se

Other books by Scott Semegran

THE BENEVOLENT LORDS OF SOMETIMES ISLAND

TO SQUEEZE A PRAIRIE DOG

SAMMIE & BUDGIE

BOYS

THE SPECTACULAR SIMON BURCHWOOD

MODICUM

MR. GRIEVES

THE METEORIC RISE OF SIMON BURCHWOOD

THE CODGER
AND
THE SPARROW

A NOVEL

SCOTT SEMEGRAN

TCU
Press

FORT WORTH, TEXAS

Library of Congress Cataloging-in-Publication Data

Names: Semegran, Scott, author.

Title: The codger and the sparrow : a novel / Scott Semegran.

Description: Fort Worth, Texas : TCU Press, [2024] | Summary: "Hank O'Sullivan, a 65-year-old widower, lives a routine life, nursing his loneliness with cocktails at his favorite local bar in Austin, Texas. A brawl lands him in jail, and he's sentenced to community service, picking up trash beside the highway. Luis Delgado lives with his single father in a small apartment. The 16-year-old troublemaker has remarkable artistic abilities, but his penchant for sneaking out and trespassing onto rooftops late at night also lands him in community service. These loners form an unlikely friendship, and when Hank tells Luis about his desire to drive to Houston to reconnect with an old flame, Luis asks to tag along. Luis's estranged mother lives in Houston, and he has been saving money for a trip, dreaming of reconnecting with her. Hank agrees, setting in motion a raucous road trip in a hot pink 1970 Plymouth Barracuda. The Codger and the Sparrow is a rambunctious story about an unusual friendship stretching across the generations"— Provided by publisher.

Identifiers: LCCN 2023049066 (print) | LCCN 2023049067 (ebook) | ISBN 9780875658681 (paperback) | ISBN 9780875658759 (ebook)

Subjects: LCSH: Teenagers and adults—Fiction. | Teenage boys—Family relationships—Fiction. | Older men—Travel—Fiction. | Loneliness in old age—Fiction. | Community service (Punishment)—Fiction. | Austin (Tex.)—Fiction. | LCGFT: Novels. | Humorous fiction. | Psychological fiction.

Classification: LCC PS3619.E4697 C63 2024 (print) | LCC PS3619.E4697 (ebook) | DDC 813/.6—dc23/eng/20231107

LC record available at https://lccn.loc.gov/2023049066

LC ebook record available at https://lccn.loc.gov/2023049067

TCU Box 298300
Fort Worth, Texas 76129
817.257.7822
www.tcupress.com

Design by Julie Rushing

For my friend
LARRY BRILL

"Everyone is a moon, and has a dark side
which he never shows to anybody."
—**MARK TWAIN**, *Following the Equator:
A Journey Around the World*

"I tell you, we are here on Earth to fart around,
and don't let anybody tell you different."
—**KURT VONNEGUT**, *A Man Without a Country*

PART I

PART I

1.

A wise old woman once told Hank, "The only two women who should ever bear witness to your pecker are your mother—when you're a baby—and your wife—when you're married. Anyone else is just asking for trouble." This was, of course, Hank's grandmother who told him this, although he could never think of the reason *why* she told him this. He often thought of this nugget of wisdom—more so now that he was becoming as old as dirt, day by day—whenever he had thoughts of other women besides his mother or his wife. Both were gone now—his mother and his wife—as well as his grandmother. But whenever he thought about a woman, he thought of what his Irish grandmother had told him.

Trouble? he chuckled to himself. He rolled the question around in his mouth, along with the last swig of a whiskey old-fashioned. *Hogwash,* he concluded.

Hank sat at the bar of his favorite neighborhood hangout, Home Runs—cigarette smoke in the air, one barstool occupied down the bar from him, distorted karaoke singers serenading strangers in another room out of sight, yellowed ceiling tiles sagging. Like a gargoyle, Hank slumped on his stool, his fists like boulders on either side of his empty lowball glass, tufts of white hair below his weathered knuckles. Jack the bartender wiped bar glasses with a dish rag. He was at least half Hank's age, twice as tall with twice as much hair, but that didn't bother Hank. He liked the guy despite his youth and nice head of hair. When Jack was a teenager, his hair was long and shiny and all the girls at his high school swooned over his hair. When Hank was in high school, all the girls swooned over the hair of the four lads from Liverpool, the Beatles, which was nothing like his own military-style buzz cut.

"Want another?" Jack said to him.

Hank nodded. "Yup."

"Coming up," Jack said, grabbing a bottle of top-shelf whiskey from behind him, then beginning his ritual of concocting Hank's favorite drink: whiskey old-fashioned. He mixed simple syrup with an ounce and a half of whiskey and a dash of orange bitters in a stirring glass. He rubbed orange peel along the rim of the drinking glass, topped it with one amarena cherry with a dribble of syrup, and finished it off with a single large ice cube. There was only one problem: Jack's jar of amarena cherries was empty, and he knew Hank despised maraschino cherries, a lowly replacement for the rich, darker berry. Hatred wasn't a strong enough word for Hank's ill feelings toward maraschino cherries. "I've got to get a new jar from the back," he told Hank, thumbing toward the storeroom. "And I've something to ask you when I get back. Okay?"

Hank nodded. Jack quickly vanished.

But Hank wasn't alone. At the other end of the bar sat Ernie, a drunk Hank rarely conversed with nowadays but saw regularly at Home Runs, one of about a dozen familiar faces that Hank recognized in his favorite hangout. Ernie's facial features were undeniable—bent, crumpled, and bashed like the wreckage of an auto accident. He glared at Hank as if he knew Hank's deepest, darkest secret, which had something to do with Hank's involvement in a plot to overthrow the US federal government. Or possibly that Hank was putting the moves on Ernie's wife or his ugly sister—the other half of the familial wreckage. It was hard to say. Ernie grunted something. Hank shrugged. A woman pretending to be Donna Summers squealed from the other room, working extra hard for her money. Ernie's face burned red. Jack returned, placing the new jar of dark Italian cherries on the bar, then continued with his concoction.

"The last time you were here," Jack began, opening the jar of cherries, then smiling at Hank. "You were telling me about reconnecting with an old flame. Is that right?" He spooned out a cherry and a bit of burgundy syrup, dropping it in the lowball glass. Hank's hands merged, fingers interlacing. He was longing to hold that next cocktail.

"Yup," Hank said, then snorted. "High school sweetheart."

"Really? That's wild." Jack stirred the whiskey, bitters, and simple syrup, then poured it into Hank's glass. He set the cocktail on a black bar napkin.

Hank toasted Jack, then took a slurp of his cocktail. Satisfied, he carefully set the glass back on the napkin.

"She lives near Houston. Found her online a few months ago. She seems to still be fond of me. At least I think so."

Jack's face lit up with astonishment. "Really? You contacted her?!"

"Yup," Hank began, then stammered. "Well, I wanted to, but . . ."

A grin slid across Jack's face. "You sly son of a—"

Suddenly, Ernie cleared his throat, a harsh sound like an envelope being ripped open. "You gonna tell her how your wife and kid *died*?" Ernie blurted, then smirked, the lame attempt at a smile appearing on his mangled mug like a gash in a potato.

Hank turned to Ernie, angrier than a trapped raccoon. Now, *that* was Hank's deepest, darkest secret—not overthrowing the US government or boinking Ernie's wife or ugly sister. Had he said it aloud at Home Runs after drinking one too many cocktails? Had he drunkenly confessed his darkest hours, days, and weeks after his loved ones' untimely and unfortunate deaths to anyone who would listen at the bar and simply forgotten? Hank couldn't remember how Ernie knew this about his lovely wife or his beautiful daughter, but he wasn't in the mood to engage with Ernie either. He wanted to punch that smug face, but he knew better. He could destroy him with one decisive punch. He knew that much. Just knowing that satisfied him, but he wasn't going to let this slight on Ernie's part go unremedied.

"Suck a donkey dingle," Hank pronounced, then turned back to his drink, placing his protective fists on either side of his sweating glass.

Jack bellowed. "Burn! You hear that, Ernie?" He placed his hands over his stomach, quelling his laughter. "Oh my god. That's the best."

Hank's propensity to not curse—no matter the circumstances—was legendary at this point, and his colorful replacements for the run-of-the-mill vulgarities offered whoever was listening a humorous respite from profanity. Ernie's face burned red again—a hotter and more malicious shade than before—then he abruptly left the building, scurrying away like a rodent without finishing his light beer or paying Jack for his tab.

Hank slurped some more of his cocktail with a carefree tilt of his glass.

Jack chuckled. "I can't believe you just told Ernie to suck a donkey dick."

"Dingle. I don't cuss."

"Dick. Dingle. Whatever. That was awesome. Your next drink is on me!"

"Put it on my tab. I've got to go after I finish this one," he said, taking another sip.

"You got it," Jack said, scribbling Hank's request on a pad of paper. "You going home?"

"Yup."

"See you next time, then."

Hank nodded, finished his drink, carefully set his glass on the napkin, then lumbered out the door.

It was late, the tarp of night having already lain over the strip mall where Home Runs resided, right outside his neighborhood, Wells Port. The sordid nightlife business of Home Runs occupied the building's left end, staying open long past the other family businesses had closed. Hank's lugubrious march to his car was accompanied by the jangle of his keys in his pocket. He wondered how he got his meaty hand in his cramped pocket in the first place as he struggled to pull it out, then stopped to concentrate when he heard a familiar voice call out.

"Hey!" the voice hollered, cracking at the tail end.

With his hand still trapped in his pocket, Hank looked up to discover Ernie standing several feet away—his stiff arms by his sides, a knife in his right hand, his left hand clenched in a taut fist, and the mostly empty parking lot spreading out behind him. The four-inch blade twinkled like a distant star. No one else seemed to be around except for a gleaming black car idling in front of the convenience store at the end of the strip mall. The air was still and humid. The interstate hummed on the horizon. Cicadas chirped from the surrounding oak and ash trees, filling the night with a distant lively buzz. Hank's hand came out of his pocket—finally—without a struggle, rolling into an angry fist. He planted his feet like he was trained long ago to do, while a young man on a team of varsity pugilists, in an era like ancient history. But the lessons were sturdy, like his fighting stance.

"You embarrassed me . . . " Ernie said, adjusting the handle of the knife in his shaky hand.

Hank didn't move. He examined Ernie's stance—the wobble in his knees, his fidgety hands, and the way his bloodshot eyes darted away and back at him. Ernie had been in a few fights in his life, but Hank had been in a thousand fights and would be in many, many more.

Ernie continued, ". . . in front of everybody."

"Just Jack," Hank said.

"That's *everybody,*" Ernie said, and lunged.

In a split second, Hank landed a swift, decisive punch into Ernie's bulbous nose, sending him backward, his arms flailing, his feet dancing an uncoordinated two-step, the knife clanking on the asphalt a few feet away. Soon after Ernie's body hit the ground, red and blue lights flashed from the grill of the black car parked at the convenience store. The unmarked car chirped a couple of times, then rolled toward the street fighters. Once it reached them, headlights glaring, the car chirped once more. A plain-clothes cop popped out, a silver badge attached to his shirt, a neatly trimmed mustache above his slit of a mouth.

"All right, turn around. Put your hands above your head," the officer in plain clothes said.

Hank, a man who respected authority, complied. He sighed. "I was only protecting myself. He attacked *me.*"

"We'll let the court see the dashcam video, but I've got to take you downtown nonetheless," the officer said, cuffing Hank's thick wrists. "Jesus, these cuffs barely fit."

"Yup," Hank replied.

The officer placed a hand on Hank's head as he pushed him into the back of the unmarked police car.

"We'll wait until EMS comes for your friend, then I'll drive you downtown."

Hank sighed again. "He's not my friend."

He sat in the backseat and watched through the tinted window until the ambulance came and took stinky Ernie away. He then watched out the window as the police car drove south on I-35, past parts of Austin he hadn't seen in a while: the 183 flyover, Airport Boulevard, Darrell K Royal Texas Memorial Stadium, the University of Texas Tower, the Texas Capitol, the changing skyline of downtown, all of which sailed by within reflections of orange, pink, and yellow neon. The whiskey Hank consumed that night penetrated every artery, vein, and capillary in his body, stretching time into nonexistence. He wasn't aware of how long it took to get downtown, or how long it took to get through jail processing. He answered when he was asked questions, things like his name and where he lived, any other declarations they requested. He was fingerprinted and photographed. An officer asked him to take off his clothes, bend over, and spread his butt cheeks. When he stood back up, he could see his lumpy, pasty reflection in the officer's glasses. From a distance, he looked like The Thing—the deformed, orange, rocky strongman from the superhero group the Fantastic Four. His torso was short and stocky like an oak tree trunk, his hands and feet massive and bulbous with craggy knuckles, and his silver hair sticking straight up as if electrically shocked. When he was a child, his mother had to custom order his shoes, as his feet were massive then. He preferred sneakers to loafers, even now. He looked down at his shriveled pecker and wondered if the wisdom his grandmother imparted on him included a curious police officer witnessing his wilted carrot in a holding cell. He blinked, then found himself in a pink jumpsuit and rubber flip-flops, being escorted—handcuffed again—to where he would spend the night. A cell door opened. His cuffs were removed. He was asked to step inside—the concrete chamber smelling dank and putrid— then the door slammed closed behind him.

Hank quickly discovered the small cinderblock room's bunk beds were already occupied—the lower one by a motionless lump, the upper one by a wheezing monster—so he sat on the concrete floor, his back against the cold wall, his legs splayed out in front of him.

This isn't how I imagined this night would end, he thought. *Hogwash.*

He remembered serene evenings with his wife and daughter, roasted chicken for dinner, board games afterwards, the routine of it sometimes numbing then, but the placidity of these family dinners seemed heavenly now. He sighed.

He closed his eyes and tried to sleep.

When the sun's orange glow illuminated the cell through a tiny, grimy window, a small opening appeared in the middle of the cell door and three brown paper bags were shoved through, plopping on the floor. Hank grabbed one and opened it, finding a peanut butter sandwich, a bruised apple, and a carton of two-percent milk inside. But he wasn't hungry, nor did he care to try the offerings from the jail guards. He set the bag on the floor and waited for someone to get him—his cellmates still snoring, his mind racing with uncertainty. It took a couple of hours, but they eventually came for him.

Hank was handcuffed to five other criminals and led down a concrete hallway to a large service elevator. They descended to the second floor—accompanied by a tall and lanky police officer—and led down another hallway to court room number two, the place where Hank might find justice or punishment; it could go either way, really. On his left was a sweaty young Latino man with halitosis and a scraggly goatee who muttered in Spanish. On his right was a Black man who Hank surmised was about the same age as he was, the man's hair mostly white, his eyes yellowed, and his shoulders rigid, tendons stringing his neck like an old steel bridge.

"This is some bullshit," the Black man declared.

"Yup," Hank agreed.

They didn't wait long before being led into court room number two. The six men sat in a pew to themselves. Hank looked around and most of the other pews were occupied by a similar group of miscreants, all colors and all men, not a single woman among them. It was like a church for the condemned; a chapel for male convicts. Hank didn't think he was a convict, but that wouldn't be up to him.

A door at the back of the courtroom opened and the court reporter quickly stood up, the bailiff ordering the accused to rise for the judge, an elderly woman so short and slight that she appeared to levitate to the judge's bench.

"Please be seated," Judge Richards ordered them, her name etched in gold letters on a block of dark, lacquered wood. A streak of white ran the length of her black hair. Gold glasses daintily sat on her pointy nose. The courtroom deputy, a young man who looked like a teenager, handed Judge Richards a stack of papers. She sighed, then called out, "Malarkey!"

Hank chuckled. She peered in his direction.

Judge Richards cleared her throat. "This is how it's going down on this beautiful morning. I'll call out a name and you will stand. I'll read your charge and you will declare your plea: guilty or not guilty. If you plead guilty, then I will sentence you accordingly. If you plead *not* guilty—"

The room erupted with hoots and hollers. Judge Richards smacked her gavel against the sound block on her desk.

"Silence, you knuckleheads!" she said, then sighed. "If you plead not guilty, then a court date will be set for your trial. Understood?"

The knuckleheads hummed an acknowledgement. Judge Richards shuffled the papers on her desk, then lifted one.

"Jackson, Melvin," she called out.

The Black man on Hank's right stood up, his left hand cuffed to Hank's right. He smelled of farts, menthol cigarettes, and WD-40. As a kid, he smelled of farts, bubblegum, and WD-40. He had never done anything in his life that would've gotten him in trouble with the law. Ever. He was as good as a person can be, except he had atrocious luck. And he was a Black man.

Judge Richards continued. "Mr. Jackson, you've been accused of stealing loaves of bread at a bakery. How do you plead?"

"Ma'am, I didn't steal no loaves of bread. The police are always accusing me of wrongdoing when there was no wrongdoing."

"Mr. Jackson—"

"Ma'am, I thought I paid for all the bread. Honest to God!"

"Mr. Jackson!" she cut in.

"Yes, ma'am. Sorry ma'am."

"Mr. Jackson, how do you plead?"

"Not guilty, your honor."

"Fine. Your court date is September twelfth. If you can make bail, then you can go."

"Thank you, ma'am," Melvin said, then sat back down next to Hank. He shook his head.

Judge Richards cleared her throat. "O'Sullivan, Henry."

Hank stood up, Melvin's hand rising with him. "Hank, ma'am. I prefer to be called Hank."

The judge stared at Hank, then read the sheet of paper aloud. "Mr. O'Sullivan, you've been charged with assault and disorderly conduct. How do you plead?"

"Well, your honor, I am guilty of punching Ernie, but he deserved it. Besides, he had a knife, so it was self-defense."

The knuckleheads hummed in agreement.

"But you're still pleading guilty?"

"Yes, I did punch him. That's true."

Judge Richards looked up from the piece of paper while the court deputy returned with a different sheet of paper in hand. He gave it to the judge, who then read it. After considering what was on it, she said, "There's a statement from the arresting police officer corroborating that the other perpetrator had a knife."

"Yup."

The knuckleheads chuckled.

The judge picked up the other sheet of paper and read it. "And it appears you have a clean record."

"That's right," Hank agreed.

"But in the end, the guilty must pay. So I sentence you to forty hours of community service. Do you have anything else to say?"

"No ma'am," Hank said.

"All righty then," she said, then handed the sheets of paper concerning Henry "Hank" O'Sullivan to the court deputy. "Next up: Salazar, Marco."

The sweaty young Latino man to Hank's left stood up, lifting Hank's left hand with him. "*Sí*," he answered.

On Hank's right, Melvin elbowed him, then leaned in.

"I told you. This is some bullshit," Melvin whispered.

"Yup," Hank agreed. "I hope it doesn't cost me much."

"You know it."

Then they listened to Judge Richards tell the court how Marco Salazar showed his pecker to the cleaning lady at the warehouse where he worked as a forklift driver. Hank wondered if Marco's grandmother would be disappointed.

2.

*H*ank drove his '70 Plymouth Barracuda southbound on I-35, then pulled off just north of San Marcos, Texas, and followed the access road—riding his clutch while he gripped the gear shift, slowing down to a more appropriate speed—until he reached his destination: the meeting site for his court-appointed community service. He was assigned trash duty when he registered, something he didn't think he'd mind doing because he loved doing yard work at his house, and this was the closest thing to yard work among the list of services he had to choose from. What were his other choices? Handing out soup at a homeless shelter? No good; he didn't want to be around bums. Shelving returned books at the public library? Too boring; he didn't like books. When he was a young man, his grandmother tried to instill in him a sense of purpose toward his community and insisted he give back whenever he could, but as he grew older, his patience for those around him grew thin. In this sense, community service was an appropriately harsh sentence. If he wasn't doing this, then he probably would be at his home doing yard work, so trash duty wasn't much different from his typical daily routine. When orange cones appeared on the side of the road along with signs declaring where to park, he knew he'd reached his destination. He slowed the 'Cuda—the preferred moniker for his hot pink hot rod with a black vinyl top and black leather seats—by downshifting into second gear, then turned right into a grassy clearing, following more orange cones to a designated parking area. He parked among the jalopies and low riders of his community service comrades.

After the Barracuda's brutish Can-Am engine cut off, Hank looked around, seeing a group of men huddled a short way ahead into the clearing. Hank sighed, got out of his car, slammed the door, and approached the group of men. The door slam caught the attention of a couple of guys who turned, then gawked at Hank's pink yet burly 'Cuda.

One of them—a middle-aged Latino man wearing a sleeveless white undershirt, khaki chinos rolled up into cuffs, and a hairnet stretched over his shellacked black hair—catcalled Hank while he approached. "Damn! That's a badass ride. That yours?"

Hank stood next to him, sliding his hands in his pants pockets. "I got out of it, didn't I?"

The guy stared back blankly, then replied with a dismissive *pssst* as if to say, *You're just messing with me, right? Right?!* He turned back to the group to listen for instructions. In the middle of the gaggle of convicts stood Anderson, as shown by a name tag on his button-down, short-sleeved shirt—the supervisor of the ragtag crew. He was an average-sized man with an average-sized build and an average haircut of light-brown hair. Everything about him screamed *average*, down to his navy slacks and starched white shirt. But little did these convicts know that Anderson enjoyed getting drunk on home-brewed hefeweizen most Sundays and blasting metal silhouettes of animals with his trusty Thirty-Eight Special. Draped over one arm were a dozen or so reflective work vests—astringent yellow with white iridescent stripes sewn into the seams. He stood next to a dingy white plastic barrel filled with what appeared to be wooden broom handles without bristles, instead ending in a point for impaling litter.

Anderson cleared his throat, spitting a loogie into the grass, before continuing with his instructions while handing out work vests. "Now, please put on your reflective vest. The last thing I need is for one of you to get run over. Or worse, to be mistaken for good citizens!" He chuckled, handed a vest to Hank, then to the next guy, and so on. "After you have your vests on, then I will hand out the trash pickers."

He hocked a larger, phlegmier loogie from deep in his throat, then spat. He handed out trash pickers to each worker. "Now, don't go murdering each other with these pickers. I'm watching you!"

An uneasy chuckle came from the group.

"Okay, see that guy over there," Anderson said, pointing to a distant figure in a navy-blue jumpsuit with a clipboard in his hand. The group turned to look. "That's Nelson. You will check in with him, and he'll give you a trash bag. Once you fill the trash bag, return it to him, and he'll check you out. Then your community service for the day is done. That's it. It's not rocket science! Any questions?"

The man next to Hank raised his hand. Anderson nodded.

"What if we have to take a leak?"

Anderson rolled his eyes. "Then whiz in the woods. Any other questions?"

No one asked a question, but there was a general bit of grumbling and feet shuffling, a sort of confused hum among the group.

"Okay then. Everyone go check in with Nelson."

The group formed a single file line with Hank at the tail end. He watched as each worker checked in with Nelson, who gave a black trash bag in return. Judging by appearance only, Nelson could've been a first or second cousin to Anderson, both men drenched in their white-guy averageness: light-brown hair, chalky-colored skin, and exuberant awkwardness. As the line slowly shuffled forward, Hank took a gander at his surroundings. Just past the grassy clearing was a line of trees—tall, majestic, and swooshing in the cool, Hill Country breeze; spring was in full swing and the brutal heat of summer would come whether he liked it or not. Soon enough, Hank found himself in front of Nelson.

Nelson masticated a sticky piece of cinnamon gum. "Name?"

"O'Sullivan, Henry. But I prefer to be called Hank."

Nelson's chomping stopped while he examined Hank. "Okay then. Here's your trash bag."

He scribbled something on his clipboard, then walked away without saying another word, so he could join Anderson. Hank turned to look at the other workers walking toward the highway, pairing off in small groups as if they were clusters of long-lost friends, poking trash on the ground with their pickers and commiserating. Hank turned back to see Anderson and Nelson sitting on the tailgate of a pickup truck, drinking coffee from government-issued, insulated mugs and laughing. He then turned to the line of trees, a serene place with an alluring presence. He meandered to the tree line, as if he was actually going to the highway with the others, but slowly drifted toward the wooded area. He occasionally looked over his shoulder to see if Anderson and Nelson were watching, but they were consumed in conversation, so Hank beelined to the trees.

Once he reached the wooded area, the sound of the highway quieted to a distant hum, and the dry leaves and twigs crunched under his feet with each step, reminding him that he was walking farther and farther away from civilization. He was on the lookout for trash to pick up, but found little, occasionally spotting grease-stained french-fry paper sacks or crumpled lottery scratch tickets with their silvery coverings desperately scratched off. He stabbed these pieces of trash with his picker and put them in his trash bag, realizing at this pace he'd be poking trash for over a week to fill his bag. But he didn't care. He was alone, away from his supervisors, the other convicts, and the rest of society. He listened to the "tweet tweet tweet" of some birds fluttering in the tree canopies and stepped around mounds of fire ants, as he made his way farther from the grassy clearing.

Soon, he heard a rustling from above, like the sound of a raccoon or possum scurrying for leverage on a teetering branch. Hank stopped and looked up, not seeing anything. He readjusted the picker and trash bag and continued his serene duty, when something fell from above and thumped in front of him. He knelt down—leaving the picker and the trash bag on the ground—and picked up what appeared to be a leather-bound notebook, a red satin ribbon hanging out the bottom as a bookmark. He opened it where the ribbon streamed out and discovered that it was actually a sketchbook, containing dozens of pencil drawings. On one page, a sketch of what appeared to be a car dealership parking lot—finely detailed, lightly shaded in pencil, with a little bird beautifully illustrated in the bottom corner. Another sketch appeared to be the view of gas pumps in front of a convenience store, as if the artist was perched on the roof of the store, the same little illustrated bird in the lower corner. He flipped the pages, finding more scenes, when someone fell to the ground with a thud, right in front of him.

"Holy schnikes!" Hank cried out, dropping the sketchbook and standing up, his knees creaking and popping. A boy quickly jumped to his feet, swatting grass and dirt from his blue jeans and black hoodie, then picked up the sketchbook. Hank kicked his right leg back and forth, as if the motion self-lubricated his creaky knee. He glared at the kid. "You scared the bejesus out of me."

"Sorry," the boy said. He was a lanky and tall Black teen, his short-cropped hair with blades of grass in it, a tawny complexion of pimples and divots, eyes brown like inky wells, wearing a green canvas backpack. He nestled the sketchbook in the nook of his arm. "Didn't mean to—"

"Didn't mean to *what*? Crash land?" Hank said, then chuckled. "What the heck were you doing up there?" He attempted to point up to the tree branch from where the boy fell but swung his hand down to his knee to help adjust it instead.

"Drawing, I guess."

"I saw those," Hank said, nodding toward the notebook.

The boy looked over his shoulder, as if on the lookout for angry pursuers. Hank did the same in the other direction, not seeing anyone. He straightened his creaky leg, popped his stiff back.

Satisfied, Hank continued. "You live around here?"

The boy looked surprised. "Live out *here*? Nah, just doing community service."

"Community service?!" Hank blurted. "I didn't see you in the group with the other men."

"*Men*?" the boy replied. "We're kids. You know, from juvie?"

"Kids, huh?" Hank mused, realizing the boy was from another group of miscreants and not the group watched over by Anderson and Nelson. He extended his hand to the boy for a shake. "The name is Hank."

The boy shook his hand. "Luis," he replied.

"Louie?" Hank said, drawing out the "oo" vowel sound.

"No, the Spanish way of saying it. *Luis*."

Hank's face squinched. "I'll just call you Louie. Okay? I need to sit down. My knee may be sprained."

"Uh, okay."

Hank hobbled to a large granite rock and sat down. Luis sat next to him. Hank rubbed his right knee while Luis put his backpack on his lap and rummaged through it. Hank watched while Luis pulled a juice box from his backpack, impaled it with a short plastic straw, then sucked the juice out.

"You got any beer in there?" Hank said.

"Nah, but I've got one more. Want it?"

"Sure," Hank said. Luis handed him another juice box and he stabbed it with its little straw. "Why you in juvie?"

"Trespassing. What did you do?"

"Fighting, although I told the judge it was self-defense. The guy who came at me had a knife," he said, then slurped the juice. For some reason, Hank thought of his daughter as he swallowed the overly sweet beverage.

Luis noticed the crusty scabs and purple bruises on Hank's hand as he held the juice box to his face. Hank sucked the last of the juice, crumpled the box, then put it in his trash bag.

"Just five hundred more of these boxes and my bag will be full," Hank said, then chuckled. He rubbed his sore knee some more, his face scrunching.

"You okay?" Luis said.

"Yup. I'm fine. Your noggin okay from falling from that tree?"

Luis smiled, then noticed something: two white garbage bags on the ground, not too far away.

"Hey, we could put those full bags of garbage into our bags, then we can turn them in and go home. What do you think?"

Hank thought about it for a second, then rubbed his creaky knee a bit more. "Sounds good to me, kid. I think I need to put some ice on this knee."

"Yeah, let's do it!"

Luis helped Hank stand up, then they walked together to where the two white garbage bags were on the ground, nestled within dried leaves. Luis pulled his work garbage bag from his backpack, shaking it open.

"Watch this!" Luis said, quickly picking up one of the white trash bags, so he could put it inside his own garbage bag, but the bottom of the white trash bag ruptured. Its putrid contents spilled to the ground: rotten garbage covered in maggots. Hank instinctively stepped back two steps, while Luis dropped the remnants of the trash bag as quickly as he could, joining Hank a few feet away.

"Not a good idea after all," Hank mused. "Why don't you fill these bags with leaves and rocks, then we can turn them in. Can you do it, though, while I stretch my knee?"

Luis agreed. He knelt down to fill both garbage bags, gladly scooping large clumps of leaves and compost into both bags. Once done, he cinched the tops.

"How's that?" Luis said, handing one to Hank, who was kicking his leg back and forth, happy that his knee seemed to be working normally again.

"Easy as pie," Hank said. "Let's hit the road."

They slowly trudged back the way Hank had come.

"Can I ask a favor?" Luis said, rubbing the back of his neck with his free hand.

"Shoot."

"Can I get a ride to my place?"

"I don't think so."

Luis sighed. "Crap. I guess I'll be stuck down here until dark since my dad's at work."

Hank felt a bit annoyed, but relented. "Fine. Where do you live?"

"Dominion Apartments in Wells Port."

"Seriously? Wells Port is my neighborhood."

"So you'll give me a ride then?"

"Sure thing, kid."

Hank and Luis walked out of the wooded area and approached Anderson and Nelson, who were still sitting on the tailgate, cracking each other up with dirty jokes. When they saw Luis with Hank, they stopped laughing.

"Who is this, O'Sullivan?" Nelson said, picking up his clipboard, a little confused.

"My grandson," Hank replied. Luis shot him a surprised look.

"Grandson?" Anderson asked. "Where did he come from?"

"You got me. He just found me and decided to help bag some garbage. Good kid. Can I go now?"

Anderson and Nelson gawked at the two full garbage bags they were lugging. Nelson scribbled something next to Hank's name on the clipboard. Anderson pointed to a dumpster in the distance.

"Yeah, sure. Throw the bags over there. And leave the vest and trash picker with me." Hank gladly handed them to Anderson. "See you tomorrow then, O'Sullivan?"

"Yup. And I like to be called Hank."

"Fine. Hank," Anderson said.

Luis followed Hank to the dumpster, where they tossed the two garbage bags, then he led Luis to the parking lot—hobbling on his gimp knee—where the 'Cuda was parked. When he stopped next to the hot pink muscle car, Luis was shocked.

"*This* is your ride?" he said.

"Yup. You coming?" Hank said, opening his door and getting inside.

Luis ran around to the other side and got in, too.

"Your car is pink?" Luis said, buckling his seat belt.

"Yup. You got a problem with that?"

"Not at all," Luis replied, reluctant to anger his charitable yet grumpy driver. "Just glad to get a ride back home."

"Good to hear."

The engine roared as Hank cranked the ignition. He backed up the 'Cuda and left the parking lot in an angry cloud of dust.

3.

*H*ank parked the 'Cuda in the circle drive in front of the Dominion Apartments, the place Luis told him he lived with his father.

"Thanks for the ride," Luis said, unbuckling his seat belt.

"No problem, kid. You gonna be picking up more trash tomorrow?"

Luis got out of the car, closed the door, then leaned on the passenger door. "Yeah, my advocate says I gotta do it every weekend for a long time."

"I'll look for you. Where will you be?"

"Same place in the trees. Later."

"See ya."

Luis turned and headed for a wrought iron gate to the left of the circle drive. Hank watched him press a sequence into a combination lock, open the gate, and disappeared behind a tall hedge just beyond it.

Hank's hood, Wells Port, was built in the late seventies and early eighties, a planned development for the burgeoning northside of Austin, Texas. Not long after the last house was built, the housebuilder declared bankruptcy and was never heard from again, but the company left behind a neighborhood of sturdy three- and four-bedroom homes decorated inside with builder-grade beige carpet, eggshell walls, and what was later learned to be asbestos-filled siding on the outside. Hank bought his tiny home for his then-pregnant wife in hopes of starting a family. He never imagined he would one day be occupying their home as a widower, without children or grandchildren. Every time he drove up the main road into Wells Port, he thought of that day he drove his wife—her belly large, her skin glowing, her smile effervescent—to look at the house for the first time. It was a beautiful day, one to remember; one he would remember until the day he died. He thought of her as he turned right onto his street—named after a German family somehow associated with the neighborhood, a name that was constantly mispronounced—then turned left onto his driveway.

With the motor still idling, he clicked the garage door opener clipped to his visor, gandering at his lawn as the door rose, the blades of grass still shorn neat, the edges of the lawn still tight and straight, and the bushes green and sculpted. He beamed with pride, then parked the 'Cuda in the garage and closed the door. He killed the engine and hopped out of the car. The garage was immaculately kept, almost clean enough to eat off the concrete floor. All the tools were organized in tall, gleaming tool boxes. Power tools were hung up on peg boards. There was a photograph of him sitting with his late wife and angelic daughter in a field of bluebonnets, evidence of the perfect family that once existed. He opened the brand-new fridge—fully stocked with beers and sodas—and grabbed a cold brewsky. He popped the top, took a swig, and considered changing the spark plugs in the 'Cuda but thought better of it. The engine would take a while to cool down. His stomach growled, so lunch seemed like a better idea. Or was it dinner time? He wiped his mouth with his forearm, then opened the door to the house.

Inside, he entered the messy living room, which was quite a different realm from the clean garage. In short, it appeared as if rascally hoarders had occupied the house while a well-oiled, military regiment occupied the garage. What happened inside? Why was it such a pigsty? The answer was simple. Once Hank's wife and daughter passed away, he neglected to take care of the inside of their home. The outside—well, that was easy for Hank. It had been his domain from the start, from the very minute the ink dried on the sales contract, and taking care of the yard was a job that was much less a chore and much more a lovely pastime. *I'll clean up this place someday*, he thought to himself. *Someday*. There were boxes stacked in the living room and piles of laundry, newspapers, and mail on most of the furniture. On a good day, the house inside smelled something akin to a mildewed gym sock, left to dry to a crisp, but it smelled like home to Hank. He walked through a dusty maze of unused belongings—film cameras, rotary phones, VCRs, all fossils from a bygone time—holding his arms close to his sides.

In the kitchen, things weren't much better. Moldy dishes were piled high in the sink—flies circling and buzzing—and old pizza boxes and frozen dinner cartons were stacked on most of the counter space. The linoleum floor was sticky from drips of spilled beer and soda, his shoes making the sound of ripped cardboard as he walked to the indoor fridge. Inside it, his food was waiting: a two-day-old sub sandwich from a shop in the same shopping center as Home Runs. He picked it up and sniffed.

"Bingo," he said, then walked back to the living room. He swept mail and magazines from his La-Z-Boy and plunked down.

As he unwrapped his stale sandwich, a framed photo on the side table caught his eye: his beautiful wife. She smiled back. Pangs of guilt mingled uncomfortably with his hunger pangs. It had been so long since he felt the touch of his wife's hand on his arm—as she would do whenever they went out for dinner or to the movies together—and he missed her companionship. He missed her love and affection. He missed the pies she used to bake for him on his birthday. He remembered the night she and their daughter died in a car accident, which was partly his fault. Too much alcohol. He felt a tear well up in one of his eyes when a familiar sound interrupted his sad dinner, a rhythmic knock on the front door: a secret knock. It could only be one person. Hank laid his sandwich on the side table next to an extra-large bottle of Tylenol (capsules he gobbled to hamper the pain in his knee), wiped the tear away, and got up to answer the door.

He slowly opened it, then sighed. "Hello, Bill."

"Hello, Hank. Busy?" Bill peeked over Hank's shoulder. "You don't *look* busy."

"Just eating dinner."

"Dinner?!" Bill exclaimed. "It's still afternoon."

"It's dinner to me. What do you need, Bill?"

"Your lawn trimmer. Can I borrow it?"

"My trimmer, you say?"

"Yes, sir!"

"But what about my leaf blower?" Hank said.

Bill's left eye twitched. He wasn't much older than Hank, judging by the number of wrinkles on his mug and the lack of hair on his crown. Both neighbors hid a similarly sized ball underneath their button-down shirts, with blue jeans from two generations ago. "Leaf blower?" Bill said.

"You heard me. You still got it. Maybe if you bring it back, then I'll let you borrow my trimmer."

"But—"

"No buts. This ain't a lending library. This ain't no hippie *commune*."

"Who you calling a *hippie*?!"

Hank chuckled. "Don't get your undies in a bunch. Just bring my leaf blower back and I'll lend you the trimmer. Is that all?"

Hank started to close the door, but Bill jammed it with his left foot.

"Vera has a friend . . ." Bill began, then cleared his throat. "She likes to play poker."

Hank opened the door and returned a blank stare.

Bill continued. "She's outdoorsy. Has a hell of a figure!"

Bill grinned, his eyebrows dancing as if saying, *Trust me. She's a hottie!* Hank continued to return his stone-cold blank stare. What Hank didn't know—or didn't even *care* to know—was that Bill was once a world-class salesman in his previous life, long before he was simply Hank's annoying neighbor. He led the team of inside salesmen at Hewlett Packard for over two decades, selling millions of dollars in network servers and computer peripherals, which generated annual salaries in the upper six-figures for Bill. He even sold luxury European sports cars, including Ferrari and Lamborghini models for a downtown dealership, to the same corporate computer inside salesman he had cavorted with for over two decades, banking large commissions to pad his retirement. But none of this sales experience prepared Bill to negotiate with his cantankerous neighbor. It was once said Bill could sell anyone ocean front property in the desert. But Bill's sales skills couldn't charm a stubborn Hank.

"Tell your wife thanks, but no thanks, Bill."

"We know you're lonely, buddy."

"Yup. Bring back the blower and you can have the trimmer," Hank said, pushing the door shut without regard to Bill's foot. When the door slammed, he heard a yelp outside. He returned to his La-Z-Boy to finish his dinner. He thought of what Bill told him about being lonely, then said to himself, "Hogwash."

He gladly finished his sandwich alone.

Afterwards, he wadded the sandwich wrapper and set it on the side table next to the photo of his wife. He glanced around the living room and half-heartedly considered a new project to clean up the mess. He knew better than to start a project like that. He'd never finish it. But something caught his attention across the living room, something at the top of a jammed, three-shelf bookcase. The bottom shelf contained auto repair manuals. The second shelf contained his wife's old cookbooks. But the top shelf contained a hodgepodge of books: travel books about places he had never been, novels he'd never read, and inspirational books that would never inspire him. But one book's silvery spine stood out, so he got up to fetch it, walking through the maze of stacked boxes and periodicals. He slid the large book out and opened it: his high school yearbook.

He flipped through the glossy black-and-white pages with headshots of students, photos of sporting events and teams gathered for group photos, sober faculty mug shots, and random ballpoint pen notations in margins. Casual flipping eventually landed on a page dedicated to his varsity wrestling team—the spine creased as if that page had been reviewed numerous times in days of old—Hank's younger self standing with his teammates while he wore a singlet bearing the image of the school's mascot. Hank's face lacked any signs of the beard, mustache, or wily nose hairs of his older years. He flipped some more, finding photos of pep rallies and smiling club members. He found himself at the back of the yearbook, the place where friends and acquaintances would leave salutations, goofy remarks, and words of wisdom. One of them said:

What a crazy year! Thanks for being the best prom date ever! What a night!! I hope to see you again after graduation. That would be swell. Best, Nancy

Nancy. *What was her last name?* he thought. He couldn't remember, nor could he remember what she looked like. He flipped to the senior section with the grid of headshots—boys sporting flat tops and greaser slicks, girls styling long hair with bows on top and flipped ends. Names were in alphabetical order by last name, but he scanned through all the first names on the first page, then the second, and eventually found her on the third page. Nancy Holzmann. *That's it,* he thought. *Nancy Holzmann.* He looked at her photo. She wore a bright smile and a headband. It seemed as if she was peering through time back at Hank and saying, *I hope to see you again after graduation. That would be swell.* He studied her small nose and the blush on her cheeks. He read her name again: Nancy Holzmann.

He reentered the maze of boxes and periodicals—the yearbook still in hand and opened to the page where Nancy's photo appeared—and walked down the hall to his study, his creaky knee popping again. He pulled an office chair out from a desk and swept papers off the desktop to find a computer keyboard. He turned on his computer—its boxy monitor covered in dust, cobwebs, and coffee splatters—and watched the eight hundred by six hundred-pixel color display shimmy to life. He double-clicked "AOL" and listened to the dial-up modem screech and hiss, then searched Nancy Holzmann. He read line after line of results from all over the US: Hershey, Pennsylvania, and Duluth, Minnesota, various Nancy Holzmanns or Holzmans or Hulzmans. It was confusing and disheartening, just the sheer amount of information brought back with one click. Discouraged, he unceremoniously jabbed the power button on the computer, killing it, the monitor screen fading to black. He looked down at her smiling face once more, then closed the yearbook.

"Hogwash," he said, then set it on the desk.

He decided that even though the 'Cuda's engine was still warm, he'd change the spark plugs anyway. It seemed like a more enjoyable way to spend the rest of his day than thumbing through a dusty old yearbook or searching for old flames on a worthless old computer.

4.

*T*he next morning, when all the men of Community Service Collective Number Two gathered around their manager—the one named Anderson—to receive their trash pickers and bags, Hank was in a noticeably better mood than the day before. He had sat up late into the night reminiscing about Nancy Holzmann, as well as debating whether thinking about Nancy Holzmann was a sin or not. When his wife was alive, she was a devout Irish Catholic and mentioned several times that married men simply *thinking* about other women was a sin. Now, you may be thinking to yourself, *well Hank, your wife is dead.* And you would be right about that. *Why feel guilty about a dead person's feelings?* But that didn't keep Hank from feeling immense guilt over thinking about Nancy—another woman. Hank thought of himself as a devoted husband, even long after his wife and daughter's unfortunate accident. It wasn't her fault that she had passed on too soon; their marriage wasn't split by acrimonious divorce. But loneliness strangled his heart some days, feeling like a vice on a metal pipe, cranking ever tighter as the days went by. When Hank woke up this particular morning, his mental debate had landed on the conclusion that his wife wouldn't want him to be lonely any longer, so he felt good about that. He stood next to the man from the day before—the one who catcalled about the 'Cuda—smiling from ear to ear.

The man noticed Hank's grin and took it as an invitation to chat. He leaned closer to Hank and whispered. "Your hot rod can smoke fools, right?"

Hank tilted his head forward, as if whispering to his chest. "Yup."

"Fucking awesome!" the man replied gleefully.

This caught Anderson's attention. "No talking until I hand out all these pickers and bags," he said, then noticed he had just handed out the last picker and bag to Hank. "Right. Any questions?"

The man raised his hand. "Why is our group called Collective Number Two? Where's Number One?"

Anderson thumbed over his shoulder. "Number One is on the other side of that wooded area where O'Sullivan's grandson is performing his court-sanctioned community service." A collective "oh" came from the group of miscreants. Anderson looked at Hank. "Ain't that right, O'Sullivan?"

"The name's Hank," he replied, gritting his teeth.

"All righty then. Everybody line up to check in with Nelson."

The group did as they were told. Hank was at the tail end. He looked at the wooded area to see if he could see Luis, but he didn't see him. The line trudged forward. When he finally reached Nelson to check in, he smiled at the man.

"Someone's in a good mood," Nelson commented.

"Yup."

"Have a good morning, Hank," Nelson said, writing something next to Hank's name on the clipboard. Hank watched the rest of the group shuffle toward the access road of IH-35 as he snuck away to the wooded area. No one seemed to notice.

Once he was among the trees, the hum of engine noise from the highway mingled with the rustling of the tree canopies, singing a breathy duet about the magical wonders of nature coexisting with the technological marvels of humans. Dried leaves and twigs crunched under his feet as he walked farther into the wooded area. He occasionally looked up at some large tree branches, half expecting to see Luis perched on one like a buzzard or a great horned owl, patiently waiting to snatch itself some rodent lunch. But he didn't see him. He did feel some comfort that he was holding a trash picker, which he could implement as a defensive weapon, if needed. His big fist wouldn't help him against a wild animal or lunatic murderer. He soon found the large granite rock he and Luis had sat on the day before, and decided to sit down and take a break. His right knee was still a little stiff and he wasn't in a hurry to get anywhere. Maybe massaging his knee would make it feel better.

As soon as his rump hit the rock, a loud noise from behind startled him.

"Boo!" Luis cried out, jumping out from behind an oak tree where he had been hiding, waiting for Hank to arrive. Hank unconsciously took a swing at Luis, barely missing his midsection. The young man fell backwards onto the ground but jumped back up on his feet almost as quickly as he fell. He swatted leaves and blades of grass from his jeans. "Hey! You almost hit me!"

Hank harrumphed. "Serves you right, Louie, scaring an old man like me."

Luis sat down next to Hank. "Is your knee feeling better?"

"Still stiff," he said, rubbing it some more. "Sucks getting old."

"Sounds like it," Luis said.

"You'll be old someday."

"*Someday*. Not today. And my name is *Luis*, not Louie," he said, setting his backpack in his lap and rummaging through it. He pulled out two juice boxes. "Want one?"

"Do you have any vodka in there, Louie?" Hank said. A sly grin appeared on his wrinkled face.

"You wish," Luis said, handing him the one labeled apple juice. When Hank grabbed it, Luis noticed Hank's bruised and scabbed knuckles, just like he did the day before. He decided to broach the subject this time. "What happened?"

Hank glanced at his hand, forgetting that it was wounded, then jabbed the juice box with a tiny straw. "Got into a scrap," he said, then slurped some juice.

"And that's why you're out here? For fighting?"

"Yup."

"Did you get him good?"

"Yup."

"That's good," Luis said, then slurped some of his juice.

"What about you?"

"Me?" Luis said, placing a hand on his chest.

"Yup."

"Trespassing. Remember? I told you already."

"No, I don't remember things so good sometimes. I'm old. Trespassing, huh? Why would you do that?" Hank said, then finished the last bit of his apple juice, crushing the box and tossing it in his trash bag. "Bored or something?"

"So I can draw." Luis finished his juice and tossed his box into his trash bag.

"Did you say *draw*?"

"Yeah!" Luis said, then opened his backpack again, pulling out a sketchbook. He flipped through its pages, looking for something in particular. Then he held it up. "See?"

He handed the sketchbook to Hank, who examined the pencil drawing. It was the detailed sketch of a gas station parking lot Hank had seen the day before. The lot was surrounded by lamp posts and ornamental shrubbery, along with a covered area for the gas pumps. The perspective of the drawing was as if Luis was on the roof of the gas station, looking down. He even drew the sign displaying the various gas prices underneath the corporate logo of the station. Hank was impressed with the level of artistry as well as the detail Luis put into the drawing. At the bottom right corner of the drawing was a plump little cartoon bird, sitting slightly askew of the drawing, like a signature.

"Nice drawing. Cute bird," Hank said, handing the sketchbook back.

Luis put it back into his backpack.

"Your knee better?" he asked Hank.

"Yup. Let's fill these bags with something."

"Okay."

Luis stood first and helped Hank stand up. As they walked farther into the wooded area, leaves and twigs crunched under their feet. Birds twittered above. A couple of squirrels played a mating game that looked more like a race. Every few feet Luis or Hank would jab a fast-food wrapper or the cardboard from a twelve-pack of soda and stuff it into his trash bag. Hank started whistling a tune that he quickly forgot the rest of, the end of the song descending into silence.

Luis cleared his throat. "Do you have a wife?"

Hank stabbed a flattened aluminum can. "Not anymore. She died."

"Oh, sorry," Luis said, rubbing the back of his neck. "I didn't know."

"How would you?"

"Do you have any kids?"

"Again, not anymore. She died, too. Are you going to keep asking me painful questions?"

Luis's face flushed. "I'm so sorry, I didn't—"

Hank chuckled. "Take it easy kid, I'm just joking. Are *you* married?"

Luis cackled. "Me?! I'm only sixteen. I'm not *married!*"

"That's good. You got plenty of time. I don't have much more time since I'm one hundred and sixty-five."

"Dang! That's old!"

"You wish. I'm only sixty-five, barely old, practically middle-aged." Hank chuckled. He knew this wasn't true because his body told him so on a daily basis. "You live with your folks?"

"I just live with my dad. My mom lives in Houston," Luis said, stabbing an empty Camel cigarette pack and putting it in his trash bag. "A neighborhood in Houston called Montrose, actually."

"Your parents divorced?" Hank said, propping his picker on his shoulder.

"Yeah, I guess. Something like that."

"Sorry, kid. That stuff happens."

"I know."

They eventually walked up to a large mound—almost three feet high and mostly covered in dried leaves. A small pile of what appeared to be black dirt crowned the top. Hank placed his hands on his hips as he examined it.

"Wazzup?" Luis said, looking at the mound, then back at Hank.

"Holy schnikes!" Hank said.

"What is it?"

"Fire ants. And a mighty big fortress, too. It'd take three cartons of Amdro to kill that mound."

"Really?" Luis said, knowing nothing about fire ants or what exactly Amdro was.

"Don't disturb it. Let's walk around," Hank said, moving around the mound. Luis followed, then looked back.

"You should probably head back the other way soon. My group is that way," Luis said, looking in the direction they were going.

Hank examined Luis's profile: his dark skin, his straight, short-cropped hair, and his pimples. He couldn't make heads or tails of what or who he was looking at. Hank couldn't help himself; he just had to know.

"Are you Black or something?" Hank said.

Luis turned to face him. "*Something?*"

"Or African American, as they like to say nowadays."

Luis laughed. "I'm Puerto Rican."

"Ahhh, makes sense now. You're a mutt."

Luis's face twisted into a question mark. "What?"

"Puerto Ricans are half African, half Spanish. Or sometimes half African, half Indian. Mutts."

"And what are you? All honky?!" Luis retorted.

Hank chuckled. "I'm a mutt, too. Half Irish, half Jewish."

"I figured you were just plain ol' white."

"That, too," Hank said, then chuckled some more.

"I better get going," Luis said, waving at Hank and turning to run back to his work site. "I can't screw around every time for community service. I'll find you again next Saturday."

"Wait!" Hank said. "I . . . need your help with something."

This statement prodded Luis's curiosity. He stepped closer to Hank. "What do you need help with?"

"Do you have a cell phone?"

"Yeah, in my backpack. Why?"

"Do you know how to find people online?"

Luis's head tilted to the side as he examined Hank's face: the look of helplessness there. Or maybe it was desperation. Either way, it appeared that he genuinely needed Luis's help.

"I can pay you. Or do something—" Hank added.

"Yeah, I know how to do that. Who are you looking for?"

Hank rubbed his burly neck. "Her name is Nancy Holzmann. Can we go back to the rock and sit down? Maybe you can show me how to do it."

"Okay," Luis said.

They trudged back to the rock, sat down, and Luis opened his backpack. He pulled out a cell phone and brought up a search screen.

"What's her name again?" Luis said.

Hank told him her name as well as all the info he knew: where she was from, her approximate age. Then he watched Luis jab and swipe at the phone's screen for a few minutes, looking at this and that, until finally, he showed the screen to Hank.

"Is this her?"

Hank examined the visage on the screen. Her hair wasn't how he remembered it, and her clothes weren't what he imagined she would be wearing, but he recognized her smile, the dimple in her chin, and the twinkle in her eyes. It was her: Nancy Holzmann, only much older.

"Yup."

"Really?" Luis said, surprised at his own ingenuity.

"That's her, all right. How can you get that to me? That information. What we're looking at on your screen."

"You got an email?"

"Yup. AOL or something?"

"Give me your email and I'll send you the link."

"But what if I need more help?" Hank said, standing back up, ready to fill his trash bag with something—anything—so he could finish his community service and go back home.

"I'll email you my cell number, too. You can call me if you need more help."

"Really?" Hank was caught off guard by Luis's lack of self-awareness and immediate kindness, given out without even a thought.

"Yeah, really. I better go, though," Luis said, standing up.

"All right, kid. Thanks for helping me." Hank smiled awkwardly. "You need a ride home?"

"No, my dad is picking me up today. Gotta run!"

Luis ran back toward where Community Service Collective Number One was supposed to be working, on the other side of the wooded area. Hank watched him until he disappeared behind a cluster of trees, then headed toward Community Service Collective Number Two working along the access road, under the not-so-watchful eyes of Anderson and Nelson, the card-playing wankers who were supposed to be managing the group. He looked at his trash bag and realized he hadn't filled it with more garbage, or anything resembling garbage. He hit the side of his leg with a clenched fist.

"Hogwash," Hank said, then put the next piece of litter he found on the ground into the bag with the picker. He thought of going back into the woods and filling the bag with leaves like he did the day before with Luis, but thought better of it and joined the rest of Community Service Collective Number Two by the highway. As he stood within earshot of the others, many retelling the questionable incidents that had landed them in community service, Hank wondered if he should join a boxing gym. Training again would do wonders for his mind, body, and soul, and just the thought of punching a bag brought the serenity he needed to pick up trash. He also thought about the night he punched Ernie and wondered what happened to him. Did he also go to jail? Or did he spend the night in the hospital? Either way, Hank was certain he'd encounter Ernie again. Next time, he hoped to knock Ernie's block off.

5.

*L*uis sat in the living room of the two-bedroom apartment he shared with his father, staring at dust particles floating within shafts of late sunlight stabbing through mini blinds while his father cooked dinner. He was making a pan of Hamburger Helper Cheesy Hamburger, one of Luis's favorite dishes from the limited selection of choices his father offered. He rarely made a dinner that didn't come from a box, preferring the nonthinking method of something like Hamburger Helper. He was just too busy with work and paying bills to cook a more elaborate dinner. Luis often wondered if the dinner selection would be different if his mother lived with them, but he rarely mentioned his mother to his father. The subject of her always seemed too painful to broach. Even at that moment while he watched the dust dance in the air—the smell of frying ground beef and processed cheese along with the scent of an overflowing ash tray on the balcony—he wondered about her and her current situation. But he didn't dare tell his father that.

"Do you have homework due tomorrow?" his father said from the kitchen, over the sound of a plastic spatula pushing around the Hamburger Helper mixture in a banged-up frying pan.

"Probably," Luis said.

"You should work on that after dinner."

"All right."

"Gotta stay on top of your school work."

"You're right."

Luis's gaze fell on the coffee table, one with a brass frame and a beveled glass top that had seen better days, its surface covered in sports magazines and comic books. It once probably looked beautiful in a furniture showroom but now looked dingy and sad. Just past it sat a television that seemed to be from another generation—boxy with a rear end that stuck out like a fender on a car from the 1950s, perched on top of four plastic milk crates, two red and two blue, all held together by zip ties. Below that was soiled carpet that looked middling brown but was revealed as light beige if you moved any of the furniture.

The sound of the spatula tapping dishes could be heard as his father plopped some dinner on two plates, then set them on a small dining table in the corner, a spot called "the breakfast nook" by the fine folks who managed the Dominion Apartments.

His father called out, "Dinner is served."

Luis joined him at the table. In front of him sat his plate of Hamburger Helper and a cup of red Kool-Aid, its flavor a mystery, the cup emblazoned with the logo of the convenience store down the street. His father—a burly man named Roberto Sanchez, although his friends called him Berto, who had wild curls of black hair and black bushy eyebrows—also sat down, setting a leftover napkin from a fast-food burger place in his lap. His bulky build was in striking contrast to Luis's thin frame and Luis was glad to not have his father's curly locks. He handed Luis a paper napkin from a fried-chicken joint, then nodded to him.

Luis put his hands together in prayer. "Rub-a-dub-dub, thanks for the grub. Amen!"

His father slugged him in the arm for the reference to the hasty prayer of Bart Simpson. "Can't always be joking about the Lord."

"Sorry," Luis said, rubbing his arm.

"You know better."

"All right."

They commenced eating. His father's hulking presence always intimidated Luis. His biceps were thick like oak tree trunks and his meaty hands often were clenched into angry fists even when he was relaxing. When his father slugged his arm, it wasn't with the playfulness his friends employed at school. A few dents in the drywall around the apartment were evidence of the storms that often brewed within him. His father's booming voice could shrivel Luis's self-esteem instantly. Luis treaded lightly, as usual. For a minute or two, they shoveled spoonfuls of cheesy food into their mouths. When

Luis finally picked up his cup of Kool-Aid for a drink to wash it down, his father cleared his throat.

He said, "I got a call from your advocate this morning. She said you disappeared from the group yesterday."

Luis finished his Kool-Aid, set the cup on the table, then wiped his mouth with the back of his hand. He didn't respond.

"To get out of this mess, you have to show up and do the work. Anything less is unacceptable. Got it?"

Luis watched as his father clinched a fist on the tabletop, so he nodded.

"Do you have anything to say for yourself?" his father said, wiping his mouth with his paper napkin, then setting his implacable gaze on Luis.

He froze whenever his father stared like that at him. And whenever he did, Luis's mind flashed to images of his mother greeting him with hugs and kisses, images of what he believed his mother might look like and act like now. He wasn't really sure, since he hadn't seen her in person for a very long time, but it was a seductive mental movie filled with positive emotion. He couldn't help it; it just happened.

"You can send me to Houston," Luis said, mentioning the faraway city where he knew his mother resided now. He knew that was a risky hand to play with his father.

"Luis *Delgado*. How many times have I told you—"

Delgado. That's all Luis had to hear: his and his mother's last name. Every time his father said it in that tone—that cynical, sneering tone—it was like a shock to his system. Luis jumped up from the table and stormed to his room, slamming the door behind him. He sat on his bed and put his backpack on his lap. He knew his father wouldn't come into his room or even knock on the door. He never did such things after disagreements or arguments. His father simply left him to his own devices. So Luis filled his backpack with things he wanted to take with him: his cell phone (someone had called him several times, but he didn't recognize the number), his sketch book, some pens and pencils, a flashlight, a juice box, and a blow gun with feathered darts. He pulled his black hoodie on over his head. Once he had everything he needed, he waited on his bed and listened. Like clockwork, his father cleaned off the dinner table, threw leftovers in the trash, and loaded the dishwasher. Finally

Luis heard the sound of his plodding footsteps to his own bedroom, then the slam of his door. Luis knew, without a doubt, that once his father was in there and on the phone with his girlfriend, Claudia, that the rest of the night was his; his father wouldn't come out again until the morning. The door slam was his signal to skedaddle. The sun had dipped below the horizon, turning the sky eggplant purple.

He put his backpack on, slid the bedroom window open, and grabbed a drainage pipe next to the second-story window, setting his feet one after the other on the pipe brackets. The pipe creaked a bit, but he knew the best places to put his hands and feet to minimize squeakiness. Once close to the ground, he jumped onto the grass and ran for the wrought iron fence that surrounded the apartment complex. Soon enough, he was at an exit gate and punching in the combination lock to open it. Once through, he ran as fast as he could across a drainage field toward a business park across the street.

Behind a warehouse he ascended a roof access ladder and walked across the flat roof—past turbine ventilators, air-conditioning units, and solar panels—to the front of the building, where he sat on a mysterious metal box. It was cool to his rump when he sat down, and the perfect height from which to watch the parking lot below, but someone on the ground would really have to be examining the roof line carefully to see him, especially in the dark of night. And he rarely saw police cars, something he didn't have to worry about in such a remote place; it was almost like the business park had been abandoned. He took off his backpack and opened it, dumping the contents at his feet. He grabbed his sketchbook and a pencil and began sketching the empty parking lot and its accompanying illuminated lamp posts. His cell phone vibrated, but he ignored it, acknowledging the possibility that his father *could* be calling him. He continued to draw, sketching the yellow delineating lines of the parking lot and the signs stuck in the neatly shorn lawn surrounding it.

Suddenly, some movement caught his eye and he stopped sketching. In the glow of a lamp post on the asphalt, he could see a small animal scurrying, maybe a possum or cat. On further inspection, it was definitely a possum and a potential moving target. Luis tossed the sketchbook and pencil to his feet, then grabbed his blow gun. He quickly dropped a feathered dart in the front of it and placed it to his pursed lips. He inhaled sharply, then blew as hard as he could, sending the dart quickly through the air, hitting the possum in its behind. It yelped, then darted back in the direction it came from. Luis snickered.

His cell phone vibrated again, and his curiosity got the best of him. He just had to see if it was his father calling him, even though he didn't want to talk to him. He picked up the phone and didn't recognize the number on the screen, but he answered it anyway.

"Hello?" he said. Nothing on the other end. "Who's this?"

"Louie?" a voice said on the phone. "It's me."

Hearing the grumbly voice, Luis knew exactly who it was. He placed his phone between his ear and right shoulder, grabbed the sketchbook and pencil and continued shading his drawing.

"Yeah. What do ya need?"

"I need your help. Got a minute to help an old codger?"

6.

*T*his one phone call in the middle of the night from Hank to Luis initiated a daily routine between the two new friends. Hank would call Luis
with all kinds of questions about the internet at all times of the day. *How
do I use a search engine? What's a social media website? Is it illegal to look
for information about people? What do you mean, I'm a snoop?!* And since
Luis was at school most of the day, he'd return Hank's calls between class
or during his lunch break. Most days, Luis had the urge to skip school. But
once Hank started calling, that deviant urge soon dissipated. He no longer
wanted to escape the confines of school. Instead, he used his free time to
answer Hank's questions while sitting on the floor in the hallways or in his
preferred spot under an oak tree at the back of campus.

"You still looking for stuff about that lady?" Luis said into his cell phone
as it sat on his lap, then taking a bite from a peanut butter and jelly sandwich
with strawberry jam: his favorite. It was set to speaker phone, so he could eat
while he talked.

"Yup," Hank replied, his voice staticky and tinny.

"What's her name again?"

"Nancy. Nancy Holzmann."

"Do you really think she wants you to find her?"

"She said it would be swell to see me again after graduation."

"Graduation?!" Luis said, then laughed. "Didn't you go to school with
Jesus or something?"

"Ha ha. Very funny. What are *you*? A comedian?"

"Nah. Just an ordinary, dumb kid."

"You're not dumb, Louie. Thanks for helping a crotchety old man like me
use the intrawebs and such. I appreciate it."

"So . . ." Luis started, before taking a large bite from his sandwich. He continued talking with his mouth full. "You-thhh gonna call-thhh her?"

"Already did."

Luis choked on his sandwich, then coughed roughly, spitting out what was in his mouth into the grass. He wiped his face with his forearm, then said, "What did she say?"

"She said it would be nice to see me sometime."

"Really?" Luis said, surprised.

"Yup."

"When is that going to be?" Luis said, examining the rest of his sandwich, then deciding to finish it after the phone call, when it was safer to eat without fear of choking.

"Dunno. Maybe I'll hit the road this Saturday after community service. I haven't decided yet."

"But that's in *two* days?!"

"Yup."

"And she knows you're coming?" Luis said, then was met with silence for a bit from the other end of the line.

Hank cleared his throat. "Nope. Wouldn't be romantic to tell her I'm coming, now would it?"

Luis considered this with his young, inexperienced mind, then said, "I guess not. And where does she live again?"

"Near Houston. A suburb called Sugar Land."

"Near *Houston*?" Luis said. The word Houston conjured images of his mother, her face young and happy, like in the photo he had of the two of them: Luis a baby and his mother a young woman cradling him in her arms. His father wasn't in this photo, nor was he in any of the images Luis conjured from when he was young. Hank continued to talk to himself while Luis ruminated.

"You still there, Louie?" he asked Luis.

Hank's gruff voice snapped Luis out of his hypnotic state. "Yeah, sorry. Just thinking."

"I gotta go, Louie. I'll talk to you later. All right?"

"Okay. Later," Luis said, then disconnected the call. He gathered his things and headed back inside the school. For once in his life, he felt needed, which was a revelation to him, and it felt pretty good.

Luis thought about his mother again during the bus ride home from school. *Would she be surprised if I just showed up in Houston? Would she be happy to see me?* he thought. He then wondered why he was even asking himself such questions, since it was Hank that was going to Houston, and not him. Maybe he had more pressing questions to ask first, like *Would Hank let me tag along? Would my dad allow me to go visit her?* He was deep in thought when he felt an elbow jab his ribs. It was the girl sitting next to him. She wore oversized glasses, an ill-fitting sweatshirt, and had a messy bun of auburn hair loosely held to the back of her head.

She gave him a slow blink, then said, "Better get off or you'll miss your stop."

Luis looked out the window and saw the front office of his apartment complex—other kids who lived there milling about and lighting up cigarettes instead of going to the apartments where their families lived—then realized the driver was impatiently waiting for him to get off the bus. He jumped up.

"You're welcome!" the girl cried out after him.

"Thanks!" he said as he jumped down the exit steps.

As he punched in the combination to the wrought iron gate, he knew what he was going to have to do that night. He was going to have to convince Hank to let him tag along to Houston so he could visit his mother, and to see if maybe she would allow him to live there with her. *She would at least consider it, right?* he thought. *Right?!* He opened the gate and bolted toward the swimming pool. The gate slammed behind him and rattled the metal fence. It was a crisp spring day, still too early in the year for anyone to swim in the pool. From the fall through the spring, the pool was mostly decorative, although leaves collected on the water's surface, along with a variety of dead bugs and trash. The barbecue grills surrounding the pool were caked over with last summer's soot. The beige patio furniture was dusty and yellowed. The only soul around was Jesús, one of the maintenance men, who was scooping the pool with a skimmer net. He always took the opportunity to greet Luis whenever he saw him.

"*Qué pasa*, holmes?" he called out to Luis.

"Jesús! How's it hanging?" Luis replied, waving a hand above his head.

"Living the dream, *compadre!*" He whistled a *conjunto* tune as he skimmed more leaves out of the pool.

Luis and his father lived in the building behind the pool—Building Nine—on the third floor. Luis bounded up the stairs, two steps at a time, to their apartment. Inside, everything was left as he remembered. Dishes and pans from breakfast were in the sink. Empty milk and juice cartons were on the kitchen counter. The musky smell of the two men hung thick in the air. His father was still at work and not there to greet him, as usual. Luis was a latchkey kid, through and through. But he was fine with that, particularly at this moment, when he wanted to give Hank a call in private. He went into his room, closing the door.

After tossing his backpack on the floor, he lay on the bed, one of the few pieces of furniture in his room besides a stack of plastic bins he used as a dresser and a secondhand side table that he used as a desk, but since he didn't have a chair to go with it, he rarely used it except to stack things on. The carpet was matted in the middle of the room from Luis sitting on it. The walls were bare and the ceiling fan was missing the glass globe, its light bulb exposed. They had been living there for what seemed like forever, but Luis wasn't interested in making himself at home. He imagined the day he would be able to pack his stuff and go find the place where he belonged, so why decorate his room? A chunky laptop computer sat on the table, its screen projecting dancing geometric shapes in primary colors. Next to the monitor sat a photo of Luis as a baby with his mother behind glass in a brass frame, the glass covered in fingerprints. He grabbed his cell phone from his backpack and called Hank. The line rang a dozen times before the old man answered.

"Hello?" he said, exasperated.

"It's me."

Silence followed by heavy breathing as if Hank had jogged around the block. Then he said, "Who's this?"

"It's Luis. You know?"

More silence. Then, "Ah, Louie. This is a surprise. I thought I only called you. I wasn't expecting you to call *me*."

"Surprise!"

"Ha ha. Very funny. This is a surprise. What can I do for you, Louie?"

"Uh . . ." Luis said, then set the phone on his comforter, pressing the speaker phone button.

Hank cleared his throat. "Spit it out, kid!"

"Right! Okay, then. So, remember when you were telling me you were going to Houston to see that lady—"

"Nancy?"

"Yes, Nancy. Would you mind if I tagged along with you?"

"Tag along?" Hank snapped, then coughed roughly. After clearing his throat, he said, "Why would you want to hang around a couple of old folks?"

"I don't think I want to hang around you and Nancy."

"Then what in blazes—"

"I want to see my mother," Luis said. Then silence. He rubbed his neck, then continued. "She lives in Houston and I need to see her."

"Then why doesn't your dad take you?"

"He doesn't want to do that."

"What?" Hank exclaimed. "And why not?"

"It's complicated."

"Complicated? What's complicated about a son seeing his mother?!"

"Exactly," Luis agreed.

"What?!" Hank said, confused. He took a deep breath, then said, "So, you're asking me to take you to Houston to see your mother?"

"I won't be any trouble. I've got money. Lots of money. I've been saving—"

"I don't know," Hank began. He wasn't sure what to make of this request. "My plan was to see Nancy, not—"

"Please. My mom misses me," he said, lying through his teeth. "I haven't seen her in almost five years."

"Five years? Holy schnikes!"

Luis realized he found his way into Hank's emotional core. "Yes, more than five years. Almost six!"

"Six years? Well, I'll be. That's terrible."

"Plus, she's been having health problems, too. Something with her diabetes . . . or cervical something or other. I don't know. Like I said, it's complicated."

Luis looked up at the blank white walls in his room and projected a vision of Hank sitting in a recliner, a look of deep concern on his face, maybe a beer in his hand. He wasn't quite sure since he had never been in Hank's house. The vision was fuzzy.

Hank sighed. "Well, if it's all right with your father and all. Can you ask him?"

"Sure!" Luis said, excited at the prospects of visiting his mother at last. "I'll ask him. No problem."

"Right now," Hank demanded. "Ask him now, so I know for sure."

"Now?"

"Is he there?"

Luis looked around his room, then stood up from the bed, shaking his hands as if the motion would unlock a plan in his mind of what to do. It worked.

"Yeah, he's here," Luis said, lifting his head and talking toward the ceiling, giving his voice some distance from the phone receiver. "Let me go get him!"

Luis opened the door to his room and called out for his father, who of course wasn't there, but Hank didn't know that.

"Dad!" Luis called out.

Then he turned and hunched over, flexing his arms and tightening his core, pretending to transform into his father's burly shape. He lowered his voice to simulate his father's. "Yes, son?"

He quickly covered his mouth to stifle a laugh, then turned back, transforming his voice back to his own. "Can I go on a field trip to Houston? It's for school."

He smothered another laugh, then said gruffly, "Sure son! You have the permission forms for me to sign?"

"Yep!"

"Well, anything for school. Right, son?"

"Yeah, dad!"

"Great! Give me the forms after dinner. I'll be happy to sign them."

"Okay! Thanks dad!"

Then he slammed his bedroom door shut and hopped back on the bed.

"How's that?" he said to the phone, a smile stretched wide on his face.

Hank cleared his throat. "Sounds good to me. Well then, pack a bag with a change of clothes. Bring a toothbrush. You know the drill since we have to stay in a hotel Saturday night."

"Okay. I will."

"We can leave right after we're done with community service. Sound good?"

"Yeah! And thank you so much. My mom will be so happy."

"I hope so. Bye now," Hank said, then hung up the phone.

Luis lay back on his bed, then shook his head in astonishment, amazed at his ability to fool Hank. But this feeling of amazement was intertwined with feelings of guilt for having lied to his new friend at the spur of the moment. It was too late now to change things, unless he wanted to back out of going to Houston, which he didn't. So, as he thought of ways to make it up to Hank—ways to make it right, as they say—he heard a noise from the other side of the apartment: a slamming door. It must've been his father, home from a long day at work. Heavy footsteps approached Luis's room, then a knock at the door.

Luis sat up in his bed. "Yeah?"

The door opened unexpectedly. "How was school?" his father said. He looked around the room like someone else might be in there, maybe hiding in the closet or under the desk.

"Good," Luis replied. He looked around his room, too, wondering what his father was looking for. He was quite surprised that his father opened the door at all.

"That's good. Hamburgers for dinner?"

"Sounds good."

"Okay," his father said, closing the door.

"Dad?"

"Yes?" his father said, opening the door again.

Luis nervously ran his fingers through his hair. "Can I spend the night at Jack's house Saturday night?"

His father's face scrunched. "Jack? Who's that?"

"A friend at community service. He said his mom could give me a ride back here Sunday. Is that cool?"

"Yeah, I don't know—"

Luis worried that his plan was about to crumble. If his dad said no, then what would he tell Hank? Was he willing to miss this opportunity to finally be reunited with his mother after all this time? Luis thought fast.

"But you said I should be making friends, right? I should be making the best of my situation. That's what you said."

His father was astonished that some bit of his lecturing seemed to have taken hold. Had Luis been listening to him this whole time? It was an unexpected revelation. He smiled. "That's fine. Just leave his mom's number on a sticky note on the fridge. All right?"

"Cool! Thanks, dad."

"Cool. I'll go pick up some burgers. Want fries, too?"

"Yeah!"

"Okay. Be back," he said, then closed the door.

Luis fell back on his bed again, looking up at the dusty ceiling fan. He raised his legs and kicked his feet triumphantly as if quickly pedaling a bicycle, then dropped his legs back down. He turned and looked at the photo of him and his mother. *See you soon*, he thought. He sat up and reached for the framed photo, pulling it close, flipping it over, and disassembling the brass frame from its brittle, brown cardboard backing. He tossed the frame on his bed and examined the photo some more, turning it over to reveal something written on the back: his mother's home address and phone number. He had been hiding the fact that he knew his mother's location for a while now, ever since Luis found the address and number while snooping through his father's phone one afternoon. His father was slumbering on the couch, snoring like a hibernating monster, when Luis decided to excavate the precious information from the unlocked phone, just in case he ever needed it. Luis had considered putting his mother's information in his own cell phone address book but worried his father would find it somehow. He knew his father would never find it written on the back of this photograph, a treasured memento he never dared to touch or remove from Luis's bedroom, so Luis scrawled it there with a permanent-ink pen. He smiled at his ingenuity, placed the photograph in his backpack, then began packing the rest of his things for the trip.

7.

*H*ank woke up early Saturday morning, packed a bag for the trip, turned the coffee maker on, and took a quick shower. While getting dressed in his bedroom—a room equally as messy as the living room, with piles of clothes on the floor and stacks of empty pizza boxes in one corner—he caught his wife staring at him from a framed photo on the nightstand. When the photo was taken many years before, she teased Hank with sensual words instead of saying "cheese" like Hank had requested, and her sexy mischievousness was caught on film. But at that moment in the bedroom, her sultry look could be interpreted as scrutiny, and for the first time Hank wondered if driving to Houston to see Nancy Holzmann was such a good idea. Even though it had been a long time since his wife's unfortunate accident, he always felt a wave of guilt whenever the thought of finding a new love crossed his mind. He still loved his wife and daughter very much, but his loneliness was beginning to wear on him, hollowing out his tough shell, making his heart feel brittle. He wasn't quite sure what to do, so he simply turned away from her photo to avoid her probing eyes.

Once dressed, he left the bedroom for the living room, where he sat on his La-Z-Boy chair, his duffle bag in one hand and a pair of brown leather loafers in the other. He set the bag on the carpet, then put his shoes on—the black wool sock on his right foot with a hole in it for his big toe to receive fresh air, the cotton sock on the left the shade of coffee with heavy cream. Again, his wife stared at him from the framed photo on the side table. Although her hair and manner of dress were different from the photo in the bedroom, her look of scrutiny was the same. The pangs of guilt he felt inside pounded his heart.

"Forgive me, sweetheart," he said, then sniffled. "A man can take only so much."

He put his duffle bag on his lap. He gazed at his wife and remembered the way she would gently touch his arm to soothe him when he was angry, the delicious pies she would bake for him on special days instead of wasting money at the department store for gifts he wouldn't want anyway, or the lovely things she would whisper in his ear at unexpected times—even when they were meeting with a tax consultant or when he haggled with a car salesman to lower the price of their new station wagon. He missed her dearly.

"You will always be my true love," he said, water gathering at the corners of his eyes. "*Always.*"

He stood up, hung the duffle bag over one shoulder, and walked to the door. Before he went through it, he turned to the photo of his wife and said, "Do I have your permission to go?"

The mischievous look seemed to return to her face.

"Thank you, sweetheart," he said.

In the garage, Hank walked around to the back of the 'Cuda and popped the trunk. As he was putting in the duffle bag, his neighbor Bill appeared as if out of thin air. He jabbed Hank in the ribs with a stiff finger.

"Stick 'em up!" Bill said, then snickered.

Hank turned around with a clenched fist, his scabbed knuckles exposed. "Don't scare a man like that. You could get clobbered."

Bill gasped. He quickly raised a hand to surrender. "Just jokes, neighbor. That's all!"

Hank saw his leaf blower in Bill's other hand. "Thanks for bringing it back."

He closed the trunk, grabbed the leaf blower, then walked around the 'Cuda to the front of the garage where his work bench sat with a variety of tools, engine parts, and gardening equipment on top. Even though it appeared to be somewhat disorganized, there was a methodology to Hank's madness.

Bill guffawed. "I don't know if I've ever seen your workbench this messy," he said, wiping his forehead.

"Got a lot of projects," Hank replied. "And my weekends have been . . . compromised."

"I see. You going somewhere?"

"What?" Hank said, setting the leaf blower on the work table. He then turned to Bill. "What'd you say?"

Bill took a step back, still worried about unwittingly being clobbered by his grouchy neighbor. "You put a bag in your trunk. You going on a trip or something?"

"Yup," Hank said, then walked past Bill, rifling through his front pockets for his car keys. "Can you keep an eye on the place until I get back? Should be back tomorrow night."

"Sure, neighbor! No *problemo*," Bill said, beginning to reach out to pat Hank's shoulder, as some friends like to do, but thought better of it and retracted his hand. "I'll keep an eye on things for you."

"Thanks, Bill," Hank said, maneuvering around Bill and getting into the driver's seat. He tried to close the door, but Bill kept it open, his left hip leaning on the door edge.

"Hey, Hank. Do you remember what I told you about the other day?" he said, beads of sweat now clinging to his forehead. "About my wife's friend?"

"The one with the nice figure?"

"Yeah, that's the one! You've got a memory like a steel trap. Anyhoo, her name's Doris. She's a nurse over at the hospital on Loop 1. Works in the ICU, I think. Happens to be a widow, too. Her husband died in Afghanistan."

"Is that right?" Hank said, grabbing the door and attempting to close it whether Bill moved or not. "Sorry to hear that."

Bill held fast to the car door the best he could. "She's a little younger than you, but her kids are grown up and out of the house. Could be someone you could go on hikes with. Maybe play some cards for nickels and quarters and laugh with. Who knows?!"

Hank looked up at Bill, a look of consternation on his face, his eyelids narrowing to slits. "Tell your wife thanks, but no thanks, Bill."

Hank tilted his head toward the door, as if to say, *Do you mind?* Bill moved aside. Hank slammed the car door shut. He jabbed the key into the ignition and cranked it. As the car rumbled and gurgled in the garage, Hank hung his elbow out the window.

"If there's an emergency, like the house is on fire, and you need to get in, there's a key under the flower pot by the front door. The one with daisies in it," Hank said, then rolled the window up with the window crank.

He put the 'Cuda in reverse and slowly backed out of the garage. Bill followed him out onto the driveway. Once in the street, Hank closed the garage door with the clicker and drove away. As he shifted the car from second to third, he thought of Nancy and hoped she'd be as excited to see him as he was to be going on this trip.

Bill waved as Hank drove away. He watched the pink 'Cuda disappear into the distance. He stopped waving and shook his head.

"Grouchy bastard," he said aloud to himself, then walked back to the safety of his own house.

— — —

That same morning, not too far away, Luis was finishing a bowl of Lucky Charms at the dining table in the breakfast nook, waiting for his father to give him a ride to community service. His backpack sat at his feet and was packed for the trip to Houston, with spare clothes and his toothbrush as well as his usual necessities: his sketchbook, dart gun, headphones, some pens and pencils, a bag of marbles, a bag of Haribo Happy Cherries gummi candies, his cell phone charger, and the photo of him and his mother. Surprisingly, he had a couple hundred dollars in his pocket, money he earned from selling commissioned sketches at school to classmates and even teachers—comic book characters for students and portraits for faculty. It was a lucrative gig once word of his talent got out. Some days, he could barely keep up with all the commission requests, but he didn't mind. He liked making some cash. As he took the last bite of cereal, his father walked into the kitchen and tossed a pad of pink post-it notes onto the dining table, hitting the bowl and splashing a bit of sugary milk on the table.

"Write Jack's mom's phone number on that," his father said, pouring himself a cup of black coffee at the counter, then taking a sip. It burned his lips. "Oh, hot!"

Luis wiped the bit of milk off the table top with his hand, wiping it onto his jeans. He grabbed a pen from his backpack and scribbled a random, made-up phone number on the pad of paper. "Here's her number."

"Leave it on the table. We gotta go," his father said, blowing on his hot coffee while searching for his keys, patting his pants pockets. "Where are my—"

"Keys?" Luis interjected.

"Yeah, my keys."

"They're by the door." *Where you put them yesterday*, he thought, but didn't say it.

"Put the bowl in the sink and grab your backpack. Hurry up. Claudia is waiting for me."

They walked together down the stairs, some of the concrete steps shifting and squeaky, to the parking lot.

"You and your lady have plans?" Luis said, acting casual, putting one strap of his backpack over his shoulder, distancing himself as hot coffee splashed from his father's mug at each step. Luis had met his father's girl-friend a time or two but didn't know her well enough to call her by name.

"Yup. Going to Fredericksburg for the night. Staying at a bed and break-fast. You know? Romantic shit."

"So, you won't even be around this weekend?"

"Nah. If you're spending that night with a friend, I figured so should I. Right?"

"Oh, right," Luis replied, wondering why his father asked him to write Jack's mother's number on the pad of paper, then left it behind. It was a good thing, since his friend Jack as well as his mother and her cell phone didn't even exist. Luis grinned. "Romantic shit."

"I say shit, you say *stuff*."

"Romantic *stuff*," Luis repeated.

"I'll be back before you get home Sunday. No worries," his father said, unlocking his car, a mid-nineties Honda Accord that had seen better days. All four tires looked dry and slightly deflated. The paint job was sunbleached and chipped. Once a shimmery silver, the jalopy now looked like a shabby beige, covered in dust, tree pollen, and splattered bugs. They got in and closed the creaky doors. "You said Jack's mom would bring you back, right?"

"Yep," Luis said, putting on his seatbelt. His father never wore his seatbelt.

"Then we're good," his father said, starting the car.

It coughed and wheezed to life. He backed out of the parking space and tore off, the car misfiring as they headed to IH-35, dried leaves and twigs that were once trapped under the windshield wipers now brittle shrapnel to the cars behind them. Luis looked out the window as his father turned on the radio to a station playing disco music, a white man singing falsetto like a Black man, an earworm about staying alive in the city. Luis watched the fast-food restaurants as they whizzed by, the smell of fried foods coming through the air vents, and he couldn't help but imagine scarfing down a cheeseburger and fries, followed by a Coke. The daydream was hypnotic, and he could've lived in that dreamworld forever, eating burgers to his heart's content, except that it was rudely interrupted by the rumbling sound of a souped-up car: a hot rod, a muscle car, an eight-barreled behemoth. It zoomed by them without a care for safety or rules of the road.

His father yelped. "You see that?!"

A hot pink, classic sports car with a black vinyl top raced ahead of them, zigzagging between and around all the other cars, pushing its way through traffic. It was out of sight as quickly as it appeared, like a neon UFO disappearing into the distance, except the sound of its burly engine could be heard far away, along with faint car horn honks and beeps. Luis's father was astonished, but Luis wasn't, just mildly amused. He knew the driver of that hot rod, although he wasn't going to admit it to his father.

"Damn! What a car!" his father declared, excited now. "I'd give my left nut to have a car like that again." He whistled a descending note of regret.

Surprised, Luis turned to his father. "*Again?*"

"Yeah, boy! When I was a young man back in Puerto Rico, me and my friends had hot cars like that. Wild colors, too, just like that one. We were hot shit!" He slapped the steering wheel and hooted.

"Really?" Luis noticed a tint of glee he hadn't seen on his father's face before. It was quite shocking to witness.

"I used to cruise around San Juan with your mother. She loved it!"

"My mom?" Luis said, astonished. He had never heard this from his father before, either. He placed his hand over his heart. "*My* mom?"

"Yup. She had these skintight leather pants—"

"No way," Luis demanded. "This is too much!"

His father laughed, overcome with a joyous nostalgia that Luis had never seen before. Luis really wanted to hear more about this incredible secret history with classic cars, driving his mother around Puerto Rico, but figured it wasn't the appropriate time. Maybe when he was reunited with his mother he could mention some of these tantalizing family details to her and see what else she had to say about their time in Puerto Rico many years ago. After five more disco jams, his father exited the highway, slowing the car down. They were getting close to where Luis needed to be, but not close enough to stop just yet.

"Everything all right?" Luis said. In his mind he could see where the Community Service Collective Number One check-in station was, but it was at least a mile away.

"You mind if I drop you off here? I don't want to be late. Claudia is expecting me shortly. You understand, right?"

Luis sighed. "I guess."

"Good kid."

They approached a gas station, one his father had stopped at many times before to buy Luis a stale donut and small carton of chocolate milk for breakfast, and quickly turned in, parking next to a gas pump.

"Need some cash?" his father said, pulling out his wallet.

Luis could see a tiny bit of remorse on his father's face, so he took advantage of the situation. "Yeah, sure."

His father pulled out some bills: several ones, a five, and a twenty. Luis snatched the largest denomination.

"Of course you take the twenty. See you Sunday night."

"All right," Luis said and got out of the car.

He slammed the door, then leaned over to say something, but his father drove away. He watched the jalopy disappear into the distance, then turned and examined the gas station. The parking lot was empty and all the gas pumps were unattended. A faint scent of fried foods hung in the air, and for a moment, Luis considered going inside to buy something to eat, but thought better of it. He decided to keep the twenty for another time—he may need it for an emergency during the trip—and walked around the building to the back, his backpack slung over one shoulder. About a half mile away, past an unkempt pasture surrounded by barbed wire, he could see the line of trees he needed to walk through to get to Community Service Collective Number One. He sighed, then began his journey on foot.

Twenty minutes later, he emerged on the other side of the trees and quickly got in the group to receive his trash bag and picker. A man with a striking resemblance to Anderson from Community Service Collective Number Two—Hank's group—was handing out trash bags and pickers, and not far from him was another man with a striking resemblance to Nelson with a line of juvenile delinquents waiting to check in for their community service. Luis was the last kid to receive his bag and picker.

The manager smirked. His name was Boudreaux, as was indicated by a name tag on his rumpled shirt. "Where were you walking here from?" he said to Luis. He looked out to the trees in the distance, then back.

Luis was taken aback. "Me?"

"Yeah. Saw you walking out of the trees. That's a little . . . different."

"Yep. Different," Luis said, grabbing the picker and trash bag. He then got in line with the other kids, waiting to check in.

Once he reached Chadwick—the assistant manager with the clipboard— he gave his name, which Chadwick checked off on his list, then was told to join the other kids. But he didn't do what he was told. Instead, Luis made his way back into the trees while the other kids meandered to the farm road, the place they were tasked with cleaning up for the past month or so. Neither Boudreaux nor Chadwick ever went after him, and they never asked him why he didn't stay with the other kids while they picked up trash by the road. There really was no recourse if Luis didn't perform his community service in a certain amount of time. He just needed to collect his hours at his own pace; no one was going to force him to do it.

In the trees, the crackle of the dried leaves and twigs beneath his footsteps grew louder as he walked farther from the highway. And just like clockwork, dependable as the sun coming up each morning, Hank stood waiting for him in the same place as the last time—his trash bag in one hand, the picker in the other, and a shit-eating grin on his face.

"Good morning, sunshine," he said to Luis.

Luis scowled. "Nothing good about it. Had to walk all the way over here from the highway."

"From the highway? Why's that?" Hank replied, looking past Luis as if he could see the highway, although he couldn't.

"My dad was late meeting his girlfriend."

"Huh," Hank said. "A tad harsh."

"Yeah, harsh," Luis agreed.

"So, your dad is cool with our road trip, right? Just want to make sure."

"Yeah," Luis said, adjusting his backpack on his shoulder. "He's cool with it."

"And you packed your bag for the trip?"

"Yep."

"Good. Do you know how to get to your mother's house?"

"Well, not really," Luis said, looking sheepish. "But I've got her address."

Hank pshawed. "No problem. Got a map in the glove box. We'll find it."

"The lady you want to see still doesn't know we're coming?"

"Nope. It's gonna be a big surprise."

"That's for sure," Luis said, then snickered.

"What's that supposed to mean?"

"Nothing!" Luis replied.

Hank groaned. "Hogwash." He placed his trash bag under his arm while he swept a hand over his white hair. "Let's fill up our bags, then hit the road."

Luis groaned. "Let's just go. No one will notice."

"We will do nothing of the sort. Might as well get credit for coming all the way down here. I didn't drive all this way to waste precious gas. It's just one bag of trash."

Hank pulled his bag open and began stabbing trash with his picker. Luis did the same.

"My dad and I saw you on the highway. You zoomed past us."

Hank chuckled. "Yeah, the 'Cuda can sure move."

"My dad even said he and his friends had cars like yours when he was a teenager back home."

"Really?" Hank said, jabbing an aluminum can. "Where was his home?"

"San Juan, Puerto Rico."

"Ah, great classic cars in the Caribbean, especially Cuba. I've heard there are some cool car clubs in Puerto Rico. I need to go down there."

"I can barely remember being down there. I was born there, but came here as a kid. I hear it's beautiful."

"That's what they say," Hank said, then stopped in his tracks. He looked down in astonishment. "What the heck?"

Hank and Luis stood over a makeshift campground consisting of empty cans of soda with bullet holes in them, an assortment of pornographic magazines, candy bar wrappers, cigarette butts, playing cards, a few wood crates, and the remnants of a campfire, still smoldering. They both looked around as if they were possibly being watched by the partygoers, then turned their attention back to their scurrilous archeological find. Hank began to bend down to rummage through the remnants of someone's recent fun, but his creaky knees protested, and he quickly thought better of it. They both used their trash pickers to push around and flip over the evidence left behind by a group of disaffected boys, no doubt.

Hank chuckled. "Looks like we've discovered the He-Man Women Hater's Club," Hank said, referring to the boys club in *Our Gang*, popular in movie theaters from the late nineteen-twenties to the early nineteen-forties, then syndicated for television as *The Little Rascals*.

"The what?" Luis said, puzzled. He never watched anything on television that was released before the nineteen-nineties, the earlier era of film entertainment considered prehistoric and pretty much unwatchable. If it wasn't Japanese- or comic book-inspired, then it wasn't worth watching.

"Never mind. Let's just clean this up and we should be done for the day. Whoever did this left a lot." Hank used his picker, impaling empty soda cans and candy wrappers.

Luis picked up a nudie magazine and flipped through it, snickering at the assortment of naked women, all shapes and sizes, many of whom posed in unnatural positions in unnatural locales. "Lots of fuzzy bushes. This one has a machine gun!" he squealed, pointing at the centerfold, which flopped down as he held out the magazine for Hank to see.

"Quit your slacking and get a move on. We gotta hit the road."

"Okay," Luis said, tossing the porno magazine in his trash bag.

After a few minutes, both of their bags were full. They stood up and looked around.

"Go turn your bag in and I'll pick you up in the 'Cuda," Hank said. "You gotta get credit for your service."

"All right, captain," Luis said, lifting a stiff, flat hand to his forehead and saluting.

"Very funny. Don't make me regret taking you with me," Hank said, turning and trudging back to Community Service Collective Number Two, his full bag slung over his shoulder.

"You won't regret it!" Luis called out. Then he headed to Collective Number One.

Once there, Luis tossed his trash bag into a dumpster, then found Boudreaux and Chadwick sitting on the tailgate of Boudreaux's pickup truck, eating donuts and sipping coffee from thermoses, laughing without a care in the world. They seemed surprised to see Luis back so soon.

"That was fast," Boudreaux said, looking to the line of trees, then back at Luis. "Need another trash bag? You've got all day to pick up more trash."

"Nah, I gotta go. Just wanted my hour of credit," Luis said, handing the picker to Chadwick.

"Ok then," Chadwick said.

A rumbling could be heard in the distance, like the sound of a nineteen-fifties movie monster grumbling—lying in wait, ready to leap out and ransack an unsuspecting community of do-gooders—and the sound got louder and louder as the monster approached the camp. Soon enough, the loud beast revealed itself in the parking area for Community Service Collective Number One: Hank's pink hot rod adorned with a black vinyl top.

Boudreaux was astonished. "That's not your dad's car, is it?"

"Nope," Luis called out, slinging his backpack over his shoulder. "But I sure wish it was!"

Luis jogged over to Hank's 'Cuda and hopped in. As Hank drove the muscle car out of the parking area, the 'Cuda's rear tires launched dirt and pebbles like shrapnel toward Boudreaux's pickup truck, the V8 engine roaring as Hank stomped the accelerator and veered onto farm road toward IH-35. Boudreaux and Chadwick shaded their eyes with their hands as Hank and Luis drove away. As the dust lifted, they could see a scrawny arm raised in the air from the passenger side of the car with what appeared to be a middle digit raised even higher.

"Did he just shoot me *the bird*?!" Boudreaux exclaimed.

"Yup, sure seems he did," Chadwick agreed.

"Son of a—"

The 'Cuda quickly disappeared in the distance, a cloud of gray dust and exhaust rising into the cornflower blue sky, the rumble of the engine morphing into the late morning chorus of cicadas.

PART II

8.

*H*ank took the exit from IH-35 to SH-71 like a sharp turn at the Le Mans Grand Prix—a race he used to fantasize about competing in as a young man—and soon he and Luis were on their way east toward Houston, Texas. Luis gripped the passenger door armrest, as it seemed Hank was taking the exit turn a little too fast, which he was. Hank just couldn't help himself. He loved to drive his Barracuda. It made him feel young and alive. He pulled and pushed on the shifter like he wanted to snap it off. When Luis wasn't closing his eyes and praying for his life, he'd watch Hank yank the shifter—a black, shiny sphere like an eight ball from a billiards table sitting atop a chrome shaft that extended down into a black, rubber base that huffed and puffed like a cheap accordion—which made the engine moan and howl. For a brief moment, Luis had a sinking feeling in his gut that he had put his faith in the wrong adult, and the engine roared so loudly that it intimidated the young passenger into silence. Hank noticed Luis gripping the armrest and laughed.

"Once we're on seventy-one and out of town, you'll get used to the noise," he said to Luis, who realized how he must've looked to Hank: scared, feeble, and pathetic. He tried to relax and be cool, even though it was difficult. "We'll stop in Columbus for a pitstop. It's about halfway to Houston. There's a big gas station there. They've got one hundred pumps outside and five-pound bags of gummy bears inside. You won't believe it!"

"Okay! I like gummy bears," Luis called out.

Hank returned a puzzled look, then cupped his right ear, so he could hear Luis better.

"I said, okay!" Luis yelled.

Hank returned a grin and a thumbs up.

As they reached the outskirts of town, the businesses slowly transformed from family-friendly national retailers to surly establishments like saloons, strip clubs, and diners that served pancakes and omelets to truckers twenty-four hours a day. It being late in the morning, most of these places were closed, except for the diners, of course. It wasn't quite time for adult-oriented shenanigans, but there was always time for pancakes. Luis smiled as he gawked at the diners.

"You like pancakes?" Hank said.

One corner of Luis's mouth turned upwards, then he nodded.

"I bet the hotel will have all-you-can-eat pancakes tomorrow morning."

Hank returned his attention to driving while Luis examined the inside of the car. It was apparent that Hank took really good care of it. In a lot of ways, it looked like it was straight off the lot. The seats and door panels were black to match the vinyl top. The dash and carpet on the floor boards were clean and black as night. Dark wood paneling snaked along the center console between the seats and slithered up into the dash between the speedometer and tachometer. In the middle of the dash, a factory-installed AM/FM radio was mounted within a frame of wood paneling. No tape deck, no CD player, no frills, it only had silver station buttons along the bottom. Luis extended his hand to turn it on, but Hank stopped him, putting his meaty hand on top of Luis's bony one.

"I only have a few rules for the radio. You have to find something classic, and it has to be fun. No sad ballads. No songs with curse words. Okay?"

Luis returned a puzzled look.

"Okay," he said, then turned the power knob to the right.

A Beatles song crackled from the speakers in the two doors, a song about the sun coming up after a long, cold, lonely winter. Hank grinned.

"That's a good one," he said, then whistled along to the song's melody. Luis turned the other dial to tune the radio to a different station. "Hey now!"

A variety of songs played through the static: a country song, a Tejano one, a classical tune. But when Luis reached the station he was looking for, a jazzy, hip-hop song bounced through the tinny speakers. The bass of the song rattled the paper-thin woofers. At first, Hank recognized the song, a Lou Reed sample that sounded like a lonely singer's walk on the wild side was about to begin. But once the rapper named Q-Tip began to rap, asking if he could kick it, Hank looked confused.

"What is *this*?" Hank said.

"You said only classics. This is classic! This channel plays old-school rap."

"But where's the singer? You know? The guy with the deep voice."

"There's no singing on this song. Only Q-Tip and Phife Dawg rapping. Like it?"

"Fife *dog*?" Hank said, then listened as the song played for a bit. A smile appeared on his wrinkly face. He snapped his fingers. "I think I like it!"

Luis nodded to the beat of the song as Hank drove. "Can I Kick It?" was a classic rap song, one from the early 1990s, so long ago that Luis assumed Hank must know it. But for a teenager like Luis, all time before he was born was like a jumbled blur, and it didn't matter that Hank was already in his late forties by the time the early 1990s came around, and the rap group A Tribe Called Quest wasn't in his repertoire. He was too busy with his life: working, husbanding, parenting.

"There are jazzy bits in this song. Do you like jazz?" Hank said, reaching for the tuning knob.

Luis shrugged. Once the song was over, Hank turned the dial to another station, one that played bebop jazz. It was John Coltrane's turn to serenade them, playing a melody through his alto sax of all his favorite things. The melody was so familiar, even Luis recognized it.

"I know this song," he said to Hank.

"Coltrane is one of my favorites. The guy could play."

Luis listened for a bit as the scaling notes galloped into his imagination, the hum of the engine underpinning the music. He looked out the window at the various ranch properties—mesmerized by the song—many of the parcels of land surrounded by barbed wire fences, one with a herd of cattle, another property home to a herd of ponies with patterns in their coats like splatter paintings, all the roaming animals nibbling at the wild grass. One property had a large sign with the words "PECANS and more!" on it, with a massive orchard of pecan trees stretching out behind a small shop. Luis contemplated asking Hank to pull the car over so they could buy some pecan treats for the trip—or maybe get some as a gift for his mother. Instead, he asked a question about the car.

"How long have you had this car?" he said, turning toward the driver.

Hank caressed the steering wheel. "I bought it new. I had it special ordered."

"You ordered a *pink* car? That's kinda weird."

"I didn't originally buy it pink. I wanted a navy-blue Barracuda, and that's exactly what I ordered. You see, when I was a young man, I was in the navy. I enlisted so I wouldn't be drafted to go to 'Nam. I thought enlisting would give me more say, but it didn't."

Luis turned back to look out the passenger window while Hank spoke. Now past the pecan farm, he watched as other ranch-style homes whizzed by, one with a large paddock and a lone horse and rider trotting the length of it.

Hank continued. "I got stationed at Seal Beach in California, where there's not much to see or do. In fact, it seemed the base was in a constant state of shutting down. I counted down the days to when I could get out and that day wouldn't come fast enough. But one benefit of getting out of the military was being able to custom order an American car at a discounted price. They sent me a catalog to look at. But I didn't need no catalog. I already knew what I wanted. A navy-blue Plymouth Barracuda with a Can-Am engine. That was the car for me."

Luis turned to Hank. "So you ordered that one?"

"Yup."

"So why is it *pink*?"

"I'll get to that in a sec."

"Okay."

"So, I ordered a navy-blue, Plymouth Barracuda with a Can-Am engine before I got on the flight back home and wrote a check for the down payment. They said I'd get a confirmation of my order in the mail in four to six weeks. That way, I'd know the car was mine. I said fine. They said *have a nice flight*."

Hank paused, then looked out the side window. In the distance, a farm house sat on top of a hill at the end of a long straight gravel driveway. Hank turned his attention back to the road and continued.

"So, I flew back to Texas. When I got home, I waited patiently for that confirmation to come in the mail. I checked that darn mail box every day.

And when it finally came, I was so happy. My folks even said they'd never seen me so happy."

"You really wanted that car, huh?"

"Darn tootin' I did. The letter said that my car was waiting to get loaded on a truck in Amarillo, Texas. The truck would bring my car to the dealership close to my house. That's where I would sign the paperwork and drive it away."

"I bet you were excited."

"Very much so. I couldn't wait. And later that night, I could barely sleep. I lay in bed thinking about all the places I wanted to drive to in my new car and the girls I wanted to take out. All that jazz. But it wasn't meant to be. You see, the next morning while I was eating a bowl of corn flakes, I was listening to the countdown of the popular songs on the radio when a news flash bulletin said a tornado ripped through Amarillo, Texas, and that many businesses had been wiped out. My heart sank."

"Oh no," Luis said, a hand covering his mouth.

"Oh, yes. My worst fear was that something happened to my new car. But in those days, news wasn't on at all times. I had to wait until five o'clock for it come on the TV. Once the news program started, the tornado that ripped through Amarillo was the top story, and right there on the screen was a camera shot of a Plymouth dealership. At the front of the lot was a navy blue Plymouth Barracuda with a telephone pole lying across the hood. I knew it was my car. It just had to be."

"What did you do?"

"I called the eight hundred number for the military program where I bought the car, and they confirmed that yes, it was my car. I was devastated. I asked if there was another navy blue Plymouth Barracuda with a Can-Am engine, and the woman on the phone said that the only other Barracuda with a Can-Am engine that I could have right away was one with a hot pink paint job and a black vinyl roof—this here automobile we're in at this very moment."

"Wow! And you didn't care that it was pink?"

"Nah. I wanted the Can-Am engine. I didn't really care about the color. I thought maybe one day I'd paint it a different color, but never did. This pink hot rod became like . . . my calling card. People knew it was mine. It was one of a kind. Just like me," Hank said, smiling at Luis.

"Cool story," Luis said, then reached for the glove box, opening it with a turn of the chrome knob. Inside, a small stack of papers sat with a color photograph on top. Luis pulled out the photo and examined it. A beautiful woman wearing large, white-framed sunglasses sat on a lawn chair with a little girl sitting on her lap. They both smiled brightly at the camera. The photo felt brittle. Luis showed the photo to Hank. "Is this your wife and daughter?"

Hank nodded.

"What happened to them?"

Hank sighed. "I don't want to talk about it, if that's okay with you."

"I'm sorry," Luis said, placing the photo back in the glove box, then closing it.

Hank cleared his throat. "It's all right, kid. It's just sad, that's all. I'm really just focused on going to Houston and meeting up with Nancy."

Luis looked back out the window, a little embarrassed. "Why do you want to meet Nancy?"

"Well, you ever been in love? I mean, *really* in love?"

Luis turned to Hank and shook his head.

"Then you wouldn't understand," Hank said.

"So, you want to fall in love?"

"Don't you? One day, a woman will look at you—*really* look at you—and you'll know what I'm talking about."

Luis turned his attention back out his window. On the side of the road, among wild grasses dotted with blue and orange flowers, was a parked station wagon with a family standing at the rear of it: a father, a mother, and a teenaged daughter with a canary yellow ribbon in her ponytail, wearing tiny blue shorts and a tie-dye tank top. Out in the grass a few feet away was a little boy—probably her little brother, no older than four or five years old, with his shorts pulled down to his ankles—peeing in the grass. He waved the urine stream back and forth like he was watering the grass, as if it was the most amazing thing he had ever experienced. His family cheered him on, shouting and pumping their fists in the air.

Luis waved at the family as he and Hank drove by. The girl with the yellow ribbon in her hair waved back to him. Luis blushed.

9.

"Time for a pit stop," Hank said. "We need fuel. Gas for the 'Cuda and a sandwich for me. You hungry?"

Luis nodded. "I'm always hungry."

"Figures. You being a teenager and all."

"Sorry. I can't help it." Luis turned sullen.

Hank sighed. "Don't get your tighty-whities in a wad. I'm just pulling your chain."

Hank took the next exit and followed the access road to Buc-ee's. It was the kind of bat-shit megastore that could only be created in the great state of Texas, a massive, one-hundred-pump gas station and extra-large convenience store that catered to the most gluttonous travelers with loose wallets, offering Jesus-themed household knickknacks for faithful housewives, neon and camouflaged-colored hunting accessories for their outdoorsy husbands, and five-pound bags of candy or cheese-flavored chips to go along with sixty-four-ounce fountain Cokes for their children. In short, it was a spectacle. If you wanted to fill your gullet with the largest available size of whatever convenience food was bad for your health, then Buc-ee's was the place for you. If you wanted to gawk at random strangers you'd hope to never, ever see again, critiquing the ridiculousness of their purchasing choices, then Buc-ee's was the place for you. Hank enjoyed both aspects of Buc-ee's: the amazing yet stupefying selection of snacks and bric-a-brac, and the traveling weirdos spending wads of cash on them. He couldn't wait to be among it all and made it a point to stop in a Buc-ee's whenever he was traveling across Texas. He maneuvered the Barracuda through the maze of waiting cars, most of the gas pumps occupied by minivans and pickup trucks, but he drove with purpose. At the end was an unoccupied pump, so he parked next to it. Luis was surprised.

He looked around, then turned to Hank. "Why isn't anyone at this pump?"

Hank thumbed at a red and yellow sign above the pump. "This one's for classic cars. You can buy an additive for older cars with engines that run with what we used to call regular gas."

"Regular?" Luis said, puzzled.

"It's—" Hank began, then sighed. "It's a long story."

Hank got out of the car and fumbled for his wallet, flexing his right knee to loosen it up. He pulled a credit card from the overstuffed taco he called a wallet and mashed buttons on the gas pump, pulling the nozzle out and spilling some gas on his shoes.

"For crying out loud!" he barked. Fuming, he jammed the gas nozzle in the tank and engaged the lock on the lever, so it would pump gasoline without him holding it. He stood with his hands on his hips, shaking his head, as he examined his shoes doused with malodorous gasoline. "Hogwash."

A man from the next pump over gawked at Hank's car, his eyes wide like saucers, a big shit-eating grin on his face, astonished that he was looking at such an eye-catching hot rod. He looked at his own boring minivan with disgust, then looked back at Hank, his eyebrows dancing up and down.

He skipped over to the 'Cuda, leaving his own gas nozzle unattended in his sad van, and whistled a high-pitched note of approval. "Hot damn! That's a hot car!"

The man wore baggy, khaki pants with brown loafers and a matching brown belt, his short-sleeved Hawaiian-style shirt neatly tucked into his starched pants, his stick-thin arms covered with a fuzzy layer of black hair. He couldn't contain his excitement. Hank gazed at the man's vehicle: a late model American minivan. Pearl white. Tinted windows. Boring.

"Yup," Hank replied. He placed his hand on the gas nozzle as if his touch would make the gasoline spew into his car faster. It didn't.

"I'm going to get me a ride like this one of these days," the man said, placing his left hand on the hood of the 'Cuda. This simple action made Hank clinch his free hand into an angry fist.

"Please don't—" Hank started.

The man persisted. "You know, sell the family vehicle and get a mean machine. Cruise for chicks. Burn some rubber!" the man cackled, jiggling his fuzzy arms.

Hank peered at the passenger-side mirror of the minivan. The passenger window was down and he could see the sour puss on the man's wife's face. A couple of kids could be heard bickering over who sat in which chair first inside the van.

"That's the dream," Hank mused.

"What's a sweet ride like this cost?" the man said, knocking the hood of the 'Cuda with his knuckles.

Hank's face burned red. "Sir, please don't touch my car."

The man's grin expanded. "Come on, dude! What's it cost? Twenty grand?"

"Couldn't tell you. I bought it new."

The lock on the lever of the gas nozzle disengaged, the loud click indicating that the tank was full. The man placed both of his hands on the hood of Hank's car. One of the man's feet jabbed the asphalt with excitement.

"Come on! Help a guy out. I live a boring life. Give me something to live for."

"Sir, I'm only going to tell you one more time."

Hank pulled the nozzle out and unconsciously aimed it at the spastic man, as if he was holding a Colt 45 to thwart his advance. He wasn't going to intentionally blast the man, but the nozzle knew nothing of intent or decorum. The last bit of gasoline spewed out of the nozzle's tip and splashed the man's crotch, a stinky, dark brown stain appearing on his starched pants.

"Hey!" he cried out, attempting to wipe his pants, but stopping short, as if he knew the stain would cause his hands to stink. "You . . . squirted me with gas. What the hell?!"

Hank was mortified. Even though the man irritated him to no end—touching his car without permission—he didn't intend for the gasoline to spray the man's pants like that. He looked over to the passenger-side mirror. A blissful smirk appeared on the wife's face as her window slid up.

Hank tried to apologize. "I'm—"

"You!" the thin man called out, pointing at Hank with an angry index finger, the last digit askew from a break long ago. "You ruined my pants!"

"—sorry," Hank continued.

The man scurried back to his minivan and pulled the nozzle out of his vehicle. More gasoline leaked onto his shoes. He slammed the nozzle into its holder on the pump.

"Damn it!" he yelled. "I'm not having a good day!"

He ripped the paper receipt from the front of the gas pump, jumped in the minivan, slammed his door, then drove away, his front wheels screeching.

Hank shrugged, then replaced the nozzle on his pump and ripped off his own receipt. He put it in his taco wallet and got back in his car.

Luis smirked. "What's up with that guy?"

"Who knows. Wound too tight, I think."

Hank pulled away from the gas pump and parked in a bit of shade right next to the store.

"Let's get a snack," he told Luis, who agreed. He picked up his backpack off the floorboard and set it on his lap.

Hank paused. "You can leave that in the car if you want."

Luis shook his head. "I'd rather take it."

Hank shrugged. "Okay."

They walked to the entrance together. The glass doors slid open, the sound of conditioned air swooshing them inside. They were immediately greeted by enthusiastic cashiers.

"Welcome to Buc-ee's!" a chorus of employees called out.

"Howdy," Hank replied. He and Luis walked past them.

Within the store, their noses were greeted by the scents and smells of the various food-vendor kiosks deep inside: barbecue, fresh roasted nuts, popcorn, tacos, and more. It was a scintillating aroma of so many different things to eat. Hank found himself walking alone and turned back to find Luis, who was standing at the endcap of an aisle of T-shirts with ridiculous puns, slogans, and cartoons on them, reading one: a pink T-shirt with a black silhouette of a pig on the front. The pig's body was sectioned with black dotted lines to show the various parts that could be eaten, but instead of actually naming the meat cuts like what you would find at a butcher shop, each section said *Yum!* or *Tasty!* or *Meat Candy!* Luis giggled.

"You like that one?" Hank said.

"It's funny!"

Hank held his hand out. "Give it to me. I'll buy it for you."

"Dude! Really?"

"Yup. And hurry up. I need something to eat."

Luis rifled through a stack of pink T-shirts, finding his size, then handed it to Hank. Luis followed Hank as he lumbered to the brisket sandwich kiosk. There were two lines, and they were twenty to twenty-five people deep. It seemed everyone wanted one of these brisket sandwiches.

Hank sighed. "Hogwash."

"Do you want to find something else?" Luis asked him.

Hank shook his head. "Nope. These are the best sandwiches in the whole world. I get one whenever I'm on the road. You'll be glad we waited."

Luis smirked. "We don't have to *wait.*"

"What's that?" Hank said, leaning closer to Luis. "What did you say? Tell me again?"

Luis whispered in Hank's ear. "I said, we don't have to wait."

"Why's that, Louie? You got some sandwiches in that bag of yours?"

Luis motioned his hand, indicating to Hank to be quieter, as if swatting the volume of his voice down. "Shhh. Something like that."

Luis took his backpack off his shoulder and slowly unzipped it, as if quelling the loud noise the zipper might make if he pulled too fast or too hard. He reached inside and pulled out the bag of marbles he had packed for the trip.

Hank's eyebrows raised like two fighting caterpillars. "What the—"

Luis extended his arm in front of Hank and pushed him back a couple of steps. Once behind him, Luis uncinched the felt bag and released the marbles in front of him. The initial dozen or so glass orbs clicked and clacked on the tile floor, then buzzed with the inertia of gravity and physics. The marbles spilled forward into the two lines of people. A couple of heads swiveled to find out what the buzzing noise was below, but before they could figure it out, a domino effect was initiated. People began to shout and crumple to the floor, some grabbing for other bystanders, who also slipped with marbles underfoot. The lines of waiting people slowly disappeared, replaced by chaos and shouting. Most of the cashiers in the kiosk came out from behind the counter to help the unsuspecting patrons on the floor, some too rotund to stand on their own accord.

Hank was stunned. Luis wasn't surprised by his handiwork. As some of the victims looked their way, frantic eyes looking for the perpetrator, Luis knew to deflect guilt. He raised his hands toward his face in mock despair, then called out, "My marbles! My grandpa gave them to me!"

One young boy, now concerned for Luis's precious marbles despite the resulting chaos, scooped up a couple and even tried handing them back to Luis, which brought a smile to Luis's face. The boy scurried away to try and collect even more marbles.

In the kiosk stood one cashier, shocked at what had just transpired, not sure what to do or if he should help. He appeared to be only sixteen years old, if not younger. Luis hit Hank on his arm with the back of his hand, snapping Hank out of his dumbfounded state.

"You're next," Luis said.

Hank stepped up to the cashier. "Two brisket sandwiches."

"What?" the cashier said.

"I said *two* brisket sandwiches." He held up two fingers for the cashier.

"Okay. Anything else?"

Hank set the pink T-shirt from under his arm on the counter. "This, too."

As if in a trance, the cashier rang up his order, then handed Hank two brisket sandwiches wrapped in foil and sealed with a red and yellow sticker bearing the cartoon face of Buc-ee the Beaver. Hank handed Luis the T-shirt and he quickly shoved it inside his backpack. The two friends walked around the dumbstruck crowd, not sure of what happened or who released the marbles, and quickly headed for the exit before a manager came by to investigate.

As they walked past the cashiers by the exit, one of them called out, "Thanks for visiting Buc-ee's! Come again!"

Hank saluted the cashier while they hustled out the exit and back to the car.

Inside the car Hank and Luis put their seatbelts on.

Hank turned to Luis. "Why'd you do *that?!*"

The engine roared when he cranked the ignition.

"So we wouldn't have to wait. Why else?"

"You knucklehead!" Hank said, then turned to look out the back window. "Someone could've gotten hurt."

"I don't know what you mean. You've been in bar fights."

"Yeah, but I don't start 'em. I only end 'em."

Luis shrugged because he didn't know what else to say.

"Next time—" Hank began, shifting in reverse, "let me know first when you're about to start a ruckus. I like to be prepared."

"Okay," Luis said.

Soon, they were back on the highway—brisket sandwiches in their eager hands—and on their way to Houston.

10.

*N*ot long after finishing their sandwiches, Hank and Luis found themselves on the outskirts of Houston, a sprawling metropolis with over six million people in its metro area, but whose skyline and urban makeup were as generic and nondescript as could be. To Luis, the idea of Houston was tied to only two things: a professional basketball team and his mother. Besides that, Houston was as mysterious to him as the planet Mars. As they moved farther within the city limits, the urban sprawl became denser, and he marveled at the sheer volume of mattress stores, strip clubs, pawn shops, burger joints, and car title loan establishments that whizzed by. Soon enough, Hank startled him with a jab to his thigh.

"I need you to help me find Nancy's place. All right?" he said to Luis.

Luis reached into his pocket for his cell phone, but Hank stopped him.

"Nuh uh," he said, then pointed to the glove box. "There's a pile of maps in there. Get the one for Houston."

Luis scrunched his face in confusion. "But I can get directions easier on my phone. It's 2011, not 1911."

Hank shook his head. "We ain't using your gosh-dern phone. Time to learn how to use a map."

"Uh . . . okay." Luis scowled, then opened the glove box. Inside, he found a variety of random items, along with a stack of paper maps: a metal flask, a flash light, lip balm, mosquito repellent, a bag of butterscotch hard candy, and the Polaroid photo of Hank's deceased wife and daughter. Luis pulled out the photo again and held it up, thinking maybe Hank would want to talk about them now, but he was wrong. Hank snatched the photo out of Luis's hand, then slid it into his shirt pocket. He huffed.

"Rude," Luis said, then shuffled through the stack of maps. "Austin, San Antonio, Dallas, El Paso. Houston!"

He put the other maps back in the glove box and began unfolding the map of Houston. It grew into an unruly thing with dozens of folds and creases that crinkled and crackled as he tried to figure out how to unfold it properly without ripping it.

Hank snickered. "You'll figure it out. It doesn't take rocket science—"

But part of the map ripped.

"Hey!" Hank yelled. "Don't destroy the thing!"

"I've never used one of these before!"

"All right, all right. Don't have a conniption."

"A *what?*" Luis remarked, before finally getting the entire map open and mostly flat, some ends of it still folded or kinked, his hands trying to smooth it out. "How do I find an address on *this?!*"

"Okay, on the back is an index of street names. We're looking for Sweetwater Boulevard. Got that?"

"Sweetwater what?"

"Boulevard. Sweetwater Boulevard."

"Okay," Luis said awkwardly, flipping over the paper map that filled over half of the car's cabin, rubbing on the dash and Hank's arm. He found the index and used his finger to scan the names in the list. He announced several names as he scanned. "Anderson. Cooper. Fennel. Hmmm." It took him a while to find Sweetwater. It tested Hank's patience, but he knew Luis would eventually find it. "Sweetwater Boulevard!"

Hank nodded. "Great! What's the grid letter and number?"

"M4."

"All right, turn the map back over and find M4 in the grid. Letters are on the left and the numbers are on the top. Got it?"

"Yeah," Luis said. He examined the map until he found the coordinates. "Got it!"

"All right, so this is what you're going to do. Right now, we're on I-10 traveling east. That means we're moving to the right on the map. I think we may have missed our exit at 6 to go south, so you'll have to tell me the next major exit to head south. Maybe the loop. You tell me. Use your finger to guide you."

Luis examined the map, his eyes squinting. He had viewed maps on his phone and computer, but never on creased paper in his hands. It was an odd experience for him, as if he was out of his time and in a different era, one without the technology he knew. "I think we need to go down Sam Houston Tollway to Southwest Freeway to get close to M4 on the grid."

Hank smiled. "Got it. Good job, Louie. I don't know what you kids would do if you lost your phones. At least now you know how to use a real map, not that electronic stuff."

"How do you know when to turn?"

"Just follow the signs. Just *follow* the signs. That's all you gotta do. They're everywhere. You just have to look."

"Okay," Luis said, folding the top of the map down so he could see out the windows. A sense of calm overtook him as Hank drove, a feeling as if a sure hand was guiding him through this particular day, something he occasionally felt from his father, though not always. His relationship with his father seemed tenuous at best, at least in Luis's mind. He wasn't sure why; it just was. For once in a very long while, he enjoyed the serenity that came from a confident admiral of this ship, or classic car, to be more precise. That's what Luis noticed most about Hank; his confidence was serene.

Luis felt so good that he pulled his sketchbook and a pencil out of his backpack and began to sketch Hank as he drove, turning sideways to face his elderly driver. Hank noticed with a quick side glance that he was being examined by the young artist. He even got a good look at the drawing, Luis's hand scratching and slashing the pencil across it, an image slowly spreading out like coffee infiltrating a paper filter. Hank didn't say a word. He just let Luis be. Soon, he found the street sign for the Sam Houston Tollway suspended above the highway—bright, grasshopper-green background with iridescent white lettering—which eventually led him to Southwest Parkway. He really didn't need Luis's help finding where they needed to go. He had studied the map in advance over cold cups of black coffee while sitting in the comfort of his La-Z-Boy and had the route memorized, but it was quite enjoyable explaining to Luis how to use a paper map, even if he wasn't as enthusiastic about it as Hank had hoped.

After driving for some time, Hank put on his turn signal, and Luis put his sketchbook and pencil away. As they merged onto the access road, Hank pointed to a building.

"See that," he said, his hand in front of Luis's face, his wrinkly index finger extended. A sign on the front of the building said *Holiday Inn Express*. "That's where we're going to stay tonight. Got us a reservation. Non-smoking. Free breakfast included."

Luis examined the hotel and, as far as he could tell, it seemed like a very nice place to stay the night. Next door sat a steak house called Longhorn Steakhouse. And next to that, an International House of Pancakes. Luis licked his lips, which made Hank laugh.

"Boy, I think your brain and your stomach are both in your gut. Don't blame you, though."

"Hotel looks nice. Food sounds nice, too."

"Maybe after Nancy's, I'll get you something to eat. Sound good?"

"Sounds good."

"We're on a mission now, though."

"Aye aye, captain!" Luis said, saluting Hank.

"Oh, for crying out loud. Stop that!"

At the first intersection, Hank took a quick right and soon they were close to Nancy's neighborhood: Plantation Oaks.

Luis began to unfold the map again. "Do you need my help finding her house?"

Hank put his hand on the paper map, stopping him from unfolding it.

"No, Louie. I know where to go. I studied that map already."

Hank turned into Plantation Oaks and they both noticed the immediate opulence of the neighborhood: large front lawns of deep green St. Augustine grass, tall majestic oak trees with massive canopies, carefully manicured shrubs lining pebblestone walkways connected to driveways in front of two- and three-car garages, two-story mini mansions of brick or limestone. In whichever home Nancy Holzmann resided, it was clear to the two of them that Nancy wasn't hurting. Would she be open to a modest gentleman caller like Hank? It was hard to say. Hank wasn't too concerned with that. In fact, he was miffed. Each time he turned his head he muttered *huh* or *wow* or *oh jeez*. Luis didn't know what to make of Hank's astonishment.

"Is this the right neighborhood?" he asked Hank, who nodded in return. "It has a weird name, but it sure looks nice."

"Got that right," Hank replied. "Nice lawns. I like that."

"Which one is hers?"

"We're getting there. Patience is a virtue."

Another left, then another right, and Hank slowed down to a crawl. "15101, 15103, and 15105. There it is." He stopped the car.

Luis looked out his window to discover the largest house he had seen in the entirety of Plantation Oaks so far. A massive oak tree sat nestled in a sea of St. Augustine grass, the blades of which were freshly cut and watered, the scent permeating the cab of the 'Cuda, as alluring to Hank as the smell of fresh baked goods to children. There was a variety of post-modern statuary littered about the yard, rectangular and triangular stone pieces polished to a gloss, that appeared to protrude up from the grass like evidence of an alien civilization. On the left sat a cedar deck covered by a matching cedar pergola, wrought iron chairs and tables underneath its shade, party streamers of a variety of pastel colors still wrapped around the railing of the deck. A herringbone-patterned walkway of red brick snaked through the yard and around the oak tree, through a matching driveway that curved around the right side of the property, then landed at the front door of the humongous two-story—maybe three-story—mansion. Or, as some people referred to such indistinctly designed gargantuan homes, a McMansion, its features garish and unnecessary. A pearl-white, late model Cadillac convertible—shiny as the day it rolled off the car lot—sat on the driveway in front of the three-car garage.

Luis turned to Hank. "You gonna park in the driveway or on the street?"

Hank cranked the wheel to the right and slowly drove up the driveway, then parked behind the Cadillac. He cut the engine, then sighed.

"Here goes nothing. Coming?"

"Yeah, I'm coming," Luis replied, grabbing his backpack. "I wouldn't miss this for the world."

They got out of the car. Hank's knee seized up again, turning his entire leg into a stiff plank. He winced, then sucked in air through pursed lips and clenched teeth.

"Son of a biscuit!" he cried out, hopping on his good leg. "Sucks getting old."

He lumbered around the car and limped to the front door. Luis followed a few steps behind him. At the door, Hank could see in the reflection of the beveled glass a few of his stray hairs slithering toward the sky. He licked his fingers and smoothed them down in an attempt to look more presentable, less desperate or frantic. Luis winked at him, as he hoped things would go well between Hank and Nancy. Then after taking a deep breath, Hank pushed the doorbell button. It dinged a familiar show tune, maybe *The Sound of Music* or *Oklahoma*, he didn't know it for sure exactly. He was filled with hope.

Soon enough, the door opened and there stood Nancy Holzmann. After all these years, Hank still recognized her; he couldn't miss her, even if he tried. Her face was burned into his brain like a cattle brand. Thin in stature with long, straight silver hair in a ponytail, she was beautiful and regal, standing with her back straight, her smile beaming, her slacks pressed, and her silk blouse shimmering in the midday sunlight. She was well put together, as if several boutique employees had selected her outfit exclusively for her, then styled her for this day. She didn't have a single hair out of place, unlike Hank, who appeared flustered and embarrassed. He wasn't well put together. He was a mess inside, his guts swirling like a tornado of self-doubt and anxiety.

He sucked in his gut, and said, "It's me, Hank." He smiled, then motioned to Luis. "And this is Louie."

"It's *Luis*, not Louie," Luis said.

"Hello there," she said, still smiling, her arm anchored to the door. She cleared her throat, then thumbed over her shoulder. "All the lawn equipment is in the shed in the backyard."

Hank's smile vanished. In fact, his face wilted. "Lawn equipment?"

Luis chuckled. Hank elbowed him.

Embarrassed, Nancy covered her mouth with her left hand. "Oh my! Aren't you the fertilizer guys? The lawn guys said another crew would be out to fertilize the yard today."

"Sorry, we're not the fertilizer guys," Hank said. He placed his hand over his heart to quell the pounding in his chest. "Nancy, it's me. *Hank*. Hank O'Sullivan."

Nancy's left hand dropped from her face as she examined Hank's own wrinkled face. His reddish blond hair was gone. His jowls sagged. His neck folded in a number of weird creases and crevices where manly odors and hairs hid from the light of day. His gut pushed his shirt in weird and bulgy ways. But one thing remained: his steely blue eyes. In them, she saw a boy from her distant past, the one she talked to on the phone the week before but never expected to see in person. In his eyes, she saw a part of herself from a very long time ago.

She covered her mouth again with her left hand. "Hank? From high school?"

He nodded. "In the flesh."

"I don't know what to say. I can't believe it. Really."

He presented both of his hands to her—palms up, like a magician—as if to say, *Ta-da!* "Believe it," he replied.

"Oh. My. God," she mused, then examined him from head to toe, and what looked like horror flickered briefly across her face, as if a long-deceased acquaintance had been reanimated and trudged to her doorstep. "What are you doing here?"

"Why, I came to see you."

"Me?" she replied, placing a hand over her heart.

At that moment, a rowdy leaf blower blared from next door as the lawn crew made its way to the next house in the neighborhood, shouting to each other in Spanish.

Hank nervously swept his hand over his wily hair. "Yup."

"*Me?*" she repeated, a little confused.

"Yup. You said it would be nice to see me. Remember? When we talked on the phone?"

"Oh, right. I didn't mean—"

"Can we come in? Drove a long way to see ya. And it's loud out here."

Nancy hesitated, then looked around as if someone might see them together. Finally, she acquiesced and opened the door. "Of course. Please, come in."

Hank and Luis stepped inside. Nancy closed the door behind them.

— — —

Hank's shoes clacked on the white marble floor. Luis's sneakers squeaked. The foyer of Nancy Holzmann's mini mansion seemed larger than the entirety of

Hank's modest home and Luis's cramped apartment both put together, and then some. A massive white staircase with a streak of beige carpet down the middle spilled from the second floor like a glacier. The ceiling with crown molding and gold air vents seemed three stories tall. Everything was white and beige, edged with gold. The air smelled of pumpkin pie that might have been baked in a plastics manufacturing plant. The clacks and squeaks from Hank and Luis's shoes echoed throughout the space, warning the rest of the house that an invasion of less fortunate people had begun. The breech of the Community Service Collective from Austin, Texas. The infiltration of the uninvited lowlifes. Hank and Luis felt like two country bumpkins in a metropolitan hotel suite. Nancy stopped and turned, presenting the entrance to her home with a slowly sweeping arm like that of a nineteen-seventies game show hostess.

"We had it custom made," she said, taking a gander at the opulence of her home. "It took three months just to select the fixtures."

"Nifty," Hank replied, without a lick of sarcasm.

Luis nodded. "That's cool."

"Follow me this way." And they did.

She led them into a room the size of a basketball court with a number of brown leather couches and chairs floating on a sea of beige carpet. White built-in bookcases lined the right side of the room, filled with what appeared to be sets of encyclopedias or sets of classic literature that had never been cracked open, their spines lettered in gold leaf; white French doors lined the left wall, looking out to a fenced-in yard, doors which also had never been cracked open. The far wall featured a red brick, herringbone-patterned fireplace like the driveway and walkway out front, with a prominent, highly polished white mantel, like the front bumper of a vintage car. There were photos of family vacations, Caribbean beach resorts, and graduations from prestigious colleges framed in gold. Nancy was the center of attention in all of them.

"This is the first reception room," she said.

"The first?" Hank replied. "Fancy."

Nancy counted three fingers, then said, "The first of three on the first floor. There's another reception room upstairs."

"Can't have too many reception rooms," he cracked.

Nancy smiled. "Would you two like a seat?"

Luis didn't hesitate and plopped in the first available leather chair, kicking his legs up on the arm rest. Hank frowned at his young companion, but it didn't affect Luis. He quickly pulled out his sketchbook and began documenting their visit like an astute courtroom sketch artist.

"We'd love to sit down," Hank said, limping around a couch, then finding a spot at the far end. He noticed her watching him limp, a look of concern on her face. "Bum knee. Getting old," he added.

Nancy sat on the opposite end of the couch, wiping imaginary dust off the seat cushion between them. "Aren't we all."

"Except for him," Hank continued, thumbing at Luis, who smiled, then continued sketching the scene. "Nice place you got here. Nice and . . . It's just nice, that's all."

"Thank you, Hank. I work hard to make it a home."

"By yourself?" Hank said.

She gasped, placing a hand over her bosom. "By myself? Oh no. Lord no! I have a maid service. They come out every other day."

"Ah. Makes sense," he said, unconsciously cracking his knuckles, his way of releasing the tension that was twisting his gut into a pretzel. He looked over to Luis, who was scribbling in his sketchbook, probably shading in the sweat marks that were undoubtedly under his arms. "It's a lot of house to keep up with."

"Yes," she began. "Hank?"

"Yup."

"What can I do for you?"

"Pardon?" he replied, then swallowed a gob of spit.

"Why are you here, old friend? Golly, I haven't seen you in . . . How long has it been?"

"It's been a couple of years," he said, smirking.

"Millions of years!" she squawked, then cackled.

They both sat in their uncomfortable silence, broken only by the scribbling of Luis's pencil, which sounded like the scratching of a mouse trapped within house walls. Hank cleared his throat. "Well, you see—"

She smiled. "Yes?"

"Well—"

"Is it a secret?" she said, looking over to Luis, then back to Hank.

He grinned. "Kind of."

"I see," she said, then stood up. "Luis? That is your name, correct?"

Luis stopped doodling, then looked up. "Yes, ma'am. That's my name."

"Would you mind giving Hank and I some privacy for a few minutes? You can hang out in the backyard and dip your feet in the pool. The water is temperature controlled year-round."

Luis looked over to Hank and examined the sheepish look on his face, then he sighed. "Sure, lady. No problem. How do I get there?"

"You can go through these French doors," she said, then stepped to them. She turned the door knob, but it wouldn't open. She fiddled with the knob lock and the dead bolt, eventually getting the door unlocked and opening it. "See the pool over there?"

Luis nodded and stepped outside. Nancy closed it behind him, then sat back down on the couch.

"Okay, we have a bit of privacy. Now, tell me why you're here, old friend."

"Right. You called me old friend before."

"Yes. Like I said, we haven't seen each other in a million years."

"That's true," he said, smoothing a hand over his white hair. He could feel beads of sweat on the top of his head and the back of his neck.

"And I find it unusual that you just appeared at my front door with . . . Is that your *grandson?*"

Hank pshawed. "Nah, he's just a friend."

"A friend?!" she said, aghast. "He's just a boy."

"He's mature for his age. Old soul."

"Ah," she said, then chuckled uncomfortably, as if the privacy they needed was something she would soon regret. "Well—"

"You see," Hank interrupted. "I came here . . . I came *here* to . . . woo you?"

"Excuse me," she said, surprised, both hands now on her bosom. "Say that again."

"I drove all this way to *woo* you. To see if maybe we could start—I don't know—talking again. Dating again."

"Dating? I don't think we ever—" she said, her face scrunching as she searched in her memories from a long, long time ago. "Did *we* date in high school?"

"Pretty sure you were my girl, at least for a bit. Don't you remember going to the prom with me? Senior year?"

"The prom? Are you asking me to think back to—"

"I was even looking in my senior yearbook recently. You signed it, *What a crazy year! Thanks for being the best prom date ever! What a night!! I hope to see you again after graduation. That would be swell. Best, Nancy.* Remember?"

Nancy stared back at Hank. She was completely at a loss for words. She took a deep breath, then said, "And this is the 'after graduation' part?"

"Well—" Hank said, then he looked at the fireplace. He examined the pattern of the bricks, the mortar between the bricks, the shiny white mantel, and the glistening reflections off the gold photo frames. He could hear the draft from the air conditioner coming in through the gold-plated vents in the ceiling. He could hear his pulse inside his ears, thumping louder and louder. "I guess, technically, this is *after* graduation."

"That was a million years ago, right?"

"Yup. You did say that already."

"Are you married? Do you have children?"

Hank hesitated. The conversation steered into unexpected, gloomy territory. "I was married. I had a child. They're both gone now."

Nancy gasped, both hands back over her chest. "Oh Hank! I'm so sorry. I didn't mean to—"

"That's life, as they say."

"No, that's horrible. I'm very sorry. How did they—" she stopped, then took a deep breath, composing herself. "None of my business."

"I'd prefer not to talk about it. Thank you."

"I completely understand. Sorry."

"And you?"

She pointed at her chest. "Me?"

"Married?"

She blew a raspberry from her ruby-colored lips, then said, "Widow. Jimbo passed away a few years ago."

"Oh, well, my condol—"

"No!" she stopped him, then chuckled. "It's fine. All of it. I discovered that I prefer to be by myself. I like my own company. I don't need a husband. Jimbo was kind of a handful!"

"Oh! Well . . . "

"I won't mince words. My marriage was . . . *hard.*"

"Uh huh."

"I don't need a man. Or a woman, for that matter. I'm a modern girl. I'm okay if a woman wants to be with a woman."

"I see," Hank said, smoothing out his shirt, then smoothing his hair again, ready to stand up. His mind drifted to an earlier thought of the two of them enjoying a romantic dinner together—one of several fantasies he imagined the previous week—but the scene was shrinking into the distant void of his mind, like a movie camera pulling away from two actors sitting at a patio table, end credits accompanied by sad music about to roll.

"I guess what I'm trying to say is, I like being single. I'm fine with it. Being single suits me. That's all. No offense!"

He stood up abruptly, shaking the sleep out of his good leg. "None taken!"

She stood, too. "I hope you understand." She attempted to put a hand on his shoulder, but he dodged it.

"Duly noted. Do you mind if I hit the head?"

"Pardon?"

"Can I use the can? It was a long trip, like I said."

"Oh. Of course!" she said, raising her hand in the direction he needed to go. "Yes, through that archway, down the hall, and the second door on the right."

"Thank you," he said, then went to find the bathroom.

He walked through the archway. He limped down the hall. He ducked in the second door on the right.

Hank slammed the door, then leaned his hunched back against it, looked down at the beige tile floor with fuzzy white bathroom rugs dotting it, like large patches of white mold infiltrating a loaf of grocery store bread. He sighed—a long, deep, withering sigh—then limped to the toilet. On top of the toilet tank were a number of framed photos of Nancy, mostly by herself, in a variety of beach vacation scenes. One looked like Acapulco, Mexico; another appeared to be Jamaica or some such Caribbean island, because of the Black fellow holding a frozen cocktail for her as if he was attempting to serve it, and she's insisting he get in her vacation shot like a close friend instead. Frustration consumed Hank. For a moment, he wasn't sure if he could pee. He just stood there with his pecker in his hand, the urine backed up in his stressed bladder. Conflicting thoughts flashed through his mind, including one of his wily grandmother, who shook an indignant finger at him, going on about putting his carrot back in his pants and just going home to his life of solitude, the life he built for himself now that he was alone in a small house that was like a shack compared to Nancy's mansion. He shook his head, knocking her out of his mind. He felt stupid—so, so stupid—and that feeling festered with pent-up frustration. The next thing he knew, he wanted to urinate all over this gaudy vacation display on top of the tank, all of these photos with Nancy front and center, her desire to be flashy, her need to be the center of attention wherever she roamed. He wanted to release an angry stream, but his enlarged prostate had other ideas. Nothing came out, not a single drop. Hank scowled at his privates.

"Hogwash," he said.

Now even more frustrated, he wanted to just disappear and reappear back in Austin. He impulsively zipped up his fly, catching a bit of tender skin in the metal teeth.

Hank yelped. He quickly reversed the zipper and carefully placed his mangled carrot safely back inside his pants, deliberately breathing in through his nose and out his mouth. He sighed, shaking his head, and slowly zipped his pants up.

"Perfect," he mused. "Just perfect."

He left the restroom without flushing or cleaning up. Back in the reception room, Nancy was at the French doors, looking outside and waiting for Luis to come back. Hank wiped his hands together as if removing irritable dust.

Nancy smiled at him. "Feel better?"

"Oh yes! Most definitely."

He stood next to Nancy, hoping she didn't hear him yelp in the bathroom, and looked outside, too.

"I called for Luis," she said, smiling. "I assume that—"

"We're going to go now. Sorry to bother you."

"It's not a bother—"

"Yup. Gonna go now."

"Okay," she said, a look of disappointment on her face, let down that she didn't handle the situation better, more regally, with more tact.

Soon, Luis stepped through the door.

"Ready to go, Louie?" Hank asked him.

Luis examined Hank's grizzled face. The sheepishness was gone, replaced by impatience, irritation, and a tinge of shame. Luis nodded, then put his sketchbook in his backpack. They headed to the front door with Nancy right behind them. Hank opened the door for Luis and they went through, stepping down the red brick steps toward his car. Nancy stood in the doorway watching them walk toward a hot pink muscle car, astonished by that particular color on that particular car.

"Do you sell Mary Kay?" she called out, impetuously. She instantly regretted asking the question. "I mean—"

Hank waved a limp acknowledgment in return, but didn't respond with a single word, like he was dismissing a pesky valet seeking a gratuity at a high-priced restaurant. He and Luis got in the car and closed their doors. He cranked the ignition and the trusty engine roared. He backed the 'Cuda down the driveway, the rear wheels shaving some grass off the edge of the pristine lawn as the rear of the car swung wildly from side to side in reverse.

Luis frantically latched his seat belt. "I guess this means it didn't go well?"

"Just letting you know now. After I take you to your mother's house, I'll be drinking a *lot* of whiskey tonight."

"How much is a lot?" Luis asked him, gripping his door.

"Gallons. No, more than that. *Barrels* of whiskey. I don't know. Enough to make me forget about today."

Soon the 'Cuda was in the street and tearing off, the engine roaring into the distance, the hulking pink car eventually out of Nancy's sight.

She shook her head, puzzled at what had transpired just minutes before, with an old man she hadn't seen in a million years, and the strange teenaged artist the codger claimed was his friend.

She stepped inside her mini mansion and closed the door.

11.

One of Hank's favorite things to do whenever he felt frustrated was to go for a drive. The 'Cuda's boorish engine and irascible stick shift helped him get his mind off things, allowing him to downshift his thoughts into a more basic state: gas, clutch, shift, gas, clutch, and shift. But while driving away from Nancy's house, he realized that driving his car at that moment was a chore, particularly in the traffic in the suburban area right outside of Houston. He was very irritable and yelled at the other drivers, most of whom were just trying to get home to their families.

When a blue minivan cut him off, he exploded. "Learn to drive, numb nuts!" he yelled. He considered tailgating the guy, so he could put a little irrational fear into the terrible driver, but he thought better of it after seeing the look on Luis's face. He felt bad. "Sorry, Louie. I'm just upset, I guess."

"Let's go to the place we're staying and . . . what do you call it when you get to a hotel and they give you your key?"

Hank scratched his scalp. "You mean, check in?"

"Yeah! Let's go check in."

"Sounds good, kid."

Hank gestured to the terrible driver that he was free to go—a simple act of forgiveness in the form of a limp hand wave—and instead downshifted the car, then drove them to the Holiday Inn Express, which wasn't too far away. They arrived in a matter of minutes, and Hank pulled his rowdy pink car into the parking lot, slowing to a crawl with the engine rumbling, to find a better spot toward the back of the property. He wanted to make sure to park as far away from everyone else so his car wouldn't get door dinged by an uncaring traveler, or worse, key-scratched by a pesky teenager. He found a perfect spot in a section of unoccupied parking spaces in front of a hedge row way in the back. He parked the 'Cuda in the middle spot.

"We made it," he said, cutting the engine.

"Looking forward to seeing the room. I've never stayed in a hotel before," Luis replied, then something caught his attention through the windshield. Outside, a person's head rose above the hedge, a head connected to a body wearing a maintenance crew jumpsuit with a Holiday Inn Express patch on the chest. "I think we're being watched."

The maintenance worker—wearing pitch black sunglasses that gave him the appearance of a house fly, with a grubby Astros baseball hat turned backwards on his sweaty head—gawked at Hank's car while chewing a large wad of gum and holding an orange, electric hedge trimmer.

The worker turned his head slightly, without taking his eyes off the car, and called out, "Rudy! Come here and check this out!"

Soon, Rudy—who was wearing the exact same jumpsuit with a similar pair of sunglasses and also a baseball hat turned backwards except emblazoned with a Houston Texans logo—was standing next to the other guy, both grinning at the 'Cuda.

"Daaaamn, Chuy! That's a fly ride!" he exclaimed, then slapped his coworker in the bicep with the back of his hand.

Chuy flinched, turning the hedge trimmer in the opposite direction, so as not to cut Rudy's head off. "Watch out, holmes!"

They both admired the 'Cuda as Hank and Luis got out of the car. Hank closed the door and inserted the key into the lock, ready to lock it. "Good day to you," he said to them.

"Is that a seventy-one?" Chuy asked Hank, smacking his chewing gum within rows of coffee-stained, yellow teeth.

"Seventy," Hank replied, then locked the door.

"Pretty sweet ride, old man," Rudy continued. "Super suh-weet!"

"Yup," Hank said, walking to the trunk. Luis met him back there.

"We'll keep an eye on it for you. Make sure nobody messes with it," Chuy suggested. He elbowed Rudy and they both snickered as if they were privy to a very secret matter.

Hank put the key in the trunk lock, then eyeballed Chuy and Rudy. "I'd rather you leave my car alone."

Chuy's eyes widened. "Oh, okay!" he replied, putting both hands up in mock surrender, masticating his gum. "Somebody's sensitive."

Hank unlocked the trunk, then lifted the hatch. After taking out their bags and closing the trunk, he realized the error in his comment. He knew deep down that he was being rude to the two workers. "Thanks for the offer," he acquiesced. "But you don't have to watch my car. I'm sure it will be fine."

"Whatever," Rudy added glibly. "Who knows what could happen in the middle of the night. Anything really." He shrugged, then gnashed his gum, returning a vague look that suggested equal measures of sarcasm and aloofness. It was hard for Hank to tell.

He and Luis walked toward the hotel, but not before getting one last look back over their shoulders. Chuy turned on his trimmer and shaved an errant branch from the hedge row. Rudy waved at them. "Have a nice stay!" he called out.

The two friends headed for the entrance.

Inside, Hank checked in at the front desk while Luis looked into the continental breakfast room. No one was in there, and the serving stations were empty, everything put away and cleaned earlier that morning for the next day's breakfast. He turned around to find Hank next to him, the receipt for their room in his hand.

"Do you think there will be waffles for breakfast?" Luis asked him.

"It's possible. Is that what you want?"

Luis nodded, his face lit up with excitement. "Sounds really good."

"If they don't have waffles, then I'm sure I can find you some waffles at a Waffle House or some such. Okay?"

Luis's head bobbed enthusiastically.

"Come on, Louie. We're in room 135. Down this hall and at the end, the gal said. Follow me."

Hank limped through the lobby with his duffle bag in hand, his right knee creaking. Luis followed close behind, his backpack slung over one shoulder. They passed a window that overlooked an indoor swimming pool completely devoid of any guests. They walked the full length of the hallway over a speckle-patterned carpet that looked like three cans of primary-colored paint had been dripped onto every inch of the low pile—to the last two rooms, number 135 being on the left. Hank sensed Luis's excitement and turned around to find his young friend vibrating in place to the point that he looked like he might explode. Hank rolled his eyes, then turned back to unlock the door with a key card.

Inside, they entered their suite with a lounge at the front, furnished with a gray sectional couch, a desk and matching chair, and a morning beverage station equipped with a single-pod coffee maker, electric tea kettle, and a small microwave oven. Nestled underneath that was a small refrigerator, which Luis quickly checked for snacks. He was miffed that it was empty.

"Dang it!"

Hank pshawed. "This isn't a fancy hotel. Just normal. You don't get snacks."

Luis continued through a short corridor, past the entrance to the bathroom, to the rear of the hotel room where there were two queen-sized beds, fluffy and white comforters on top of both like mounds of meringue. He tossed his backpack on a chair in the corner and launched on top of the farthest bed, turning on his back and fanning his arms and legs as if carving an angel in powdery snow.

Hank chuckled. "You're acting like you've never been in a hotel before."

Luis propped himself up on two elbows. "That's what I already told you."

"You did?" Hank said, scratching his scalp. "My memory ain't so good anymore."

"Getting old sucks," Luis said, mimicking an old man's voice, possibly Hank's. If it was, then it was a bad impression.

"You got that right," Hank said, stepping over to a dresser, then setting his duffle bag on top. He unzipped it and pulled out a wad of clothes. He considered putting the clothes in the dresser, then changed his mind, shoving the clothes back in the bag. Instead, he pulled out a stainless-steel flask and sat on the other bed. "You got the address to your mother's place?"

Luis nodded. "Yup."

Hank unscrewed the flask and took a swig, wiping his wet lips with a forearm.

Luis wasn't amused. "Can you wait on drinking until after we go to my mom's?"

Hank agreed, then put the flask in his pocket. "Sorry kid. Habit. Did you bring the map in from the car?"

"Nope."

Hank sighed. "Why not?"

"Because we ain't going to use it."

"Then how are we going to find her place?"

Luis smirked. "Modern technology." He reached into his front pocket and pulled out his cell phone. "I got the map stored on my phone."

"We're not using that doodad," Hank huffed. He was serious, too.

Luis patted a spot next to him on the bed. "You showed me how to use the paper one. Let me show you how to use a virtual one. It's cool!"

"If you say so," Hank said, sitting next to Luis. "This better be good."

With his index finger, Luis selected his mother's address from a drop-down menu. A virtual map of her section of Houston appeared on the screen, then the map zoomed in with a variety of pop-up messages asking if Luis wanted directions for walking, driving, or taking a bus. Hank watched, the look on his face turning from apprehension to curiosity to astonishment.

"She even will tell us where to turn, and when to exit."

"*She?!* Your phone is a woman?"

"Yep!"

"Hogwash," Hank replied. "I'll believe it when I see it."

Luis pressed a button on the screen that said *Start.* The phone announced, "You'll arrive at your destination in twenty minutes."

"Holy smokes, Batman!" Hank exclaimed.

"So," Luis started, then sat up. "Can I be your navigator?"

Hank smirked. "Yup."

"Then let's go!" Luis cried out, jumping up.

"Wait!" Hank said, holding an arm out, his face pained. He placed his hand over his lower abdomen.

Luis waited, not sure of the problem. "Yes?"

"I gotta hit the head. Enlarged prostate."

Luis didn't understand what that meant, but he sympathized with his old friend. He jumped back into the fluffy comforter while Hank took a whiz.

"You gotta do what you gotta do," Luis remarked, inhaling the toasty clean scent of the freshly washed bedding, content to relax for a few more minutes.

After what seemed like ten minutes of filling the toilet bowl, Hank zipped up and flushed the toilet. He told Luis he was finally ready to take him to surprise his mother. They left the suite, the door loudly clicking shut behind them.

12.

The sun angled westerly across the afternoon sky as the two friends headed back toward Houston on Southwest Freeway, which would eventually snake its way downtown and get them close enough to Montrose, the neighborhood where Luis's mother lived. When the 'Cuda reached a certain speed—which at this moment was about seventy-five miles per hour—and Hank barely pressed the accelerator with his foot, the engine hummed at a hypnotic decibel, similar to the sound of a waterfall crashing into a pool of water, along with the hum of the air-conditioning. They sat silently, lulled by the drone of the car. Luis sensed Hank was upset about the visit with Nancy, and Hank sensed Luis was nervous about seeing his mother after all these years. Hank knew what it was like to have the idea of someone special occupy every nook and cranny in your mind like an apparition, and after seeing Nancy again many decades beyond their high school graduation, he almost wished he hadn't driven to Houston to surprise her. Almost. It did provide him a modicum of closure, albeit unexpectedly terse and embarrassingly awkward. He didn't feel like talking to Luis, anyway. Besides, he was waiting for Luis's phone to speak to him again and tell him where to exit off Southwest Freeway, so they could get to Montrose. He found he liked being told what to do by the electronic female voice.

He looked at Luis, who was holding his phone in his left hand, his forearm propped on his left knee, while he gazed out the window at the passing urban scenery—fast food restaurants, car dealerships, and shopping malls.

"Is she going to tell us when to exit?" he finally asked Luis.

Luis looked at the screen. "It says we have five miles before we exit. She won't talk until we get closer."

"Ah," Hank said. "Does she have a name?"

Luis shook his head. "It's just my phone. It doesn't have a name."

"Nervous?"

Luis shook his head again.

"It'll be all right," Hank assured him. "What mother doesn't want to see her son?"

Luis shrugged.

"If you don't mind me asking, when was the last time you saw her?"

Luis sighed. "I don't want to talk about it, if that's okay with you."

"I understand," Hank replied. He set his gaze on the highway.

"I'm just kidding. I don't mind talking about it. I'm not a scrooge like you," Luis said.

Hank rolled his eyes. "As the kids say nowadays: whatever!"

Luis continued. "Anyway, the last time I saw her, I was small. Very small. I barely remember much around that time. I don't think I was even two or three years old. At least that's what my dad tells me."

"I see. What do you remember then?"

"I remember leaving the island—"

"The *island?* What island is that?"

"Puerto Rico. That's where my parents are from. I mean, I was born there, but they brought me here when I was small."

"Ah. I see."

"It's all bits and pieces. I remember the *flamboyán* trees along the streets. I remember the airport, a lady standing out front with a chicken in her arms. I remember holding my mother's hand, and she had long red fingernails. I think I remember the flight. Maybe. I don't know," Luis said, then sighed.

His phone interrupted their conversation. The female voice said, "Exit Hazard Street in less than two miles."

"There she is!" Hank blurted. "With that *sexy* robot voice."

"Eww!" Luis replied. "Calm down. It's just my phone."

"Right. Continue with your story. Something about a chicken and maybe you remember the flight."

"Yes, I remember bits and pieces about coming to Texas. My dad says my mom was only around for a short while, and then she left for Houston. That's about all I know."

"That's it?!"

"Yeah," Luis said.

"Sounds fishy to me."

"Tell me about it," Luis said, sighing some more. "My dad won't tell me anything."

"Well," Hank began, then gripped the steering wheel as if steadying himself before speaking out of turn. "I guess . . . this would be a good opportunity to ask your mother about it. Right?"

"I hope so."

"No time like the present, they say."

"Who says that?" Luis said, examining Hank.

"You got me, Louie."

The female voice interrupted again. "Take the exit for Hazard Street now."

Hank growled like a cartoon tiger. "She's sexy! Sorry, kid. Maybe I should get a phone, too."

"You could join the modern world," Luis added.

"And I could listen to her tell me where to go every day."

"That's a little weird."

Once they exited the highway, they turned left at the first intersection, then soon entered the Montrose neighborhood. They passed funky clothing stores, French patisseries, and independent bookstores. They passed a sandwich shop with a dancing man out front—shirtless, wearing skintight tiny shorts, a glistening bald head with pink earbud wires twirling down to a music player attached to his leather belt—with his arms outstretched above his head, a sandwich board spinning in his hands like a helicopter propeller as he danced to a disco anthem. Then there were the houses—old but cute with manicured lawns, which Hank appreciated very much—the lawns, that is, most with rainbow flags displayed proudly for all to see. Luis's phone instructed them to turn right on the next street—the one where his mother supposedly lived—and Luis counted down the street address numbers aloud: 101, 103, and so on. When the phone announced that they had reached their destination, Hank pulled over to the curb and parked.

Luis looked out his window. In the yard, he watched a woman mowing her lawn with an electric lawnmower, the engine sounding more like a hair dryer than lawn-care equipment. She was oblivious to their presence. She wore a tie-dyed T-shirt emblazoned with primary colors and knee-length, army-green cargo shorts, sandals, and a sunhat with a chin strap. She wore large black sunglasses like Jacqueline Kennedy Onassis would've worn, which seemed to cover a third of her dark, sundrenched face. Like the other homes in the neighborhood, hers was cute and tastefully painted, nineteen-twenties-era details painstakingly restored. The lawn and shrubbery were manicured. Luis couldn't help but think that he wouldn't mind living in a house like that, or living in exactly this house, if possible. Hank cut the engine and rested his hand on the back of Luis's headrest.

"Well?" he said to Luis. "What are you gonna do, Louie?"

Luis watched her mow. He noticed her thin body, reminiscent of his own lanky build, her skin tone similar to his, too, closer than his father's. He mulled over Hank's question, then shrugged.

Hank looked out the front window at the houses next door. "This neighborhood reminds me of Hyde Park back in Austin. Or Tarrytown."

"It's nice, right?" Luis replied. He looked at Hank.

Hank nodded. "Yeah, kid. It's nice."

Luis turned back to look at his mother. When she reached a point where she had to turn the mower back the other way and start a new cutting row, she finally looked up. At first, she appeared puzzled that there was a hot pink muscle car parked in front of her house. She released her hands from the mower's handle and placed them on her hips. The hair dryer engine cut off. But a quick bob of her head and a jiggle of her shoulders indicated that a pink car in front of her house wasn't so unusual after all. She strolled toward the car. Luis rolled down his window and waved at his mother. When she got close enough to see Luis more clearly, she stopped in her tracks, one of her hands rising to cover her heart. She slowly removed her sunglasses with her other hand and squinted. It was clear to Luis and Hank that she couldn't believe what she was seeing.

"Luis?" she said, then looked down at her feet, her head swiveling from side to side, a gesture of denial, as if they just might disappear if she looked away long enough. After a moment or two, thinking through excuses and alibies and stories ditched long ago, she realized they weren't going to disappear. She continued to approach the car. When she got close enough, she removed her hat and wiped her sweaty brow with her forearm. "Does your dad know you're here?"

Luis looked up at his mother, her face so familiar yet so different from the photos he possessed, not believing that he was sitting so close to her. It seemed like a dream, or a mirage; it definitely didn't feel real to him. He wasn't quite sure how he felt or what he was doing there. The smell of freshly cut grass and perspiration saturated the air, so he realized this moment was real and not a dream.

Hank cleared his throat. "Yes, his dad knows."

"I see," she replied, "And *you* are?"

"I'm his . . . friend."

She sighed, looking at Luis. "I figured you'd come around someday. Just not today. Do you want to come inside and have a drink?"

Luis nodded.

"I'd love a drink," Hank added.

Luis's mother looked around as if considering the possibility that she was being watched—or punked by one of those prankster-type television shows she enjoyed watching so much but never thought would feature her—then put her sunglasses back on her face as if the coast was clear and there were no cameras around.

"Well, come inside, then." She turned around and walked toward the house, her floppy sun hat bashing against her leg as she sashayed to the front door.

Luis looked at Hank, who unbuckled his seat belt. "Let's go, kid. Maybe she has a Coke to go with my whiskey."

Luis unbuckled, too, and grabbed his backpack. They got out and followed her into the house.

━━ ━━ ━━

Inside, the smell of something delicious was in the air, as though a soup or a roast was simmering in the kitchen. Luis didn't know what to make of it, as he had never inhaled the aroma of a home-cooked meal. On the other hand, Hank was visibly shaken, as he hadn't smelled anything like that since before his wife died. They both stood in the foyer, inhaling the intoxicating scent. Luis's mother called to them from another room. They followed her voice deeper into the house.

They found her in the living room, a large space with high ceilings and exposed rafters, the wooden bookcases lining the walls filled with books, vinyl albums, and framed photos (none of which contained an image of Luis), the musty yet alluring smell of vintage books and records mixing with the scent of whatever was simmering in the kitchen. A massive brown leather sectional couch wrapped around a chunky oak coffee table topped with photo books of local artists and colorful, enameled coasters. A bar separating the living room from the kitchen had four leather-clad barstools with brass legs. Fresh cut flowers like a Fourth of July fireworks display exploded from a vase on the bar. For some reason, Luis had a feeling that his mother didn't decorate the living room. She seemed more at ease when she was out front in the grass; it seemed more probable that she was in charge of the lawn. It was just a hunch he kept to himself.

His mother set her sunglasses on the bar and placed her sunhat on a bar stool. She looked Luis up and down, one corner of her mouth perking up to almost a smile.

"You're grown," she said. "Want some water or tea?"

"I'll take a Coke if you got it," Hank interjected. "Although I'd prefer a whiskey old-fashioned, if you got the fixings."

"I have Coke," she said to Hank, then looked at her son. "Luis?"

"Water is fine, thank you."

"Such a gentleman," she added, then went into the kitchen, grabbed a Coke and a cold bottle of water from the restaurant-style refrigerator, and handed the drinks to them. They thanked her. She sat on a bar stool, then motioned for them to sit down. They found spots on the sectional couch. Hank's Coke hissed when he opened it, sending a foam discharge to the crotch of his pants, which made Luis laugh. She watched both of them fidget on the couch as she shook her head. "I'm at a loss for words, really. Not sure what to say."

"I wanted to find you," Luis said, then looked down at his feet. He was worried.

"Well, you found me. My wife will be shocked by your company."

"Wife?" Luis said, puzzled.

"Your dad didn't tell you?" she started, then pshawed, shaking her head. "Figures."

"I don't mind that you're married . . . " Luis said, looking up at his mother. He realized in this moment—looking in the face of a woman who looked eerily similar to himself—that there was probably a lot more his father hadn't told him, very personal and sometimes difficult things to talk about or comprehend. "Married to another woman."

She smiled. "How kind of you. Thank you, Luis."

"You're welcome."

At this point, Hank felt he was intruding during this awkward family reunion. He decided it was time to give them some space.

"I can go out back, if you'd like. Don't mean to intrude," he said, standing up and exposing the soiled spot on the crotch of his pants. "Maybe the sun will dry this stain."

"Go through the kitchen and through the dining room until you find some French doors. They lead to the back patio."

"Perfect," he said. "And if you don't mind me asking, what's your name? I don't want to just call you Louie's mom."

"Carmen," she replied, then stuck out her hand for a shake. "My name is Carmen."

Hank shook it. "Nice to meet you, Carmen. My name is Hank," he said. "I'm going to go out back, now, and drink away my sorrows." He smiled at her, tapped the flask lodged in his front pocket with the tip of a finger, then left the living room with his Coke in hand. The French doors could be heard opening—mini blinds rattling—then closing.

"Do you know what I'm cooking for dinner?" she said, then thumbed over her shoulder toward the kitchen. "*Pollo Guisado*. Does your father ever make it for you?"

Luis shook his head. "He mostly makes Hamburger Helper. Or cooks a frozen pizza."

"Oh, god," she mused. "How awful."

Luis chuckled. "It's not that bad. I'm used to it."

"That's good. Better than nothing, right?"

Luis agreed.

She interlaced her fingers, then sat her hands in her lap. "Luis, what are you doing here?"

He looked at his feet again, not sure how to start, even though he knew exactly what he wanted to say. He had been reciting this speech all week in front of a variety of mirrors, exactly what he wanted to tell her and how he wanted to say it, but his words failed him. He stuttered, then blew a raspberry with his lips, an uncomfortable gesture that was obvious to Carmen. Luis inhaled deeply, then found the courage to say something. Anything.

"I want to live with you for a while."

She returned a blank stare.

"If that's okay," he added.

"Luis—" she began, then stopped. She looked up to the rafters as if staring at a timeline that began in Puerto Rico some seventeen years ago and ended in downtown Houston, Texas. In between, there were so many events, so many moments, and they all led to her estranged son sitting in her living room asking if he could live with her. She didn't want to hurt his feelings, even though she knew she would. She acquiesced. "I'd have to talk to my wife about it. But I really don't know. I can't make any promises."

"That's okay. Talk to her first. That's cool."

"Why do you want to live here with me?"

Luis thought of his long speech, the one that said everything, the one with years of feelings and frustration and angst. But all he said was, "I want to get to know you. I need a change."

His mother's face twisted into a question mark. "Is your father mean to you?"

"No!" Luis blurted. "No, he's not mean. He's just . . . preoccupied."

This proclamation grabbed Carmen's attention and pulled her up from her stool. She walked around the coffee table and sat next to Luis.

"With a woman?" she asked him.

"Yes. Claudia. His girlfriend."

Carmen nodded an acknowledgment, as if that was all Luis needed to say to her. She knew. She just did.

"I see," she said. "I'm not surprised. Your father has a habit of blocking out the rest of the world when he's . . . preoccupied with a woman."

Luis set his backpack in his lap and stared at it. In this moment, he realized it was a lot more beat up and shabby than he had been aware of, many of its stitches fraying, the black zipper with threads coming through it like sprouts stuck between dirty teeth.

Carmen also looked at the backpack. "What do you have in there?"

"My stuff. My drawings."

"Drawings?! Can you show me?"

A smile slid across Luis's face. "Yeah."

He opened the bag and pulled out his sketchbook. He quickly flipped through it, too fast for Carmen to see anything. So, she held out her hand for the sketchbook. Luis proudly gave it to her. She flipped to the first page and examined it, really absorbed every line and gradation on the page. Then slowly turned to the next page, also examining it carefully. Her eyes widened at the level of skill he possessed.

"Luis, you're *very* talented!"

He blushed. "Thank you."

She flipped to a few more pages—she studied and considered each one carefully—then closed the sketchbook and handed it back to him. "I understand your frustration with your father. You're growing into an adult. You probably want to see the world. You probably want to know where your place is in it."

"I guess," he said, returning his sketchbook to his backpack, then zipping it shut. "But I want to get to know you, too."

"Okay," she said, then sighed. "I understand that, too. I am your—" She hesitated to say the word *mother*, as if it was just too weird to say out loud, as if she never thought she would ever say it out loud to anyone. "Well, I certainly understand you wanting to know your family, who we are and how it relates to you. There were times when I felt my family didn't understand me. I felt like I didn't fit in."

"Really?" he said, looking at her face, looking deep into her brown eyes. He saw his face in the reflection, looking back at himself.

"Oh, yeah. My folks *never* understood me. They didn't want to admit they had a gay daughter. Catholics think being gay is a sin. Maybe the worst sin. My parents felt I was choosing the wrong path. But I didn't choose to be gay."

"I know," he said. She placed her hands on his, patted them, then held them for a few seconds. "So, you'll talk to your wife then?"

She hesitated, then took her hands back. One of the corners of her mouth perked up. "Of course I will."

"Great!" he replied, relieved. "That would be awesome."

"I bet there's a lot you want to talk about, a lot you want to know."

"So much!"

She smiled, then placed her hand on her knees and began patting them impatiently. "Where's your friend?" she said, looking around as if he might be hiding behind the couch. "The old man?"

"Uh. Out back. Remember?"

"Right. Tell you what," she began, patting his hands some more, then standing up. "Are you two staying in Houston?"

"Yeah, we have a hotel room, but we were going to leave tomorrow afternoon to go back home."

"Ah. Then why don't you come back tomorrow around lunch time. That will give me some time to talk to my wife about it. Her name is Nina."

"Nina," Luis repeated, as if trying on the name to see if it fit in his life. "*Nina*."

"Yep. Now, let's grab your friend and I'll see you two tomorrow. How's that?"

Luis stood up and quickly hugged her. He was so quick to swoop in that it caught her off guard. She gently patted his back as he hugged her tightly. She inhaled his presence. He released her, then walked through the kitchen to the French doors. Carmen followed him.

Outside, they found Hank sitting in a wicker patio chair, guzzling the last of the whiskey from his flask. When the last drop slipped into his gaping mouth, he wiped it with his forearm, then realized he was being watched.

"Sorry!" he blurted, then burped, a rough intoxicated belch. "I can't find my napkin."

Luis's face flushed. Carmen stared.

"It must be the drinking hour," she said sarcastically.

"Should've started much earlier today!" Hank replied, stumbling to his feet.

"Are you okay to drive?" she asked him.

Hank pshawed. "I'm fine. No problem-o."

"Just don't want you driving if you've had too much to—"

"Too *much?* Hogwash," Hank said. He turned to Luis. "You all right, Louie?"

Luis nodded.

"Good. Then let's go."

"You'll be back tomorrow around lunch time?" Carmen said.

Hank looked to Luis for a response. He smiled back. So, Hank said, "Yes, ma'am. We'll be back tomorrow."

"Good," she said. She leaned in to give Luis a hug, but Hank hugged her instead, which surprised her. "Oh! Okay then." She put an arm around Hank and leaned in with one shoulder, the smell of alcohol thick in the air around him.

"Shoulder hug, huh?" he said, pulling back. "Okay then."

Hank pushed open the French doors and barreled through. Luis shrugged, then followed him with Carmen close behind. They walked through the house back to the foyer.

Hank turned to Luis. "You got your back—"

Luis showed one of the straps was over his shoulder.

Hank pshawed again—his drunken, nervous tick. "Right. Let's go. See you tomorrow, *madre.*"

"Goodbye, Hank," she said, then turned to Luis. "See you tomorrow."

Luis smiled, then followed Hank out the door. Carmen watched them walk to the pink 'Cuda and get in. The engine roared when it started, and a plume of dark exhaust shot out the muffler. The car idled for a minute, then slowly pulled away, the sound of the clutch grinding as it went out of sight.

Carmen hesitated, staring down the now empty street. "*Dios mío,*" she sighed, then closed the door.

13.

*L*uis has a peculiar riddle he likes to ponder. What is the earliest memory of his childhood he can recall with clarity? He plays this game often, particularly when he is bored. If he's sitting in class at school and can't draw in his sketchbook, then he will riffle through his memories of his childhood until he uncovers snippets of the earliest memory. Once he believes he's found it, then he continues to mine for an even earlier one. When recalling memories from his childhood, Luis can remember many special moments.

He remembers the first girl he kissed in the fifth grade. Her name was Cathy with a "C," as she told everyone including Luis, right before he planted his slobbery lips on hers. The feeling he felt when he kissed her was queasiness rather than sexual delight, but there was a yearning within the queasiness that he didn't understand at such a young age. Her breath smelled of tuna fish salad, salty chips, and hard candy, an unusual combination that would seem sickly, but to Luis was delicious. Luis and Cathy would only share this one perfect moment together; they never kissed or even touched each other again, although she occasionally smiled at Luis through their middle school years. This was a remarkable memory, but definitely not his earliest one.

Digging further, he remembers when he successfully rode a bicycle for the first time—by himself—the summer before the second grade, when his father let go of the back of the seat. Luis pedaled unassisted through the apartment's empty parking lot with his dad cheering him to go farther and farther, and he felt the adrenaline rush of achieving this monumental goal. All of his friends had been bragging on the playground at school the previous spring about learning to ride their bikes on their own. At this moment, he would join the cool kids club, a worthy memory indeed.

With even more digging, he remembers making his first goal in little league soccer: his maneuvering through the other team's defenders, their goalie diving through the air for the ball, and the net undulating when the ball sailed into it, past the goalie's outstretched arms, his father cheering with the other parents on the sideline. Before this, he was an awkward, second-string defender on his own team who tripped and fell down more often than he kicked the ball downfield. After this, he would ascend to star player on his team and acquire the nickname of "Big Foot," as he was a short player with a mighty kick, an unlikely tyke with blistering offensive moves.

When each of these memories pops up in his mind, he attempts to rewind the memory film earlier in time. There are so many flashes of moments: holiday mornings filled with gifts, various costumes for different Halloweens, and Thanksgiving dinners of deli turkey sandwiches and Lays potato chips with just him and his father. First encounters with animals. First tastes of desserts. First rides at amusement parks.

But the one memory that he feels is the earliest he can recall is of his second or third birthday. He's not sure which one it is, as he doesn't have any photographic evidence of this day. But there it is in his memory bank—the chocolate birthday cake with yellow candles and pink flowers at their base, brightly colored helium balloons tied to the chair backs around the dining table, cans of Coke on a plastic birthday celebration tablecloth, and "Everybody" by the Backstreet Boys playing on a tiny boom box, the CD scratching the laser lens as the song played. Mostly, it is the birthday cake that is the center of his attention. It is the anchor of this memory: his ultimate, mental treasure. He remembers his mother cutting him a big slice, her smile while he watches her, her nails of rosy red, her shiny black hair, setting the plate in front of him, people chatting and singing along to the Backstreet Boys, and the taste of that special slice of birthday cake.

The flavor of it in his mouth.

The icing he licks off his fingers.

The second bite more delicious than the first.

He eats the cake like he's starving—like he hasn't eaten in weeks—and he beams with delight when his little friends and all of his family sing "Happy Birthday," and he is so ecstatic that he runs outside and down the Puerto

Rican street of pastel-colored, cinderblock homes with silver tin roofs attached by rusty nails. Other kids run the streets with him, cheering and laughing. He's ebullient. His feet seem to hover off the ground.

When he rewinds this memory—to study it again with the fastidiousness of an archaeologist—there it is: the chocolate cake. The scrumptious birthday dessert with yellow candles and edible pink flowers of icing at the base, cans of Coke on a table, but without a tablecloth, no balloons, "Livin' la Vida Loca" by Ricky Martin playing instead of the Backstreet Boys earworm, fewer family members singing "Happy Birthday." Is Berto arguing with an old man? Who is the old man with the white bristle-broom mustache, balding pate with white skirt of hair, wearing a maroon *guayabera* shirt with ornate silver stitching on the front?

But that cake.

It's divine.

He remembers his mother cutting him a huge slice, she's frowning as he watches her set the slice on his plate, her nails still ruby red, her hair shiny and curly from the humidity and black as night, his father standing at the far end of the table. No one is singing with Ricky Martin even though *su vida es loca.*

Again, the flavor of the cake in his mouth.

The icing he licks off his fingers.

The second bite even better than the first.

He eats the cake like he's starving—like he's never enjoyed sumptuous food before, ever—and he beams when his parents sing him "Happy Birthday," even though they're frowning while they sing, and he is so ecstatic that he runs outside, to the pool at the center of his apartment complex. He wants to jump in the water, but his mother yells at him not to.

He really, really wants to jump in the water, even though he knows he can't swim. When did he learn how to swim? He doesn't remember yet.

The apartment complex confuses Luis, so this must be a different birthday party, since it's not in Puerto Rico. They didn't live in an apartment complex then, he is told. They lived with his mother's parents in a small house on the outskirts of San Juan. Their street—lined with *flamboyán* trees, the canopies red and pink explosions above gray and tan trunks—is at the top of the hill.

An old man begs Luis to pull his finger and bellows when he farts. His laugh is infectious; Luis can't help but laugh with him. *Abue?*

And that chocolate cake.

His mother asks him what he wants for his birthday.

Mamá!, he says.

Me? she says.

He nods emphatically.

She serves him a huge slice, smiling this time, her teeth like pearls, her eyes gleaming with pride, and a love so deep it's incomprehensible to others.

He eats the cake like he's starving—like he'll never get the chance to eat it ever again—and he beams when people sing him "Happy Birthday," and is so ecstatic that he runs outside and down the street of pastel-colored, cinderblock homes with silver tin roofs and yards of gravel. Other kids run the streets with him, cheering and laughing. He's ecstatic. They weave around cars parked in the street, some with tireless, rusty wheels sitting on cinder blocks, a palm tree swaying in the humid breeze, a line of red *flamboyán* trees exploding on the hilltop. The old man farts and laughs, his teeth like clams.

Luis wants another slice of cake.

He runs home.

His mother and father are arguing inside.

He remembers his mother cutting him a huge slice, she's frowning, her nails a deep, cherry red, her hair shiny and black, his father standing at the far end of the table with his arms crossed, scowling, no one is singing with Ricky Martin because they all hate Ricky Martin.

Again, the flavor of the cake in his mouth.

The icing he licks off his fingers.

The second bite as good as the first, if not better.

He devours the cake, smiles when his parents sing him "Happy Birthday," and is so happy with himself that he runs outside, to the pool at the center of his apartment complex, the water yellow and low. He runs around the perimeter of the pool, then runs around again when his mother chases him. She's scared he'll fall in and drown in the dreary water because he can't swim.

I swim, he says. *I swim.*

She catches him and plops on a lounge chair.

No swim, she says.

Old man toots, he says.

Grandpa can't make it this time, she says.

Abue, he says. *Toots.*

Luis breaks free from his mother. He runs around the pool again, waving his arms above his head, while another kid on a balcony, three stories up, waves back. A palm tree sways in the humid Texas breeze.

This is the game Luis plays with himself.

When he tries to think farther back, he finds nothing.

But that chocolate cake, he can still taste it.

14.

hen Hank and Luis arrived back at the Holiday Inn Express, the late afternoon sun dove behind the hazy horizon, leaving a thick pink and orange blanket of twilight in its place below a gradually graying sky. Hank drove to the rear of the parking lot, back to the empty spaces in front of the hedgerow, the parking space from earlier still empty.

"The parking gods are smiling down on us!" he bragged drunkenly, as he pulled into the spot.

Luis offered a thumbs up. "What do we do now?"

"I'm hungry. That whiskey kick-started my appetite. What about you?"

"I'm always hungry."

"Attaboy! That's the spirit! Let's go find some grub," Hank said, killing the engine and getting out of the car. The smell of gasoline clung to the scent of freshly cut shrubbery.

Luis followed Hank as he walked through the parking lot toward the entrance of the hotel. "Where should we go?" he asked him. As they walked, a bright sign with neon trim rose above the hotel in the distance. The sign said: Longhorn Steakhouse.

"You like steak?" Hank said.

"Sure," Luis agreed.

"My kind of guy. Saddle up!" Hank said, putting his arm around Luis. "Maybe I'll buy you a cocktail, too."

"I'm not old enough to drink alcohol."

"Oh yeah? Says *who*?"

"The law."

Hank spat on the ground. "Hogwash."

Inside the steakhouse they were immediately greeted by two blonde young women behind a host stand, neither of them much older than Luis, both with their hair in shabby ponytails, both wearing starched, tightly fitting button-down shirts and tight black slacks. The air was cool and thick with the smell of grilled meats and fried potatoes and the sound of lazy chatter. When Luis noticed the hostesses, his face flushed and he looked away. Hank elbowed him and clicked his tongue. He took a quick gander around the restaurant as if looking for the finest seating location. One of the hostesses—the one with the name tag that said "Heather"—wiped laminated menu pages with a damp cloth. Her colleague chewed a wad of mint gum, Luis getting a whiff of its scent. Her name tag wasn't visible, as it hung sideways from her busty chest, her shirt so tight that Hank could make out the pattern of the lace on her black brassiere through the thin white material. He tried not to stare at her chest, but he found it difficult not to.

"Table for two?" Heather asked Hank, who seemed disinterested in her question.

"Can we sit at the bar?" he said, looking for the watering hole of beer and liquor somewhere past the sea of dining tables dotted with white linen napkins folded like origami.

"Seat yourself, then," she replied. Her hosting partner turned around and rose on her toes, maybe looking to the bar, maybe looking for an exit plan.

"Come on, Louie," Hank ordered Luis. They left Heather and her colleague behind.

Hank wandered through the maze of tables and tea refilling stations, past the bored wait staff and a listless bussing crew. He quickly found the bar and saddled up on a stool. Luis sat next to him. They were alone, and Hank liked it that way. Soon enough, the bartender appeared at the far end, letting himself behind the bar by raising a side section.

"Good evening, gentleman. What can I start you with?" he asked them, tossing two square napkins on the bar like a casino dealer laying out cards. "Menus, too?"

"Whiskey old-fashioned," Hank ordered. "Two menus."

"Old-fashioned is my specialty," the bartender replied. He hooked both thumbs around his leather apron strap, rocking back and forth on his heels as if he was mighty proud of his cocktail recipe.

"I couldn't be happier—" Hank began, then squinted his eyes to read the bartender's name tag. "Alan."

"And for you?" Alan asked Luis.

"Give him the same," Hank blurted.

But Luis waved him off. "Do you have any root beer?"

Alan smiled. "We make our own. Wanna try it?"

Luis nodded. Alan repeated their order aloud for accuracy, dropped two menus on the bar, then got to work.

"Not a drinker, I assume?" Hank said softly, leaning toward Luis.

"Nah."

"Okay. Got it. So, things went all right with your mother?"

"Yeah. She wants to talk to her wife about me, and asked that we go back tomorrow around lunch time. I have so much I want to ask her."

"Sounds like a plan," Hank said, pounding the bar with a fist. "Your visit was much more successful than mine. Mine—that was a total disaster. I guess I'll just die *alone*."

Hank propped up his menu and opened it, pretending to read the items. Luis could see that Hank wasn't reading the menu, but staring into nothingness. He desperately wanted to say something to Hank to comfort him, but he didn't know how. Again, his words failed him. Soon enough he didn't have to say anything, because Alan returned. He set a root beer in front of Luis. Its sweet and spicy aroma bubbled out from its foamy head.

"Try that, my man!" Alan said.

Luis took a sip and grinned. "That's good!"

"You bet it is," Alan replied, then set the items he needed on the bar to create his cocktail masterpiece. "Now, time for a proper whiskey old-fashioned."

He poured the perfect amount of whiskey and bitters into the mixing glass, along with a tablespoon of simple syrup—the clear liquid from the jar. He dropped two cherries into the lowball glass, the color of the berries and syrup such a deep burgundy that they appeared to be black holes at the bottom of the glass. Alan pulled a chrome peeler from an apron pocket and shaved off a thin slice of orange rind. He twisted the rind above the ice cube—a mist of orange essence coating the ice—then wiped the rim of the glass with the peel before dropping it inside. A Cheshire Cat grin appeared on his face as he observed Hank watching him stir the whiskey concoction with a long metal spoon, then poured it into the lowball glass. He set the cocktail on a coaster in front of Hank, then quickly wiped the bar top with a damp white towel.

"What do you think?" he asked Hank, but he already knew the answer.

Hank raised the glass to his quivering lips, then took a sip. He was overcome with joy. "Phenomenal!"

"Excellent! What can I get you two to eat?"

"I'll have your best steak. Medium rare. Loaded potato. And whatever he wants," Hank said, thumbing to Luis.

"Burger and fries," Luis added.

"You got it. I'll go put this order in and be right back."

"This place is great," Hank mused, then took another sip from his drink, a much larger one this time. "That goes down easy. How's the root beer?"

Luis took a sip. "It's great!"

"That's good, Louie. That's good."

Just then, they were abruptly joined on either side by two men—one of them slapping Hank on the back, the other grabbing Luis by the back of the neck and playfully shaking him—which surprised Hank and Luis. Some of Hank's cocktail spilled on the bar.

"Hey!" he called out. "What in the blazes do you think you're doing?!"

He turned to discover Chuy the maintenance man sitting next to him, still wearing his black, house fly sunglasses, even though it was night time, as well as still wearing his dusty work uniform. He smelled of freshly cut grass, tobacco, and musky sweat. He lifted the sunglasses and set them on top of his oil slick of hair. "If it isn't the old man with the shit-hot car."

Hank pshawed. "If it isn't Tweedledee *and* Tweedledum," he said, then slurped the rest of his cocktail before Chuy had a chance to spill anymore, and slid the empty glass forward so Alan could refill it with another of his magical concoctions.

Rudy, who was sitting on the other side of Luis and leaning on the bar with his right elbow, scoffed. "Is that how you talk to the brave men who are keeping an eye on your precious vehicle?"

Luis instinctively slid his backpack down from his lap to the top of his feet, nestled in a safe spot between his shins. He recoiled from Rudy's malodorous breath, which hinted of a daily diet of chewing tobacco, stale beer, and bologna sandwiches. If words had easily escaped Luis before, then they surely had taken a permanent vacation at this moment. He couldn't tell if Chuy and Rudy were being jovial or snarky. The line of discernment was razor thin. But he wasn't sure he wanted to find out, either. Hank, on the other hand, didn't care which side of the line these two resided on. All he wanted was to be left alone.

Hank said, "As I told you earlier, I didn't ask you to watch my car. I'd prefer you just leave it be." At this point, Alan reappeared in front of Hank and asked him if he wanted another whiskey old-fashioned. "Why, yes, my good man."

"Put a couple of brewskies for us on his tab," Chuy added, slapping Hank on the back. "The tall boys on special will be just fine."

Now, there was almost nothing more insulting to Hank than someone adding their drinks to his tab when he didn't want to pay for them, but he could see that Luis looked uncomfortable, and he didn't want there to be any trouble while they were away from home. So, Hank grudgingly agreed.

"That okay with you?" Alan asked Hank.

Hank nodded. "Yup."

"Attaboy!" Chuy called out, putting both of his hands on Hank's shoulders and giving him a squeeze. Hank brushed off his dirty hands.

Alan pulled two tall boys of beer from the cooler and handed them to Chuy and Rudy. The two maintenance workers cackled, then left to find a table.

"Sorry about that," Alan lamented.

"Take those beers off my tab," Hank demanded. "They can buy their own friggin' beers."

"Uh, okay," Alan said, then went back to the computer terminal, rubbing his temples with frustration.

"Are they messing with us?" Luis said, taking a sip from his root beer. "It seems like they are."

"Don't know. Don't care. Just want to have a nice dinner, then go back to the hotel. What about you?"

"Sounds good to me."

"Then it's done."

Alan appeared in front of them with their food: a steak with baked potato for Hank and a burger with fries for Luis. Hank tapped the rim of his glass with a fingertip, indicating he wanted another.

"Aye aye captain," Alan said, then went about his business making another whiskey old-fashioned. "And sorry about adding those tall boys to your tab."

"No problem," Hank said. "Thanks for rectifying the situation."

Hank and Luis went about their business devouring their dinners, quietly shoveling food into their mouths, when a tall man in a tan suit sat on the stool to Hank's left, bumping Hank accidently with his elbow, which caused Hank to drop his steak knife on his plate, splattering his shirt with bits of food and steak sauce. The man immediately noticed his faux pas and placed his hand on Hank's arm.

"Oh, man. So sorry! Let me buy you a drink. It was an accident. One hundred percent my fault," the man insisted. He watched Hank attempt to clean the front of his shirt with his linen napkin, then motioned to Alan. "Bring this man another of whatever he's having."

"I was already making him a cocktail," Alan replied, stirring the concoction.

"Then put it on my tab and his next one, too," he said, then turned to Hank, putting out his hand for a shake. "My name is Brad. Down here on business from Dallas. Staying at the hotel next door. What's your name?"

Hank gave him a firm shake. "I'm Hank. And this is Louie."

Hank thumbed to Luis, who waved at Brad. Luis mumbled an acknowledgment, as his mouth was full of fries. He wanted to correct Hank again and tell Brad his name was really Luis, not Louie, but he knew it was futile.

After releasing Hank's firm grip, Brad shook his hand out. "What a grip! Is that your grandson?"

"Nope," Hank replied.

Brad waited for Hank to give more information about Luis, but he didn't. He looked at what they were eating for dinner.

"That sure looks good. I'll take a steak, too," he ordered Alan. "And a light beer. Whatever is cold."

Alan finished Hank's cocktail and set it in front of him on a fresh coaster, quickly poured Brad a light beer in a pint glass—its head a thin sliver of fizz—and set it on the bar, then moved back to the terminal. Brad leaned on the bar with his elbows as he looked up to the many television screens suspended above the wall of liquor bottles. His heavy application of cologne from earlier in the day still hovered around him like a dust cloud, its pungent aroma offending Hank's nostrils. Brad reached into his inside coat pocket and pulled out a cell phone that seemed to Hank to be the size of a dinner tray, then set it on the bar, along with a few business cards. On the television screens was the visage of a coach, his face larger than life, with looks of concern and disgust in equal measure.

"You a Cowboys fan?" Brad asked Hank, then slurping his beer.

"Nah. Don't have any skin in the game." Hank started eating faster. He had been more concerned about his love life the past few years than what was going on in the NFL.

"Ah," Brad started, "you probably don't know much about their drafting plans for the fall. Huh?"

Hank shook his head and so did Luis. They wanted to eat their dinner in peace, but Brad wasn't having it.

He continued. "Well, let me tell *you*. Back in Dallas, people are ready for this guy's *fucking* head!"

Hank bristled at the curse word, the hairs on his neck standing up. He cleared his throat as a polite attempt to show his displeasure, but that didn't stop Brad.

He went on. "What we need is a quarterback and *this* guy—" Brad pointed to the television, then angrily pumped his index finger a few more times. "This *fucking* guy just goes on and on about *fucking* tight ends and *goddamn* wide receivers. Then he drafts *fucking* more linemen, like we need more *motherfucking* linemen!" Brad scoffed, then chugged his beer.

Hank took the last bite of steak and set his silverware on his plate. He dabbed the corners of his mouth with his napkin and put it on the plate, too. He looked at Luis, twisting his face into an expression that said, *Can you believe* this *guy?* Luis smirked.

Hank sipped from his fresh cocktail. Brad gulped more beer, then continued complaining with beer foam coating his upper lip. "They pay these *bastards* millions of dollars to run a *goddamn* world-class organization and they just run the *fucking* thing into the *fucking* ground. It's *fucking ri-goddamn-diculous!*"

Brad went on like this for another five minutes. Ranting. Pointing. Raving. Pontificating. Sermonizing. Slurping beer. And all of his commentary laced with his profane language. Hank couldn't take it anymore. The cursing. It was just too much. He tilted his head at Luis, indicating that it was time to go. Luis shoved the last bite of burger in his mouth, then chugged the rest of his root beer. Hank asked Alan for the check.

Brad was miffed. "You guys don't have to go," he pleaded. "I'll buy you another round. Barkeep?" Alan looked at him and blinked a couple of times. "Give these guys another round of whatever they're drinking."

Hank shook his head. "Thanks, but no thanks. I—" Hank pointed to Luis and himself. "We've had enough of your potty mouth."

Brad's face contorted with confusion. "Potty mouth? Did you just say *potty mouth?*"

"That's right." Hank confirmed, then stood up. Luis stood up, too.

Brad grabbed Hank's arm. "You can't be serious?"

Alan placed Hank's ticket on the bar. "I can close you out."

With Brad still clinging to his arm, Hank glanced at the ticket, pulled a hundred-dollar bill from his shirt pocket, and dropped it on the bar. "Keep the change."

With his right arm, Hank swept Luis away. Then he grabbed Brad's hand from his left arm, bunching Brad's long, bony fingers together like carrots, squeezing them together as hard as he possibly could. His knuckles cracked as Hank squeezed even tighter. Brad grimaced and attempted to pull his hand away, but he couldn't.

"I said, we've had enough," Hank insisted.

Brad's fingers crackled like brittle twigs. He yanked his arm, eventually his hand slipping from Hank's grasp. Brad stood up, towering at least a foot taller than Hank, if not more. He shook out the pain in his hand, then took his tan jacket off and placed it on his barstool. His face was an angry shade of red.

"I'm going to knock your block off, buddy," he said, raising a southpaw fist.

"I doubt it," Hank replied.

Alan raised both of his hands in a conciliatory fashion. He didn't want any trouble. Luis's mouth morphed into a surprised O. He certainly wasn't expecting a fistfight between Hank and a stranger, but he was about to see a side of Hank he'd never seen before.

Brad took a swing at Hank and missed. Hank crouched faster than seemed possible for a man of his advanced age, clenching his own retaliatory fist and swinging a roundhouse punch that landed squarely in Brad's bulging gut. Brad bellowed as he stumbled backwards, both of his hands over his belly and a look of genuine surprise on his face. Hank stepped forward, his angry fist still clenched. He cocked that boulder of a hand back, then sent an uppercut to Brad's chin that lifted him off the ground, sending him flying up and backwards. He landed, backside first, on a square dining table, knocking it over and sending the four surrounding chairs crashing in every direction, the origami white napkins now flapping doves. Brad lay in a clump on the floor, silverware and glass condiment containers clattering around him.

Hank wiped his hands, as if cleaning them of Brad's presence, then turned to see Luis, who was in shock—his eyes wide and his backpack held tightly to his chest—astonished to have witnessed this old and seemingly gimpy man knock the tall, belligerent businessman on his proverbial butt. Luis couldn't believe it. Alan held the crown of his head with both hands, surprised at what had just transpired. The most action he typically saw at the steak house was a server bickering with a host about seating assignments; bar fights never occurred. Ever. That was, until Hank and his chaste ears showed up. Hank felt bad for creating a mess for Alan to clean up. He pulled another hundred-dollar bill from his wallet and dropped it on the bar.

"For your trouble. Sorry for the mess. Please don't call the cops," Hank insisted.

"Well, he did start it," Alan said.

"You got that right. Mind if we go out the back door?"

"Uh, sure thing," Alan began, thumbing to the end of the bar. "Take a left and down the hall. Once through the door, you'll see the exit in the back."

Hank put his arm around Luis. "You all right?"

"You beat the sh—" Luis began. Hank raised an unapproving eyebrow. "You beat the *crap* out of that guy."

"Yup."

"Where did you learn to do that?"

"High school."

Luis looked surprised. "Bullies?"

"Nah, varsity pugilists. Let's get the heck out of here before someone calls the cops, or worse, forces us to clean up this mess."

"Okay," Luis agreed. "But let's go fast before some other crazy crap happens."

They walked the length of the bar—Hank all of a sudden limping with Luis helping him along—turned left at the end, and quickly vanished out the back door.

15.

*B*ack in their hotel room, Hank spread his suitcase open on the bed and examined its contents with discernment, trying not to sway too much to one side or the other. The alcohol was beginning to infiltrate the part of his brain where better judgment originated, as well as the other part that imparted balance and decorum. He roughly wiped his nose, then rifled through his things until he found what he was looking for: a pint of whiskey. He gleefully showed it to Luis.

"Bingo! Just what the doctor ordered."

Luis wasn't impressed. If Hank had pulled a large bag of gummy candies out of his suitcase, then Luis would have been pleased, excited even. But whiskey? Not so much. Hank considered folding the suitcase back and zipping it shut, but decided on opening the pint instead. He took a long swig.

"You okay?" Luis asked him, worried. He sat on his bed, his back against the headboard.

"Golden," Hank replied. "Want a sip?"

Luis shook his head.

"Maybe one day," he sang, like the sweet refrain from a show tune, then burped.

"Should we try to get some sleep?" Luis asked him.

Hank shook his head. "Can't. Too amped from punching that jackalope. I probably won't be able to sleep for hours."

"Hours?"

"Maybe even all night. Maybe—" Hank began, then placed a thoughtful fist under his chin. "Maybe, I should walk it off. That'll do the trick."

"You want to walk around?"

"Yup," Hank said, then took another glug from the bottle.

"I'm down with that," Luis replied, grabbing his backpack. "Sounds fun."

"Okay then. Let's go!"

With the whiskey bottle, Hank lumbered to the door and swung it open. The door slammed hard against the wall. Luis followed him out of the room, his backpack slung over one shoulder. The door slammed behind them, the noise reverberating down the empty hallway. Hank guffawed, then burped, which mutated into a series of breathy hiccups. He stumbled down the hallway with Luis right behind him, watching him sway side to side, almost like he was going to topple over, but he didn't. The bottle occasionally clinked against the wall, and Luis worried that it would break, but it also didn't. It was as if Hank was being protected by an unseen force—a better angel, if you will. When they came to the end of the hallway, which opened to the lobby of the hotel, Hank stopped in front of a large window that overlooked the indoor swimming pool. The bright-white reflection of the shimmying pool water refracted on the ceiling, dancing hypnotically, Hank watching the watery shapes twist and turn. He soon very much wanted to go inside. Next to the window was a door. He grabbed the knob and twisted. Nothing.

He blew a wet raspberry, then announced, "It's locked."

Luis tsked. "I can open it."

"You can?"

"No *problemo*," Luis told him, then pushed him aside. He opened his backpack and rummaged through it. He pulled out what looked like a long nail file.

"What's that?" Hank said.

"A stone carving tool from art class," Luis said, kneeling and inserting the tool between the door and the jam. He shimmied the tool up and down, then applied a bit of a twist, his tongue poking out of his mouth for emphasis. The door unlocked. "*Voila!*"

Luis pushed the door open. Hank barreled through. Luis closed the door behind them and followed Hank. Hank walked along the edge of the pool to the far end, where some concrete steps led down into the water. He stood at the rim of the pool at the steps, looking at the glowing water, which cast writhing, sparkly reflections back at him. For a split second, Luis believed Hank would fall in the pool as he drunkenly swayed in place, but he didn't. Again, he had a guardian presence keeping him safe. He plopped on his butt and the whiskey bottle clanked on the concrete, but miraculously didn't break. Luis wondered if the glass bottle was stronger than he assumed. *It must be drunkproof,* he thought. Hank pulled his shoes off, tossing one to the side on a lounge chair and the other in the deep end of the pool, the shoe splashing before sinking to the bottom. He set his throbbing, calloused feet into the cold water.

"Ah!" he said, then exhaled. "What a relief!"

Luis sat next to him and also removed his precious sneakers, setting them just far enough away that they wouldn't get wet, but not too far that he couldn't reach them if needed. He slipped his bare feet into the water, too.

"Feels nice, right?" Hank added. He tilted the pint vertically and took several glugs.

Luis nodded. He watched Hank set the bottle on the concrete and wipe his mouth on his forearm.

"Let me guess," Hank began, then attempted to straighten his posture, but gave up, slumping instead. "You're going to pull out that sketchbook of yours and scribble something in it."

"That's a good idea," Luis agreed, and did just that. He tossed his backpack on the lounge chair with Hank's shoe, then began scribbling in his sketchbook. Occasionally, he would examine Hank as he pressed the blunt end of his pencil to his cheek, then furiously sketched some more. His breath deepened and slowed as he drew, taking in the heavily chlorinated air.

Hank watched him draw while taking pulls from the whiskey bottle. Soon enough, Luis was finished and he showed his masterpiece to Hank, who again marveled at Luis's skill and attention to detail. He saw a beautifully rendered portrait of himself sitting by the pool with his feet in the water, a serene expression on his wrinkled face.

He chuckled. "I'm not *that* good-looking."

"I draw what I see."

"Ah."

"What's your name?" Luis asked him, ready to write it on the paper.

"You know my name," he said, then harrumphed.

"I don't know your *last* name."

This surprised Hank. He scratched his head, and pondered this a bit. "I see. My last name is O'Sullivan. My name is Hank O'Sullivan," he said, the pesky hiccups starting again. Hank pounded his chest a few times, but that didn't make the hiccups stop.

Luis wrote *Portrait of Hank O'Sullivan* in the upper right corner, then scribbled something in the bottom right. The little bird, its silhouette showing a few lines here and there to indicate gradation in the color of its plumage. The sight of the little bird made him smile.

Hank pointed at the little bird, jabbing the paper with his nubby finger. "Why this?"

Luis grinned. "I draw a little bird instead of signing my name. I guess the bird is my signature."

Hank rubbed his chin thoughtfully. "Looks like a sparrow."

"Oh. Okay. I wasn't trying to draw a particular bird."

"In Ancient Egypt—" Hank began, then took another swig from his bottle. He licked his lips with the intensity of a dehydrated soul stuck in a desert without water. He continued, "They considered sparrows soul catchers. They believed sparrows took souls to heaven. In the old days, European sailors used to tattoo sparrows on themselves to ensure safe passage to heaven, in case they died at sea. Imagine that."

"Oh," Luis mused. "That's a little . . . morbid."

"Death is only morbid if you're worried about it," Hank said, then he winked. He took a long pull from the bottle, draining the last of the amber alcohol. He belched, although his hiccups stopped. "Which I'm not. But if I had to face it, then I would want you to be my sparrow." Then he belched again. He examined the empty bottle. A look of profound anguish appeared on his face. He set the bottle carefully on the concrete. It teetered, then tipped over. "That's a bunch of . . . hogwash."

Luis felt morose all of a sudden. He grabbed his backpack from the chair and put his sketchbook inside. Then he changed the subject.

"Where did you learn to fight like that?" he asked. "You said in high school at the restaurant. That's like a million years ago. Right?"

Hank scoffed, then put up his dukes. "I can take you, too, you whipper snapper!" He jumped to his feet, danced a boxer's jig, and performed a one-two punching combination. Momentarily, he didn't seem inebriated, nor did he stumble because of his creaky knee. He floated like a hummingbird, albeit an elderly one.

Luis stood up and raised his dukes as if to guard himself. Hank jabbed at the air in front of Luis a time or two. It was obvious to Hank that when it came to fighting, Luis was as coordinated as a newborn giraffe.

"Teach me," Luis said, trying to look tough.

"Ha!" Hank called out. "Like in the movie where the old Japanese handy-man shows the young twerp how to Kung Fu those bullies?"

"You mean, *The Karate Kid?*"

"If you say so," Hank said, swinging some haymakers.

"Show me."

Hank stopped moving and examined Luis's face, the genuine interest he expressed. He sighed, then stood next to Luis. The smell of alcohol clung to him like a dense fog.

"All right. There really are only a few things you need to know. Plant your feet," he said, then adjusted his stance. He looked down at Luis's feet as he positioned them in a similar fashion. "Attaboy!"

Luis smiled. "Okay. Then what?"

"I'm getting there. Rome wasn't built in a day," he said, then belched. He raised his dukes in front of his face again. "You gotta protect your good looks. Keep your hands up in front of that *punim* of yours."

Luis mimicked Hank's stance with his hands up. "Okay. Got it. Now what?"

"Okay. Here's the most important part. You listening?"

Luis nodded. Hank turned and stood directly in front of Luis. Hank's eyes slit as he gave Luis a withering stare.

"You gotta watch the guy's eyes. They tell you everything. Where he's gonna move. Where he's gonna punch," Hank said, holding his eyes on Luis for a tense moment or two. Then, without warning, he dropped his hands and plopped back down on the concrete like a sack of potatoes. He swung his feet back into the water.

Luis sat next to his crumpled friend, propping him back up so he wouldn't fall in the pool.

"Maybe you can show me more tomorrow when you're not drunk."

"I'm *not* drunk!" Hank exclaimed, an indignant index finger rising in the air. "I'm slightly intoxicated. Just a tad sloshed." He belched again, his breath hot and rank.

Luis waved his foul breath away with a swatting hand. "I can help you get back to the room," Luis offered.

In a moment of clarity, Hank could see his current state worried Luis. In the reflection of the illuminated pool water, he could see his swaying presence, his slumped shoulders, the wild white hairs springing from his scalp. "Okay," he agreed.

Luis stood up, grabbed his backpack, and swung a strap over one shoulder. He put his arms out, offering to assist Hank. Suddenly, Hank appeared old and feeble, weak and powerless. He struggled to stand, the weight of his entire body crumpling in Luis's arms. Luis concentrated on steadying Hank as they walked together. He raised Hank's left arm over his head and draped it across his shoulders. He guided Hank out of the pool area and through the door.

On the trek down the hallway back to their room, Hank's right knee gave out again, making it difficult for him to walk, and even more difficult for Luis to help him. To Luis, Hank felt like he weighed a ton, if not more. Luis wheezed with each labored step he took while helping his friend get back to their room.

Hank cleared his dry throat. "I . . . have to tell you something," he said.

"All right," Luis said, struggling to hold Hank up.

"I'm a fraud. I'm not who I say I am." He sighed.

"You're not *Hank!*" Luis cracked.

Hank didn't laugh. "I am Hank. Just not Irish Hank. I'm not Irish at all."

Luis looked up and saw they were halfway to their room. There was hope he'd get there without falling down.

"You're not Irish," Luis repeated. "Got it. Then what are you? Just plain ol' white?"

Hank took a labored step, then another. He stopped and looked at Luis.

"My mother was Jewish. My real father was German. I didn't know my real father. I only knew my stepfather. He was the Irish one."

"Okay," Luis said, attempting to walk again. It was a struggle, but Hank eventually followed suit. "All of this is news to me."

"I'm Jewish."

"Okay, you're Jewish."

"Sorry to just drop this on you—like *this*," Hank said, hiccupping now. He hiccupped again. Then the syncopated hiccup march began anew, accompanied by a sense of shame, his confession an unbearable weight. "I hope it doesn't change our friendship. I don't like being called a liar."

"It's okay. We're almost to our room."

"Do you think I'm a liar?"

"No," Luis said.

They stood in front of their door, Hank hiccupping and Luis panting. Luis realized he didn't have the key card, so he fished in Hank's pocket for it, which made Hank giggle. He found the card at the bottom of Hank's left pocket, along with a ball of lint and a small pocket knife, which he left in there. He slid the card in the lock, pushed it open with his right knee, and they both got through. Many difficult steps later, Luis landed Hank on his bed, facedown. He turned him over onto his back and propped his head up with a pillow.

Hank wheezed. "My mother didn't want me," he admitted. It seemed as if Hank would cry—a few labored breaths hinting at a good, teary release—but he began to snore instead, a throaty, bellowing snore that rattled the lamp on the nightstand between the beds.

Luis ran a hand through his hair and sighed. He was drained. He took the key card out of the door and made sure the room was secured inside—locking the dead bolt and latching the safety lock. He walked back to the mini fridge. Inside, a single, red can of Coke glistened, somehow materializing in the once empty fridge. He plopped into a lounge chair and pulled the tab, the Coke hissing as he opened it. Savoring the first sweet gulp, he watched Hank snore, his gut rising and falling, both his arms splayed out, giving him the appearance of flying like a superhero, albeit upside down and drunk. Luis gulped more soda.

"Not Irish?" he mused quietly to himself.

He wondered why Hank confessed this to him, then concluded that he was just drunk. It could've been complete nonsense. Luis didn't know. He finished the last of the Coke and crumpled the can.

Change our friendship? he thought.

He wrestled down the comforter and sheets on his bed, slipped in underneath them, and pulled them back up to his chin. He considered sketching some more, but decided to try to sleep instead. He wanted to be fresh and well-rested for his visit with his mother the next day. He also wanted to eat waffles for breakfast.

Waffles! he thought.

Nothing sounded more heavenly to Luis than eating waffles with maple syrup and butter for breakfast.

Nothing.

He closed his eyes and listened to Hank snore, a phlegmy bellowing that came and went like a foghorn in the night. It was a strange lullaby, both grotesque and comforting at the same time. Luis thought of his mother and the possibility of what might come the next day. Would she be willing to accept him into her life again? The thought was tantalizing. He soon fell fast asleep in his cottony cocoon.

16.

*M*ost nights, if not all, when Hank lies in bed waiting to fall asleep, he thinks about the night his wife and daughter died. He should've died, too, he surmises, but he didn't. So, here we are. The circumstances surrounding the accident were never fully investigated.

Once Hank recovered from his physical injuries, he was never the same. The mental trauma lingered. Hank didn't spend time in jail. In fact, the judge overseeing his case felt the death of his family was punishment enough. *So it goes*, the judge said to him. Hank thinks about his wife and daughter so often that most nights, he settles into lucid dreams, the ones a savvy-enough dreamer can try to control. The dreamer makes choices; the choices have consequences. So, ever since Hank recognized he could experience lucid dreams, he has attempted a reconciliation with his wife and daughter ever since.

Here's an example.

Hank lies in bed, replaying the night of the accident in his mind. He imagines his wife's face: her kind smile, her effervescent eyes, and the dimple in her chin. He imagines his preteen daughter: her long, dark, curly hair, her mischievous grin, a dimple in her chin, too.

When he sees his wife's face, he says her name: Linda.

When he sees his daughter's face, he says her name: Tammy.

He repeats his mantra: Linda, Tammy, Linda, Tammy, Linda . . .

When he finally drifts into sleep, they are there.

Here's what he might see on any given night.

Hank is at a wedding with his wife and daughter, sitting at a large round table. Half-eaten meals sit on cold white dishes. Hank has been nursing the same beer for an hour and a half; he's not really a drinker. His wife, Linda, is on her third chardonnay, ready for a fourth. Their daughter, Tammy, scurries to the dance floor to join the wedding party as they dance to "YMCA," a spot-on cover of the song by the Village People, leaving her parents to themselves at the otherwise empty table. Linda chides Hank.

"You should have another beer. Loosen up! It's a wedding reception, for God's sake."

"It'll just make me sleepy. Anyway, I'm driving, for God's sake."

Linda grimaces. "You're no fun! And you never dance with me anymore."

Hank leans over to touch her shoulder, but she defiantly crosses her arms.

"But sweetheart—" Hank starts.

"Don't touch me," she snaps.

Hank retreats to the bar and orders two beers and a shot of whiskey. With his low tolerance to alcohol, he's drunk within a matter of minutes. He meanders back to the table and pulls his wife onto the dance floor. He attempts to dance with her, but they're both too drunk to dance. They decide to grab Tammy and just go home. Friends at the wedding ask Hank if he's had too much to drink. He tells them all no. Again and again: no. The valet asks him the same thing. Still no. The family of three gets in the car and leaves the wedding venue.

His wife slouches in her seat, mumbling before snoring, "You're no fun."

His daughter sits quietly in the back seat and eventually falls asleep on their way home, her face smashed against the window, her breath fogging the glass.

Hank knows he's tired, but soldiers on. *Just need to get home*, he thinks. *I'll sleep in tomorrow.*

The next thing he knows, he's in the hospital. The nurse tells him his wife and daughter are gone. Deceased. *They didn't make it*, she tells him. *So sorry.*

Hank wakes up in real life with tears on his face.

The next night, he's determined to do right.

The mantra begins again: Linda, Tammy, Linda, Tammy, Linda . . .

Here's what he sees then.

A New Year's Eve party. Hank wears his dusty tweed suit. Linda and Tammy are in their finest Sunday dresses. They're sitting at a large round table with a massive floral centerpiece. Half-eaten meals sit on cold white dishes. Hank has been nursing the same margarita for a while. Linda is on her third glass of wine, maybe her fourth. Hank knows the drill, but wants to apologize this time, before everything goes sideways. He remembers that much—the sideways part. Tammy scurries to the dance floor to join the party as they dance to "Get Down Tonight," a spot-on cover of the song by KC and the Sunshine Band, leaving her parents to themselves at the otherwise empty table. Linda chides Hank again.

"You should have another margarita. Loosen up! It's New Year's Eve, for God's sake."

"It'll just make me sleepy. I'm driving, for God's sake."

Linda grimaces. "You're no fun! And you never dance with me anymore."

Hank leans over to touch her shoulder, maybe apologize, but she defiantly crosses her arms.

"But sweetheart—" Hank starts.

"Don't touch me," she snaps.

Hank retreats to the bar and orders another margarita—a double—and a shot of tequila on the side. "No salt or lime," he tells the bartender. He's drunk within a matter of minutes. He stumbles back to the table, falls down, gets up, and drags his wife onto the dancefloor. He attempts to dance with her, but they're both too drunk to dance. They decide to grab Tammy and just go home. Friends at the party ask Hank if he's had too much to drink. He tells them all no. He tells everybody, "No, I'm not drunk!" The hotel valet asks him the same thing. Still no. The family of three gets in the car and leaves the hotel to go home.

His wife slouches in her seat, mumbling before snoring, "You're no fun."

His daughter sits quietly in the back seat and eventually falls asleep on their way home, her face smashed against the window, her breath fogging the glass.

Hank knows he's tired, but soldiers on. *Just need to get home*, he thinks. *I'll sleep in tomorrow.*

The next thing he knows, he's in the hospital again. A male doctor tells him his wife and daughter are gone. Deceased. *They didn't make it*, he coldly tells Hank.

Hank wakes up in real life, again, with tears on his face. He's aware that he initiated the dream, but is frustrated that it ended the same as before—the same as in real life.

He tries again: the mantra, a party, his wife is upset, his daughter runs off to dance, his wife chides him, Hank gets drunk, they decide to leave, they all fall asleep on the way home, Hank finds himself back at the sad hospital, a medical professional tells Hank his wife and daughter are dead, and he's startled to consciousness.

And he tries again.

He does this for years, hoping for a different outcome, but it always ends the same.

They say, "The definition of insanity is doing the same thing over and over again and expecting a different result."

But this isn't true.

The definition of insanity is knowing you didn't deserve something, yet it happens to you anyway. Insanity is hoping for the best, yet getting the worst in spades. Insanity is dreaming about a tragedy over and over again, and you can't do anything to stop it.

What Hank doesn't understand is that this traumatic event has damaged his brain. Like a computer hard drive with a bad sector or a scratch on a vinyl album or a dead pixel on an LCD screen, the place in his mind where this horrible event resides—the little cranny where it is lodged—is irreparably damaged.

He can't fix it, nor will it ever heal.

Despite this, he persists. Hope is a seductive motivator.

Hank has performed this bedtime ritual so often that, even on nights when he doesn't recite his mantra, the dream begins nonetheless. When the dream ends, he still wakes up in tears.

When he is sober, he recites his mantra, falls asleep, and tries with all his might to have a dream with a different ending.

When he is drunk and out of his mind—too inebriated to recite his mantra—the dream still comes. Its madness more potent and unsympathetic.

It's insanity.

It's trauma.

It's Hank's sorrow.

The mantra is Hank's lullaby.

The ending is Hank's regret.

"You're no fun," Linda tells him, over and over again. Her declaration is in the damaged cranny of his mind.

Hank desperately wants to tell her he's sorry, but he will never get the chance.

He desperately wants to hug Tammy, but he won't get to do that, either.

But, he has hope.

This night, after drinking too much whiskey and slugging a traveling businessman in the bar of a steakhouse, he finds himself in his dream sitting with Tammy and Linda in a different fancy steak house: tables with white linen and waitstaff in formal attire. Hank nurses a whiskey on the rocks. Linda is on her fourth Lambrusco. The family can see a parade outside through the restaurant windows. Tammy runs outside to watch the parade, leaving her parents at the table. Linda is upset, but Hank is determined to appease her. He knows something bad will happen and wants nothing more than to end this particular night on a good note.

"You should have another whiskey. Loosen up, for God's sake," Linda says.

"I don't need another whiskey. I'm fine."

Linda is surprised, then smiles. "Then that's fine, dear."

"Can we go home?" he asks her. "I want to go home with you."

"Yes," she says.

He pays for the meal and they leave together, his arm around her shoulders. Outside the restaurant, the crowd gathers to watch the parade. Hank and Linda see Tammy closer to the street, a dozen or so people between her and them, spectators—fathers with children on their shoulders, doting wives next to them. Tammy beckons for her parents to come to her, and they wade through the crowd. But no matter how many people they push aside, or how many couples they step around, they don't get any closer to Tammy. Hank hears a rumble in the distance and to his left; a locomotive barrels through the crowd and parade.

Surprised at its presence, he taps on Linda's shoulder. He points in the direction of the wicked locomotive.

When he turns back to Linda, she's not standing next to him. She's with Tammy.

Linda and Tammy embrace.

The train crashes through the parade. People fly into the air along with cars and chairs and decorations.

The train runs over Linda and Tammy, then disappears down the street, now empty: no parade, no crowd, no nothing. Only Hank and nothing else in the desolate cityscape.

Hank walks out into the empty street, looking in the direction where the locomotive vanished. There is no sign of Linda and Tammy. He walks toward an intersection. There are no cars or pedestrians, only a traffic signal hanging from a wire above him. Its green light is flashing.

On and off and on, it flashes.

Red means stop. Green means go, he thinks to himself. *Time to go.*

That's right, Hank. Time to go.

17.

When Hank woke up in the morning—his eyes damp with tears—the first thing he saw was the blink of a green light on a smoke detector attached to the ceiling in the hotel room. He wiped the tears and watched the pesky green light blink for a moment, then realized he had been dreaming again. He also realized he was naked. The chilly, air-conditioned air had pulled goosebumps up on his exposed skin and his first inclination was to cover his withered carrot with his hands. He quickly placed his hands over his crotch, but found a wadded bath towel there, keeping his dignity intact. He groaned, then sat up. He examined his bed, which was also naked, its comforter and sheets all on the floor in a sad mound. He found Luis sitting in the lounge chair in the corner, fully dressed and ready for his day with his backpack in his lap.

"Good morning," he greeted Hank.

"Good morning to you," Hank said, pressing the bath towel tighter over his crotch. He looked around. "Where are my clothes?"

"Over there," Luis said, pointing to the nightstand. "I covered your—"

"Thanks for doing that. You didn't have to," Hank said, rolling over to the side of the bed, then scooching up to the headboard, embarrassed. *What would this look like to Luis's parents?* he thought.

"That's what friends are for. Right?" Luis said.

This caught Hank's attention. He turned and looked at Luis, expecting a look insinuating sarcasm, or worse, a look of condemnation for his naked display, his unconscious act of hedonism in the night, where his clothes were enemies and were dispatched summarily by zombie limbs. But what he saw surprised him. Luis returned a kind smile, one that said everything is going to be all right. *You're going to be all right.*

One corner of Hank's mouth lifted. "Truer words . . . " he began, then bent over to pick up his clothes. "I see you're ready for breakfast."

"I want waffles," Luis chirped. Hank's pale butt suddenly revealed itself as he slipped on his briefs. Luis snapped his eyes closed.

"Of course you do. Let me get dressed and pack my bag, then we can go eat waffles."

"Yeah!"

Hank chuckled. "Keep your hat on. It may take me a few minutes."

"Okay. I'm already packed."

"I see that," Hank said, sliding his pants on, then pulling his shirt over his head. He then went to the bathroom and performed his morning routine while shoving all his belongings in his duffle bag. He put on one shoe, but couldn't find the other. He came out of the bathroom and asked Luis, "Have you seen my other shoe?"

"It's at the bottom of the deep end of the pool."

"What?" Hank said, confused.

"I'll get it on the way to breakfast."

"Okay, then."

Hank grabbed the key card off the nightstand. "Let's go."

They left the room, the door slamming behind them. When they reached the door to the swimming pool, Luis handed Hank his backpack, then went inside. Hank watched him through the window as he walked around to grab a blue metal pole with a net on the end, then fished Hank's shoe from the bottom of the pool. He emptied the shoe and carried it back to Hank.

Luis handed the sopping shoe to Hank. It smelled of chlorine. "Here you go."

They continued on to breakfast, Hank carrying the dripping shoe.

When they arrived at the continental breakfast room, the first thing they noticed was that the serving tables were full of all types of breakfast convenience foods: mini boxes of cereal, small containers of yogurt in a bowl of ice, another bowl filled with waxy, red apples, and stainless steel chafing dishes with who-knows-what inside. And at the end was the holy grail of all breakfast stations: the waffle maker.

Luis beamed. "I'm making waffles!"

He went straight for the station.

The second thing they noticed was that the continental breakfast room was completely empty—no servers and no patrons. It was just the two of them, surrounded by enough food for dozens upon dozens of hotel guests. It was a ton of food for a clientele of two.

"Nobody. Just the way I like it," Hank admitted, finding a booth and setting his duffle bag next to his damp shoe on one of the padded seats. He saw Luis standing dejectedly at the waffle station, but he wasn't doing anything, just standing there. Hank walked over to him. "How long til they're ready?" he asked Luis, placing a hand on his shoulder, looking down at the open waffle maker.

"They're out of batter," Luis said. "Out of order."

"No! There *must* be more in the back," Hank insisted. They had already agreed that they would get waffles. He looked around the continental breakfast room and saw a door with a sign that said, "Employees Only." He banged on the door. After a moment or two, he banged harder, rattling the hinges. Soon enough, the door opened and a woman just as bulky and squat and aggravated as he was—a female Hank O'Sullivan in an apron—greeted him gruffly.

"Yes?" she grumbled, eyeing his dingy tube sock on the red tile floor.

Hank cleared his throat. "Oh, sorry ma'am. But—" He pulled up at his belt as if a hidden force was constricting it. "The waffle batter is out. Do you have more?" He thumbed in Luis's direction, next to the defective waffle station, looking quite pathetic.

She squinted at Luis, then back at Hank. "Let me go check." Annoyed, she quickly closed the door.

Hank turned to Luis and shrugged. When the door opened again moments later, she had a brightly colored box the size of a shoe box in her hands.

"All we've got are Eggo waffles. Will that do?" she said, but she didn't give him time to reply. She pushed the box into Hank's chest, then closed the door.

Hank was caught off guard, but wasn't surprised. He walked back to the waffle station with the crumpled box of tiny frozen waffles in his hand. "All they got is frozen," he said to Luis, handing him the box.

"That's fine," Luis said flatly, even though it was obviously not fine. He looked like he was going to melt under his sweltering disappointment.

The two resigned themselves to gathering what they could to eat and met back at the booth. Hank prepared himself a bowl of Raisin Bran with skim milk, adding a container of coffee creamer to the bowl to thicken the watery milk. Luis toasted six Eggo waffles and stacked them on a plate, slathering them with margarine and imitation maple syrup.

Luis sighed. "My dad gives me frozen waffles sometimes before school. So weak."

"Sorry kid. I got the shaft, too. Skim milk is just white water. It's not fit for cereal. Let's just eat our grub and head out."

"Okay," Luis agreed.

"This trip's been bad enough. It can't possibly get any worse. Besides, I'm sure your mother is looking forward to seeing you."

"Maybe." Luis worried this was a bad sign, but tried not to worry too much about it.

They ate their breakfast in mutual silence like an exhausted old married couple.

When they were done, they stepped outside into the warm sunshine, Hank with his duffle bag in one hand and wet shoe in the other, Luis with his backpack slung over one shoulder, marching together through the parking lot, heading behind the hotel where the 'Cuda was safely parked. But as they got closer, Hank noticed something on the ground next to his car, something unusual, something that gave him pause. He quickened his pace.

"What the—" he said, then bent over when he reached the back of the car. He dropped his duffle bag and shoe, and picked up an empty tallboy of beer from the black asphalt, tipping the silver can upside down, a stinky dribble of stale beer dripping out. There was another can next to the rear wheel, and another one closer to the front wheel. He slowly made his way to the front of the car, tossing the can he was holding over the hedge row. Luis cautiously followed him. He had a bad feeling, which Hank confirmed rounding the front of his precious classic car. "What! The! Fuck! You goddamn sons of *bitches*!" he cried out.

Hank pressed both sides of his head together as if trying to keep his brain intact inside a volatile skull, only moments from self-destruction and certain death. Luis was shocked when he heard the profane words escape Hank's mouth, as he hadn't heard Hank utter anything close to that level of vulgarity. In fact, there was a time when Luis thought Hank was incapable of using profane language. But when Luis finally saw what Hank saw, he instantly understood.

On the hood of the 'Cuda, scrawled in the middle with a sharp object, like a knife or key, were the words "OLD FART!"

Luis turned to Hank, who was clutching his shirt over his heart, his face maroon with anger, his hair standing on end, furious tears streaming down his cheeks. Luis worried for his friend because it looked like he was having a heart attack. But it was something much worse than that.

He changed, like Bruce Banner morphing into the Incredible Hulk. He was consumed with murderous rage, the type of rage that would lead a kind man to kill someone.

"Stay here!" Hank ordered Luis, then he stomped back to the front office, both hands clenched in angry fists.

Luis didn't know what to do, so he read the etched graffiti again, his eyes going over each letter. He had a feeling he knew who had done this heartless act of disrespect and vandalism, as the empty tall boys of beer were solid evidence, but he still couldn't believe it. Luis wasn't an expert in cars, but he knew Hank's car was ruined. A new coat of paint wasn't going to fix it. And even if Hank purchased a new hood, and had it and the rest of his beloved car repainted, Luis knew this malicious act had caused permanent damage to Hank's heart and soul. Reading the words "OLD FART" hurt Luis, too. It just seemed too cruel.

After a moment or two, Hank stomped back, a white piece of paper waving in one hand as he angrily swung his arms. When he got close, he crumpled the piece of paper into a wad and threw it on the ground.

"Where are those assholes?!" Hank demanded, looking around. On the other side of the hedge row was an aluminum shed they hadn't noticed before—painted in similar colors as the hotel—a good place to store lawn equipment and the like. Hank ripped through the hedgerow like it was tissue paper and stomped to the shed. He tried to open the door, but it was padlocked shut. The shed rattled as he tried to shake the door open, but it wouldn't. So, he punched the shed a few times instead, leaving deep, round dents in the door. He stomped back over to the hedgerow, bent over, grabbed the trunk of one of the bushes, and ripped the entire bush straight out of the ground. He yelled—a guttural, primal cry—then tossed the bush as far as he could across the parking lot, dirt and leaves and broken branches raining on the asphalt.

"Hank?" Luis called out, but Hank was enraged. He didn't hear Luis.

Hank shuffled back to the front of his car to witness the vandalism again. He just couldn't believe it. "Why? *Why?!*"

"Hank?" Luis asked again.

Panting, Hank turned to Luis, his face a deep shade of furious. Droplets of sweat clung to his forehead, some taking the miserable journey down his cheeks.

"Should we call the cops?" Luis said.

Hank pshawed. "The cops aren't going to do shit!" He began to pace back and forth. "Besides, you and I are criminals in the eyes of the law. We haven't even finished our community service. What do you think the cops are going to do when they show up and ask for our IDs? *Huh?!* You think they're going to help us once they see who we are in their godforsaken system?"

Luis shrugged. He didn't know what else to say.

Hank continued ranting. "I'm screwed. The lady at the front desk said I could fill out a report, but what's that going to do? Nothing, I tell you. Not a goddamn thing!"

Hank continued to pace back and forth, huffing and puffing. Luis watched him, helpless. But after a few minutes, Hank began to calm down. He attempted to breathe normally, taking a deep breath, then exhaling. He repeated this a few more times. A more human color reappeared on his face, although he remained sweaty and flustered. He smoothed his hair, then made his way over to Luis and put both of his meaty hands on Luis's scrawny shoulders.

"Sorry you had to see that, Louie. Let's go," Hank said. He patted Luis's shoulders—giving him a wilted smile—then picked up his duffle bag and tossed it in the trunk. He picked up his wet shoe and shoved his foot into it. Then he got into the car and slammed the door shut.

Luis walked around to the other side—his head hanging low, his backpack over his drooping shoulder—and got in, too.

The engine roared to life, idled momentarily, then Hank and Luis drove away.

———   ———   ———

They didn't speak to each other as Hank drove them back to Carmen's house. Luis felt conflicted as he looked out the window, watching the businesses go by. On one hand, he was excited to speak to his mother again. He felt like he was on the precipice of something, but he wasn't sure what. On the other hand, he felt bad for Hank and what happened to his car. He didn't know what to say, so he decided it was best to say nothing. Hank didn't speak either, nor did he need the electronic female voice to guide him this time. He had an excellent sense of direction. He remembered how to get back to Carmen's house all on his own.

Hank eventually took the exit to get them back to Montrose, turning at the familiar intersection from the day before, and passing the same quirky shops and bespoke restaurants. They passed the sandwich shop with the topless, dancing man out front, still grooving to "Funky Town." They passed the same homes with the rainbow flags waving proudly in the morning breeze, and soon found themselves parked in front of Carmen's house. Luis watched his mother through the window, this time down on her knees as she pulled weeds from a garden bed, wearing the same floppy sun hat and large sunglasses. He was excited to talk to her. She eventually noticed them and waved, standing and wiping blades of grass and dirt from her bare knees. Hank cut the engine. Luis got out, and Hank followed.

Carmen extended her hand to Luis like he was a door-to-door salesman. "Good morning," she said.

"Good morning," Luis replied.

Hank also shook her hand. "Ma'am."

"Do you want to come inside? Nina will be back soon."

Luis and Hank agreed and followed her in the house.

Inside, they were greeted again by a delicious smell, although this time it was sautéed onions and garlic, maybe a chicken roasting. For some reason, Luis took this as a good sign. He wasn't quite sure why, but it just felt good. Seemed homey and inviting, he felt. He and Hank followed Carmen into the living room and again sat on the big leather sectional. Déjà vu, as they say. Carmen returned to her barstool, sitting in front of a new bouquet of flowers on the bar. She set her sunhat and sunglasses on the bar, then wiped her sweaty forehead.

She cleared her throat. "I hope your stay at the hotel was nice."

"I've stayed at better," Hank grumbled, still agitated. "Won't be going back there, that's for sure."

Carmen noticed the bottom of one of his pant legs was wet—having absorbed much of the pool water from his waterlogged shoe—and turned to Luis, worried. "Oh, no! I hope nothing bad happened."

"Bad night, bad morning. That's all," he said, then took a deep breath. "Did you think about what I asked you yesterday?"

Her face brightened. "I did! But—" The sound of the back door closing was followed by approaching footsteps, and a woman appeared in the kitchen with a grocery bag in one hand and a potted plant in the other. "And here she is!"

The woman set the bag and plant on the kitchen counter, unaware that they had company. "Babe! You won't believe this. I got us a reservation on the patio at Baba Lesbians—" She looked up, noticing the two strange men sitting on her couch, then forced a smile. "Ah."

"Luis and—" Carmen began, gesturing to Luis, then to Hank.

"Hank," he reminded her.

"Right, Hank. Babe, this is Luis and Hank. They came all the way from Austin."

Carmen's wife stepped out of the kitchen and around the bar, leaning over to offer a hand to shake. "Nice to meet you," she said, as she quickly shook each of their hands, giving a couple of vigorous pumps. Her arms were toned, her grip firm and forceful. "Sorry, I was out running some errands. Just excited to get a reservation at Baba Yega. That's a tough one to get."

"We call Baba Yega, *Baba Lesbians*," Carmen added with a grin. "Popular restaurant in our community. It's kind of a lesbo hangout."

"My name is Nina. I guess I can introduce myself," Nina said thickly.

"I was getting to it, babe," Carmen said, rolling her eyes.

"Sure you were," Nina snapped, going back into the kitchen and rattling the paper grocery bag as she emptied it, each item clunking or thudding as she plopped them on the counter. Tension suddenly hung in the room.

"I *was!*" Carmen replied, then shook her head. "Anyway, Luis and I were just talking about what he asked me yesterday."

"Oh really?" Nina replied, more interested now. She set the grocery bag aside, then made her way back to stand next to Carmen, draping a protective arm over her wife's shoulder. She seemed to tower over her. "Do tell."

"He was just asking—" Carmen began.

"I was just asking my mother if she thought about what I asked her yesterday," Luis added.

He gazed at his mother, but she looked away, seeming preoccupied. It was an unsettling observation, since he felt he had made a connection with his mother the day before. It was as if Nina's mood had infected Carmen's like a virus. Luis looked at Hank, who tilted his head as if to say, *Go on, Louie. Go on!*

Luis continued. "I would love the opportunity to get to know her better."

Nina cut in. "She already told me about your surprise visit yesterday. You want to stay *here*?" she said, pointing to the floor.

Luis nodded.

Nina continued. "You have a lot of nerve just showing up, trying to get Carmen to take you in, after everything she's done for you. You have a perfectly good home with . . . with . . . that *man*."

Carmen turned to Luis. "Nina is right. This is all very sudden. You know? Nina and I have a life here. We don't—have kids for a reason."

Luis placed his hand on his chest. "But I'm your son." He turned to Hank who returned a sober look, one that said, *This ain't going so well, Louie.* "But—"

"You know, Luis," Carmen began, squeezing Nina's arm so she wouldn't interject. "You'll be eighteen soon. You'll be done with high school. At that point, you'll be free. You'll be able to do whatever you want. Go to college—"

"I want to go to art school, not college," Luis interjected.

Carmen nodded. "That's great. You can go to art school. You're very talented. Be your own person. Live the life you want to live."

"But I've got so many questions. I don't even know my own mother."

"I understand," she said. "You and I, we can write letters. You can ask me questions and I'll be glad to answer them."

"But, but I need more than that. I need—"

"We don't *need* your drama! You can't just show up and manipulate Carmen like this. Who do you think you are?" Nina interjected, finally saying what she really wanted to say all along.

Carmen stood up. "You're not helping," she declared.

"Fine. I'll keep my mouth shut," Nina snapped, then went back into the kitchen. She slammed drawers and cupboard doors as she finished putting away groceries.

Luis continued. "I won't be a burden. I could get a job and make my own money. I won't be any trouble. I promise."

"He is a good kid," Hank added.

"I'm sure he is," Carmen said, then sighed. "It's just, we don't have the—"

"Please!" Luis said, then stammered. "*Please.*"

Nina barged back in. "Don't you get it, kid?! Nobody wants you. We don't want you here. I'm sure your *father* doesn't even want you." She paused, her anger boiling now. "He's not even your *real* father anyway."

Luis's back straightened and his face contorted into a bewildered question mark. Nina's attempt to hurt Luis worked, and her eyes suddenly filled with hot tears, as if she knew she had crossed a line. Her jab had landed directly in Luis's heart. She suddenly bolted for the back door, and seconds later they heard the screech of her tires on the drive.

"What?" Luis said, searching his mother's face. It revealed everything he needed to know. "Not my father?"

Carmen replied with a shake of her head. "Sorry, Luis."

"Why are you telling me this now?"

– 143 –

"My pregnancy wasn't planned. My parents were Catholic. I couldn't get an abortion, so I just went through with it. Your father—I mean, Berto—already had plans to come to America. He was my friend. He said he'd bring you and me here, and help us. I made a quick decision and accepted his help. It's . . . a long story."

Luis looked at Hank. He couldn't believe what he was hearing, and neither could Hank. It was a disastrous turn of events. Luis looked down at the coffee table, which the day before was covered with interesting books and curio, as if to say to guests, *Stay a while. Look at the interesting things we have to show you. Be our guest!* But at this moment, all of those things were gone. The coffee table was conspicuously empty and cold. Luis felt a chill and held both his elbows, as if embracing himself.

Hank leaned toward Luis and whispered, "We can go now, if you want. You don't have to be here."

Luis turned to his mother again, whose face was red with embarrassment.

Carmen continued. "I knew Berto liked me, but I didn't like him that way. When I finally told him who I really was, he promised me he still wanted to take care of you like you were his own. He told me he would even adopt—"

"I don't believe you," Luis told her, standing up. "I don't believe you at all. I'm sorry I came here." All the speeches he had given over the years in front of the mirror back in his room in the apartment he shared with the man he had only ever known as his father, they all raced through his mind. All the times he gazed into the eyes of the young woman he knew as his mother in a few precious, faded photos, the very few pictures his father told him to keep safe, as they were the treasures of his past, evidence of who he was and the family he came from. He angrily unzipped his backpack and plunged his hand into it, pulling out the photo he brought with him of his mother—young, hopeful, smiling—and him as a little boy—happy, loving, entranced—in her arms. He tossed it on the coffee table, then turned to Hank. "Let's go."

"Sure thing, Louie," Hank said, standing up.

Carmen moved toward Luis, as if she wanted to hold him, but he twisted away from her.

"Sorry I bothered you," Luis muttered, heading for the front door.

Hank nodded at Carmen and followed Luis.

Luis stormed outside, Hank following across the pristine lawn. They got in the 'Cuda and slammed their doors.

Hank turned to Luis. "You sure you want to leave?"

"I want to go back to Austin," Luis said, staring out the front window. He tried to swallow the lump in his throat, determined not to cry. He put on his seat belt.

"You got it," Hank said. "Me too."

He jammed his key into the ignition and started the car. The engine roared. Hank stomped the clutch, rammed the shifter into first gear, and peeled away from the house Luis's mother shared with her bitter wife. Luis looked straight ahead, his arms around his backpack. He seemed to be shrinking in his seat. Hank looked in the rearview mirror and could see Carmen running from her yard out into the street, waving both arms above her head as if she wanted him to stop, but he didn't tell Luis that. And he didn't stop. He just kept driving and kept his promise to Luis. *You don't have to be here,* he had said. And he meant it.

18.

ank took Southwest Freeway west out of Montrose, then a quick jaunt
north on Loop 610 to I-10, the Interstate Highway, which would get
them at least halfway home to Austin. Hank and Luis didn't speak. They
didn't need to. They both knew this trip was a disaster, and neither wanted
to waste precious air rehashing just how disastrous it was. As Hank would've
said, *It was as plain as the nose on your face.* Fair enough. They just wanted to
get home. Hank wanted to get home to the comfort of his cluttered burrow,
eating day-old sandwiches in his La-Z-Boy, drinking whiskey old-fashioneds
at his favorite neighborhood hangout Home Runs, cutting his lawn, and
tuning up his 'Cuda in his garage. Luis wanted to get home to his bedroom,
the quiet emptiness of his late-night walkabouts, drawing scenes in his
sketchbook, the endless slog of high school, and eating frozen waffles fixed
by his father in the mornings before school.

But his mother said he wasn't Luis's father.

So who was he, this Roberto Sanchez? Or Berto, as his friends liked to
call him. *Do I call him Berto now, too?* Luis mulled over this dilemma as he
watched the businesses whiz by: shopping malls, burger joints, taco shacks,
and gas stations. As they got closer to the outskirts of the city, these businesses soon made way for large pastures surrounded by barbed wire and
rows of cedar trees, where herds of cattle milled about trying to stay in the
shade, hoping for a respite from the hot Texas sun. Luis hoped for a break,
too. But from what exactly, he didn't know. The confusion stirred around in
his brain with the rest of the teenage angst and anxiety.

He looked over at Hank, who was staring coldly out the front window
at the highway stretching into the distance. He held the steering wheel with
his right hand as he propped his left elbow on top of the door panel, his head

leaning on his left hand. There was a weariness about him—a bold sadness—that made it difficult for Luis to look at him, so he turned away, back to his own window and his view of ranch land.

That was, until they heard the explosion.

Then the *whump whump whump* sound.

Not losing his cool, Hank took his foot off the gas pedal and steered the 'Cuda to the shoulder with a firm hand, in the same way he would've pulled into an empty spot in the grocery store parking lot. Once the car completely stopped, he cut the engine and banged the steering wheel with an angry fist.

"Hogwash," he said, taking the key out of the ignition, opening his door, and getting out. Luis watched him walk to the back of the car and unlock the trunk. The raised trunk lid obscured his view of the highway, but he could see other cars whizzing by out the driver's side window. He could hear Hank rummaging around in the trunk for the spare.

Then nothing. All Luis could hear was the passing cars.

He then noticed something he hadn't noticed before. On the other side of the highway, directly across from where they were stranded on the shoulder, was Buc-ee's, the massive gas station where they had stopped at the beginning of this godforsaken trip.

Still not hearing anything and feeling charitable, he decided to get out and see if Hank needed any help. He had no idea how he could help, but he felt he should be a good citizen of the world. It was the right thing to do. So, he got out of the car and joined Hank at the back.

What he found was Hank leaning against the opened trunk, chugging from a pint of whiskey. Luis looked in the trunk and found a flat spare tire—the shriveled tire covered in cobwebs and mildew, the wheel rusty—and a bright red first aid kit lying on top of it. The kit was splayed open, but wasn't filled with emergency medical supplies. Inside were two more pints of whiskey, a pack of Camel cigarettes, a lighter, some darts, a pack of playing cards, and a vacuum-sealed package of beef jerky, all of which looked relatively new, unlike the spare tire. Hank's priorities revealed themselves.

When Hank noticed Luis standing next to him, he wiped his mouth with his forearm, then said, "Flat tire. Flat spare. We're screwed." Hank thumbed over his shoulder to the passenger's side.

Luis turned around and saw the flat tire on the rear wheel, rubber strands spilling on the ground like the tentacles of a beached jellyfish.

"Oh," Luis remarked.

"That's all you got to say?" Hank asked him. Luis shrugged. "Figures."

"I'm just a dumb kid, remember?" Luis said, standing next to Hank.

"I never said that."

"You might as well have."

"I'm just a dumb old man," Hank mused, shaking his head. "Dumb. Dumb. Dumb."

Luis gazed at the Buc-ee's across the highway. It stood in the distance like the Taj Mahal, or the Alamo more like it: big, grand, and majestic. "Maybe we should go get help over there."

"That's a negative," Hank began, then gulped the last bit of whiskey from the pint. He tossed the bottle as far as he could over the barbed wire fence separating the highway from a cow pasture, then grabbed a new bottle from the trunk. He cracked the top and took a sip. "They probably got our photos up by the registers. We're the marble pranksters, or something like that. Probably wanted in three counties by now."

"I don't know," Luis began, looking around. "Where are we going to get help? There's nothing else out here."

"You got me, Louie," Hank said, taking another sip of whiskey. "Your guess is as good as mine."

Cars whizzed by, and nobody stopped to help them. Occasionally, a car would honk, or squeeze out a quick succession of *beep beeps* like an amusing salutation. But besides that, none of the travelers acknowledged that Hank and Luis needed help. It was like they were lepers.

"We should try something," Luis prodded.

"Nah. Just let the vultures pick my bones. I'm old. Nobody wants me anymore. The vultures probably won't even want to eat me. I'm tough and dry and pickled to the bone."

"Okay," Luis said, sarcastically, drawing out the "A" sound.

Ahead of them, he noticed the back of a small sign about ten yards away, the sign about the size of a shoe box lid. He turned around and craned his head above the car and could see a similar sign ahead in the other direction, the face of it green with white numbers on it. He pulled his cell phone from his pants pocket and dialed.

Hank watched him, then asked, "You calling Triple A?"

Luis shook his head. Hank took another pull from the bottle, then wiped his mouth again. He put the cap back on the bottle, set it back in the first aid kit, then began putting everything scattered in the trunk back where it belonged.

Someone answered Luis's call and he spoke to them. "Yes, we need help. We've got a flat tire," he said, raising a flat hand to his forehead, shading his eyes from the bright, unrelenting sunlight.

Hank continued to putter in the trunk. He had everything back to the way it was before he opened it, but decided it was best to put the pint of whiskey he had just opened into his pants pocket instead of leaving it in the trunk.

Luis continued. "Yes, ma'am. I think we're near mile marker 692. That's what's on the little green sign. Okay. Oh, okay." Luis placed his hand over the receiver and turned to Hank. "They're sending a tow truck."

"Outstanding," Hank replied. A smile bloomed on his face, a glimmer of hope with it. He elbowed Luis for him to get out of the way, then closed the trunk.

Luis took his hand off the receiver. "How long? Fifteen minutes? That's great!" He turned to Hank. "A tow truck will be here in fifteen minutes!"

"When we get back to Austin, you'll never have to see me again," Hank replied.

Luis went back to the call. "Thank you for your help. Thank you!"

Hank leaned against the back of the 'Cuda and crossed his arms. "I don't even know what we're doing together."

"What was that?" Luis said, sliding his phone back in his pocket.

"Nothing," Hank said.

"They'll be here in fifteen minutes."

"That's what you said already. I'm not deaf."

"Okay," Luis said, also crossing his arms and leaning against the back of the car. "I won't bother you again when we get back to Austin."

"That's fine."

"Sorry about the trip."

"Nothing to be sorry about, Louie. It was all my idea anyway. It's on me. The whole thing. The whole kit and caboodle. The whole, stinking, rotten enchilada."

"I think you may have a drinking problem," Luis mused, thinking aloud. He didn't mean to say it out loud, but he just did, and it almost felt good, too. Almost.

"You're probably right," Hank began, then cleared his throat. "You've got a family problem. Big time."

"I guess you're right," Luis said, raising a flat hand back to his forehead. He looked all around, seeing nothing except passing cars and the "Alamo" surrounded by gas pumps in the distance, the mirage of convenience. "I might as well be an orphan."

And that was the last thing they said to each other.

They stood there on the side of the highway—their arms crossed and their skin baking in the sun—in complete silence for almost fifteen minutes.

Until the tow truck came.

It parked in front of the 'Cuda. The burly driver got out and pulled the sad car on the back of the truck with a motorized pulley and a greasy length of chain. Even then, Hank and Luis didn't speak to each other. They only spoke to the tow truck driver. Big Dave was his name, or at least that's what he asked the two stranded travelers to call him. He had a rectangular patch stitched on his overalls over his heart that said, "Big Dave," the denim outfit struggling to contain his three-hundred-pound chassis. The white T-shirt underneath was splotched with sweat and food stains, and stretched so thin you could see the curly hairs on his shoulders and chest through the translucent cotton. He wore a trucker hat tilted on the back of his head with an ashy sweat ring around the bottom of it and a Houston Texans logo on the front. He smelled of tobacco and rank of body odor. He looked at Hank, examining him from his hair down to the tops of his shoes, sucking the wad of chewing tobacco wedged behind his lower lip and cheek.

"You must be the Old Fart," he said, spitting the most vile gob of tobacco-infused saliva that Hank and Luis had ever witnessed—in their entire lives—onto the gravelly ground.

"What?" Hank responded, then felt stupid for asking the obvious question. "Oh, right. Yup, that's me."

"Someone do that to your pretty car?" Big Dave added, chewing the tobacco wad now.

"Well, I certainly didn't carve it. Why would I do that to my own car?"

"I see. Where were you headed?" he asked them.

"Austin," Hank said.

"Still a ways," he said to both of them.

"Yup," Hank agreed. "Can you fix the flat?" He thumbed in the direction of the 'Cuda.

"Yup," Big Dave said, hocking up a blubbery loogy this time, then spitting it in the grass. "Two hundred buckaroos will get you back on the road. That'll cover the tow and the used tire. Parts and labor and whatnot. Tires pretty good, though, even if used. Lifetime warranty, I reckon."

"Fine," Hank said, then sighed.

"You two want to ride in the truck cab?"

"Do we have a choice?" Luis said.

"Well," Big Dave began, taking his hat off and wiping his bald head with a damp red handkerchief that he pulled from his back pocket with a magician's flair. "You could walk, but I wouldn't advise it in this heat."

He made the handkerchief vanish and placed his hat back on his head, askew.

"That would be suicide," Hank acknowledged.

"So, the cab then?" Big Dave said.

"Yup."

Big Dave walked to the driver's side of the tow truck and climbed up in. Hank and Luis walked to the passenger's side, where Luis watched Hank climb up into the cab, his fuzzy butt crack peeking out the top of his trousers, then followed him. Soon enough, the tow truck roared to life, a plume of black smoke rising from a smokestack. The truck shook and crawled forward with the 'Cuda on its back, then slowly eased onto the highway, its left turn signal flashing, dense diesel smoke billowing to the sky. Passing cars blared their horns at the slowly moving rig. Big Dave raised his left arm out of the driver's side window, up in the air as far as he could extend it, his profane finger standing at attention for all to see. He blared his truck horn defiantly as he drove Hank and Luis to his little auto shop in the middle of nowhere, his bastion of hope for wayward travelers and stranded motorists. Inside the shop, he kept a bowl of leftover Halloween candy next to the cash register for customers, his way of making them feel pampered.

Luis would shove a fistful of candy into his backpack.

Hank would finish the rest of the pint of whiskey outside in the shade of a tattered awning, while they waited for the tire to be replaced.

And they wouldn't get back to Austin until well after the sunset.

Finally.

PART III

19.

*L*uis sat at the dining table in the breakfast nook of his apartment, eating a frosted strawberry Pop-Tart for his dinner, his sketchbook and a variety of pencils on the tabletop before him. The sketchbook was open to the portrait of Hank O'Sullivan, the one he had sketched poolside at the hotel, and he considered tearing the page out and throwing it away. But he recognized that it was a fine portrait—maybe one of the best he had drawn that whole year—even though he wasn't enamored with the subject matter's ugly mug. He decided to keep it for his portfolio, the one he would need to apply to art schools. He inventoried in his mind all of the sketches he would include in his portfolio while he ate his sad dinner.

It had been almost a full day since Hank dropped him off in front of the apartment complex, then tore away in the pink 'Cuda without saying goodbye, leaving Luis in a cloud of exhaust and dust. He walked through the complex in the dark and tiptoed up the stairs of his building to his apartment. When he entered—trying to be as quiet as possible so as not to disturb the man he had known as his father for as long as he could remember—he discovered that his father wasn't even home. The apartment was empty, filled with stagnant air; two gnats buzzing around the trash bin were the sole signs of life inside. Luis dutifully brushed his teeth and went straight to bed, got up the next morning and ate one Pop-Tart from a double pack for breakfast (the other Pop-Tart was now his dinner), then caught a ride on the yellow school bus that stopped at the apartment complex.

Later after school, he braced himself for his father's return. He worried that his father (or should he call him Berto now?) would've somehow discovered that he and Hank drove to Houston and that Luis had surprised his estranged mother with a visit instead of spending the night at a friend's house, like he promised he would. But his father still wasn't home when evening came around. That's when Luis decided he would keep doing what he had always done: finish his homework, eat dinner, then leave the apartment after dark to find a new place to explore, maybe a grocery store rooftop, or maybe a lounge by the community pool in Hank's neighborhood. The pool was Olympic-sized, with plenty of lounge chairs around it, and vending machines with dispenser openings wide enough for Luis to snake a lanky arm up inside and snatch a can of Coke for free.

He was thinking about how to draw the twenty-five-foot-tall springboard of the community pool in the dark when his father barged into their apartment, a shit-eating grin on his face. Luis's presence at the dining table surprised him, even though it shouldn't have.

"Oh! Hey, son. How are you doing?" he said, closing the door behind him.

Luis chewed his Pop-Tart and didn't respond.

"I see you're eating dinner," Berto said, going to the kitchen sink and putting the dirty dishes in the dishwasher like he had been in the apartment the whole time. He looked over a shoulder back at Luis. "Drawing something new?"

"No," Luis answered, swallowing the last of his dinner. "Just thinking about what to put in my portfolio for art school applications."

"Right. Say—" he began, putting the last of the dishes in the washer, then closing it. "Want to have a Star Wars marathon? We can watch the DVDs in chronological order or whatever."

He turned to face Luis, putting his hands on his hips. But what he discovered was a look of contempt on Luis's face.

"What's up?" he asked Luis. "Are you upset that I'm late coming home?"

"I know you're not my real father," Luis said, definitively. It made him feel good to say this, to verbalize his anger and disappointment in such a pointed way.

Berto slowly crossed his arms. But instead of looking defiant or defensive—as Luis expected—he looked relieved. He didn't have to harbor this secret anymore.

"How did you—" he started, then chuckled, shaking his head. "It doesn't matter."

"Were you *ever* going to tell me?"

"Now Luis—"

Luis huffed, then sorted his things on the dining table so he could put them in his backpack.

"Luis! Please!"

Luis stopped and looked at him. Berto looked sad, his shoulders wilting. He fumbled for words—meaningful ones. He took a deep breath and exhaled heavily out of his mouth.

"Look, I always intended to adopt you. It was always in the back of my mind. Really. I guess I just figured I would always have time. More time. I guess I just didn't."

"Okay," Luis said, putting his pencils and sketchbook in his backpack. "That doesn't explain not telling me the truth. That you're not my *real* father."

Berto pshawed. "What's real anyway? Who has taken care of you?" he said, placing a hand over his heart. He patted his chest. "Me, that's who. I've taken care of you *like* a father. I consider myself your father."

"But you're not," Luis snapped.

"You mean, like biologically?"

"Yeah."

"Well—" Berto said, then smiled. "You're right, there. I didn't create you. But I took care of you. Doesn't that count for something?"

"I don't know," Luis said, standing up and starting to walk to his bedroom, but Berto stopped him with a hand on his chest. Luis looked down at Berto's hand, then up at his face. For some reason, Luis still expected anger, but didn't find any. Luis felt tears welling up, but he did his best to not cry. He didn't want to cry. "I just don't like being lied to."

"Now, son—"

"Please don't call me that."

Berto lifted his hand from Luis's chest, raising both hands as if surrendering. "Fair enough. What do you want to do?"

"I don't know," Luis said, and he meant it. He was confused and didn't know how to straighten it out. He looked at Berto, who again smiled back.

"You know, this weekend Claudia and I talked about getting married. She wants to move in and take your old man for a test drive," he said, then chuckled. "That sounds grosser than I meant it to."

"Claudia wants to move in here, with us?" At first, Luis wondered how she would even fit into their tiny apartment, then realized she would fit into Berto's bedroom. He hadn't considered before now how she would fit into their life, let alone in their cramped living space.

"She's down with it. We could be a real family then. A *new* kind of family. You know?"

"I guess. Then what? You'll both adopt me?" he said, searching Berto's eyes for some reassurance, but not finding any.

"Well, we didn't discuss *that* exactly. But it seems doable."

"Doable?"

Berto shrugged. "I'm just flying by the seat of my pants, son."

"Don't call me that."

"Sorry, Luis. I'll figure something out. I always do. Just think about it. Okay?"

"Okay," Luis replied. He wanted to go to his room, but Berto stood in his way. "Can I go now?"

"Sure."

He stepped aside. Luis went to his room and closed the door.

Inside, he sat on his bed, thinking about what he wanted to do that night, or where he wanted to go. It was getting late, the perfect time to roam around and look for mischief, or just a place to sit and draw, the best way he knew to let off steam. He thought about walking to a new construction site about a mile away, something he saw while riding the bus home from school. He then thought again about heading to Hank's neighborhood pool, the one with the tall springboard and the army of lounge chairs. Hank's face appeared in his mind, like a friendly ghost, and he could hear Hank talking, saying his silly cuss-word proxies, complaining about this and that—general old man stuff. The thought made Luis smile. Was Hank really mad at him? It's not like all the unfortunate things that happened on their trip were his fault. Not really, anyway. He missed Hank's amiable gruffness, his sturdy presence. He felt an insatiable desire to visit him and make amends, even though he didn't need to make amends. He just wanted to, but he didn't know where Hank lived. He could walk the entire neighborhood and try to find his house, maybe the pink 'Cuda resting from the malicious attack on its hood on a serene driveway. But he decided against it, as that would be a big waste of time, the aimlessly walking about.

Instead, he decided to go to the construction site—no, to the community pool. He would sketch the tall springboard under the glow of an even taller night lamp, casting long shadows across gray concrete, and create an imaginary scene where comic book superheroes took turns performing competitive dives, a discerning Spider-Man sitting on a lifeguard's perch, judging each dive with a display of a number from one to ten. The idea pleased him, so he unzipped his backpack, spread its contents on his bed, and gathered all the things he would need.

Then Berto knocked on the door. *Good thing I locked it,* he thought.

Berto cleared his throat. "Luis?"

He didn't respond.

"Son? I mean, Luis. Can I come in?"

Luis froze. He knew more than anything that he didn't want Berto to come in. "I want to be alone."

"Okay," Berto replied.

"Okay."

Silence. Luis expected to hear the muffled sound of feet walking away on the carpet, but he didn't hear anything.

"You'll think about what I said? About me and Claudia being your new family?" Berto said, talking through the door. Luis could sense him pressing his hulking frame against it.

"Okay," Luis replied. A vision appeared in his mind of the three of them sitting for a family portrait in a department store, a vinyl backdrop with a field of bluebonnets on it, and a cheery photographer prompting them to say *queso* instead of cheese before clicking the shutter. It was a peculiar idea to Luis, one of a family he never envisioned having.

Silence again, then muffled footsteps walking away.

Luis made sure he had the pencils he wanted, a flashlight, a package of Haribo Goldbears (just in case he needed a snack, which he always did), and considered taking his blow gun with the feathered darts (maybe he could stick a squirrel or stray cat), but decided against it. Finally, he picked up his sketchbook and thumbed through it, making sure he had empty pages to draw on, when he flipped to the portrait of Hank O'Sullivan. He flattened the page and examined his friend's face.

He read his name, written in pencil.

Hank O'Sullivan.

His name is Hank O'Sullivan, Luis thought. *That's his full name. Hank O'Sullivan.*

Luis pulled his cell phone from his pocket and opened a browser. He typed in "how to find a home address" in the search box. A variety of results were returned, an assortment of blue links, all offering the ultimate answer. One stood out. *Use property tax records to find . . .* it said in the description. It had a link to a website for the Travis County Appraisal District. He found another link for a property search and touched it with his index finger. He typed in O'Sullivan for a last name in the search form, a capital H for a first initial, then tapped enter.

A result was returned for a Henry O'Sullivan with an address and a zip code that was the same as Luis's apartment complex. *That has to be him,* Luis thought. *It has to be!*

Luis put his sketchbook and cell phone in his backpack and slung it over his shoulders. He stepped to the window and slid it open. He propped one foot up, ready to climb out the window, when Berto knocked on the door again.

Luis froze, his foot hanging in the air.

"Luis? I got a letter in the mail that said you've missed a lot of community service. Have you been ditching?" he said, then waited for Luis to answer. Another gentle rap on the door. "Luis?"

But Luis didn't answer. Instead, he continued to climb out the window, then slid it closed from outside after grabbing the trusty drainage pipe. He descended from the second story, then hit the ground running and booked it as fast as he could through the grass, across the steaming asphalt of the slumbering parking lot, and disappeared into the darkness.

20.

When Hank finally got home after dark from their miserable road trip, he wasn't relieved to be alone in an empty home like Luis was. Instead, he was livid. *Filled with piss and vinegar,* as they say, *with a dash of Tabasco for good measure.* After pulling the 'Cuda into his garage, he grabbed a cold beer from the fridge, gulped half of it, then got to work. He popped the desecrated hood open and removed the four bolts securing it to the hinges of the car, propping it against the top of his head as he unscrewed the bolts.

One. Two. Three. Four. Pop!

The hood fell on his back. He extended his arms out to support it and carried it out of the garage, teetering back and forth across the lawn like a lightning bug carrying a heavy load, and unceremoniously tossed it on the ground. The sound of the edge of it hitting the concrete curb rang out into the night, echoing past all the neighbors' homes extending down the street. When it lay flat in the grass, he read again what was inscribed there.

Old Fart!

"Good riddance," he said, wiping his hands clean of some of the anger and resentment he felt, but only some of it. The rest of it was wedged deep into his heart.

He stomped back to the garage, pressed the button to close the garage door, grabbed his half-full beer can from the tool bench and a fresh one from the fridge for good measure.

The living room was as he had left it before the trip: cluttered with stacks of boxes and periodicals, all dusty and dank, everything smelly and sad. He set the fresh beer on the side table and gazed at the framed photo of his wife.

He wiped beer foam from his mouth with his wrist. "You said if you ever died before me that I'd find love again. You promised." He belched. "You *promised.*"

He stomped through a maze of boxes to the front door and swung it open wide. Then, like a crazed army ant, he picked up the closest box to him, propped it on one shoulder, and hauled it out to the curb. He tossed it on top of the car hood, the box splitting open.

"Good riddance," he said, stomping back to the house and repeating this routine. He picked up another box, stomped to the curb, tossed it down, expressed a bitter farewell, and went back inside for another.

Occasionally, he'd stand over his wife's photo, gulping beer, and mumble his litany of grievances. She patiently listened to him, smiling the whole time.

An hour later, with the exception of his La-Z-Boy chair, the photo of his wife, and the side table it sat on, the living room was completely empty of all clutter and boxes, as well as all other furniture and electronics. His second beer was now gone, so he retrieved another one from the garage, popped it open, took a gulp, grumbled some more to his wife's photograph, then moved onto the next room: a guest bedroom. The somber routine continued. He dragged out the bedding, the mattress, the furniture, everything, and tossed it on the front lawn, cursing after each item was tossed. It took a bit, but he eventually got it all out.

Fourth beer, and he was now in his own bedroom, the one he shared with his wife. Except for a lamp he never liked and a dingy throw rug that had been peed on by a pet dog long gone, he didn't take anything from this room. Their room was still sacred. But for how long? He drained the beer, retrieved another, then moved on to the next room.

He continued in this manner until everything he didn't want was tossed onto the lawn. He marveled at his handiwork, his mound of belongings, piled high on his once pristine St. Augustine grass, waiting in shame for the garbagemen to take it away to its new home: the city dump.

"And good riddance," he finally said, wiping his hands clean of the rest of the anger that had consumed him for the last few hours.

He went inside, blew his wife's photo a kiss, and moved on to the bath-room. With the exception of a roll of toilet paper, a bar of soap, a toothbrush, and a tube of toothpaste, the bathroom was now devoid of trinkets, tchotch-kes, wall hangings, even the shower curtain. All gone. He washed his face and hands with cold water and ran a wet hand over his wild grass of hair, blown askew by his exertions. He tried to make himself look handsome, but gave up.

"Hogwash."

He had decided while emptying the kitchen of dusty appliances, brittle china with gold leaf from the nineteen-fifties, cabinets full of stiff Tupper-ware without matching lids, and drawers full of random screws and ball-point pens with the slogans of one hundred now-defunct local businesses, that he wanted to go to his favorite neighborhood hangout, Home Runs, and tie one on.

And that's exactly what he did. *Gosh darn it!*

He drove his 'Cuda—sans hood and with the driver's side window down, just in case he needed to hurl—to the bar. He barreled into the parking lot and parked haphazardly in two spots (one a handicap space, no less). He tumbled inside as quick as he could to order his favorite cocktail.

He climbed onto his favorite bar stool and sat, like a lumpy gargoyle returning from a misadventure.

Jack the bartender smiled. "The usual?" he said, wiping a wet lowball glass with a towel.

"Yup," Hank answered. "Make it a double."

"Coming up," Jack agreed, gathering the ingredients and glassware he needed.

Hank licked his lips and looked around. "Slow tonight?" he asked the bartender.

Jack poured whiskey in a mixing glass. "Kinda. Karaoke ended a little while ago and everyone split, except for Ernie—"

"What an ass," Hank interjected. "Sheesh."

Jack chuckled. "And Hilda. She's around, too."

"Floozy," Hank said, then sucked his teeth. He teetered on his stool but maintained his seat with a stiff leg to the brass footrest at the bottom of the bar.

"Someone's feisty tonight," Jack said.

"Yup."

Jack created his alcoholic masterpiece and set it on a coaster in front of Hank. It glistened underneath the Tiffany lamps suspended above the bar, several in a row like an armada of spaceships. "I have to go to the back. Out of cherries again."

"You're gonna need 'em," Hank said, then slurped his drink. "First of many."

Jack disappeared, leaving Hank to himself. Or at least he thought he was by himself. Ernie the barfly appeared at the end of the bar. *Out of thin air,* as they say. This time, it was true.

Poof!

Hank felt Ernie's stare and turned to look at his foe. Ernie glared, a pint of yellow beer in one hand. Hank looked back at the wall of liquor bottles, unperturbed by Ernie's presence. He delicately sipped his cocktail, raising a pinky for emphasis and a bit of elegance.

Jack returned, looking down the bar at Ernie, then back at Hank. "There won't be any trouble tonight, will there?" he said aloud to both of them.

Ernie grumbled, grabbed his beer, and vanished.

Hank chuckled. "Adios, knucklehead."

Jack fumbled with the new jar of cherries, trying to open it. "Say, whatever happened the night you two got into a fight? Did you get arrested?"

"Yup," Hank said, slurping the last of his drink, the shrinking ice cubes clinking the glass when he set it down closer to Jack. "Another one."

Jack still couldn't get the jar opened. Hank requested the jar with a gesture. Jack watched Hank open it with his massive mitts, as easily as ripping tissue paper. He handed the jar back to Jack.

"Did you go to jail?"

"Yup. Had to stay the night."

"Then what happened?" Jack said while preparing a fresh cocktail.

Hank sighed. "Judge gave me community service. Picking up trash on the side of the road. Et cetera."

Jack mixed the concoction in a tall mixing glass with a long metal spoon. He set the thing of beauty on a coaster in front of Hank.

"That sucks," he said to Hank.

"You're telling me. A total waste of good weekends."

Jack wiped the bar top with a white towel. "And what about Ernie? He get community service, too?"

"Beats me. He can suck toads for eternity, for all I care." Hank sipped his fresh drink and smiled. "You make a fine whiskey old-fashioned."

"That's why they pay me the big bucks," Jack reminded him, then eyed his tip jar.

Hank pulled a twenty from his back pocket and dropped it in the jar.

"You're a scholar and a gentleman," Jack said.

"Nah," Hank said.

He drank one cocktail after another over the next couple of hours, keeping his pace like a marathon runner—steady yet persistent. He watched Jack perform his closing duties. He witnessed Ernie pay his tab without even saying a word to him. *What a relief!* he thought. *Getting into it with that blockhead is the last thing I need.* And before he knew it, closing time had arrived.

Jack dropped his tab on the bar. "You don't have to go home, but you can't stay here."

Hank wanted to say *Yup*, but found that the word stuck to the roof of his mouth like a glob of peanut butter. Frustrated, he decided to pull out his wallet and drop some bills to pay his tab. *Don't need the change*, he thought. *Never do.* He left four twenties, maybe five. He didn't count them. He stumbled to the exit, a sight that concerned Jack.

"I can call you a cab. No need to drive," he said to Hank. "Come on, buddy. What do ya say?"

"I'll walk," Hank managed to say in return. "No worry . . . Walk!"

He flung the glass door open and left. Jack shook his head. He had watched Hank walk out the door in a similar fashion for a long time—too long to remember, too many times to count—and Hank always made it back to his favorite barstool in one piece. He considered running after Hank, but then thought better of it. A little voice in the back of his head whispered, *He's too strong and too stubborn.* He locked the glass door so he could finish closing up.

Outside, Hank tripped over a parking space curb but managed to keep from falling to the asphalt. The night air was cool and crisp, not a hint of humidity at all, unusual for sure. The black sky was clear and the moon bright and yellow, white stars like pinholes in the curtain of night, and Hank could even see a small plane with a red flashing light cruising across it. A short film of Santa Claus flying across the sky in his sleigh pulled by a crew of reindeer flashed in his mind, which made Hank snicker. He knew he was drunk and was enjoying it, even the weird mental films he didn't ask to see. It was better than the alternative, the thoughts he'd rather not think, the absence of loved ones, the inevitable. The parking lot was empty except for the 'Cuda, a couple of rows over. It sat alone in the sea of asphalt, a pink island floating within a maze of yellow lines. He knew he shouldn't drive, but fumbled for his keys anyway. He pulled the wad of keys from his pocket and immediately dropped them on the ground. They clinked when they hit. He pshawed at his misfortune, then looked around for any witnesses. There was no one. He smirked, then leaned over to pick them up.

When he stood back up, his index finger through the key ring and the keys swinging around the centrifugal force of his hand, a dark figure stood before him. He couldn't make out who it was.

He caught the keys in the palm of his hand, and put them back in his pocket.

The figure took one step forward, then stopped.

Hank could see the figure was clinching its fists, which hung at the end of long, thin arms.

Hank clenched his own fists without even thinking about it. Call it instinct, if you will, his fists ready for a fight.

The figure took another step closer. The light from a street lamp above fell across the figure's face. Hank's eyelids closed into slits. He knew who this was.

Ernie. That jerk.

Hank sneered. "You. Again?"

Ernie nodded. "Me. Again."

Hank sighed. "Didn't I beat enough—" he began, then stuttered, "s-sense into you last time?" he asked Ernie, then shoved a fist into his pocket and fumbled for his keys again. "I just . . . want . . . to go home."

"Oh, you're going home all right. Going home for good."

The light of the streetlamp revealed a black revolver with a large snub-nose barrel at the end of a stiff arm. Hank recognized it. It was a Smith & Wesson .357. He knew what would happen if Ernie pulled the trigger, if his aim was true. Hank lifted both of his hands as a sign of surrender, his key ring impaled on his index finger.

"Suck a—" Hank began, then roughly cleared his throat, spitting a loogy on the ground. "Donkey dingle."

Then he heard a loud bang.

Lights out.

Time to go home.

For good.

21.

*L*uis walked on the sidewalk up the main road into Wells Port—the neighborhood where Hank supposedly lived, near the apartments where Luis lived not far away—then turned right onto the street where the app on his phone told him to go: Pfeiffer Road. The name was often mispronounced, sometimes out of ignorance, other times for fun. The nearby town of Pflugerville was often called P-ville, even though the "P" was silent. Pfeiffer Road was sometimes called P-road by its residents, although Hank wasn't one to call his beloved street that. He thought P-road sounded too much like P-word, suggesting the trashy word "pussy." Hank didn't like that at all, not even the insinuation. Luis would've thought that was funny. He whistled as he walked to the address, unaware that *pfeiffer* meant whistler in German.

Luis noticed the monolith of garbage even before he knew for sure that it was sitting in front of Hank's house. He couldn't miss it. At the end of the driveway, he stopped and gazed at the sheer number of boxes and stuff, like it was Stonehenge—mysterious, imposing, and absurd—built by an unknown construction crew from an ancient era long gone. He looked at the number stenciled in black and reflective white on the curb and compared it to the number in his phone's app. They were the same. He looked at the house for any signs of life. The front porch light was off. There weren't any lights turned on inside the house; all the windows were black, reflective pools with shimmery reflections of street lamps and neighboring porches from across the street. In some ways, the house looked abandoned, as if looters had ransacked the place, then dropped everything on the lawn in fear of being arrested by the deputies of the Travis County Sheriff's Office. But Luis soon realized—without a smidgeon of doubt—that this was Hank's house. At the very front of the monolithic pile, down at the bottom and jutting out from the grass and over the curb slightly, was the pink hood from the 'Cuda. He couldn't see the words that had been scrawled on it, but he knew they were there. He slid his phone in his front pocket and sneaked over to the front porch.

He stepped up two concrete steps and made his way over to a window next to the front door, a flower pot filled with daisies at his feet. If Luis had known Hank just a little longer, he would've learned what was underneath the pot, but he hadn't. He smashed a flat hand against the window screen, wedging his forehead against his thumb and index finger to see inside, but it was too dark. He couldn't see anything or anyone. He looked back to the street. No one was outside, all inside their homes, even the street was empty of moving cars. He craned his neck to look to each side of the house and wondered if there was a gate in the fence. For a brief moment, he wondered what a cop driving by would think if he noticed a Black teenager lurking around Hank's house, but he decided to check anyway, his impetuousness overriding his concern. He stepped off the porch and went around to one side.

There was a gate in the fence for sure, but it was padlocked. That didn't stop Luis. Without a thought, he grabbed the top of the fence with both hands and gracefully flung himself over in one swooping motion. Spider-Man would've been proud. He crept through the damp grass to the covered back porch, weaving through patio furniture and lawn equipment cloaked in shadowy darkness. The toe of one shoe nudged a metal chair, making it squeal. Luis froze and waited for lights inside to come on, but they didn't. There was a sliding glass door that he was certain would've been locked, but it easily slid open. He stuck his head inside and listened for any signs of life. Except for the hum of the refrigerator, there was dead silence. Not even the air conditioning was running. He debated going inside. He knew that entering someone's house, even if the door was unlocked, was an illegal entry. But he rationalized in his mind that he knew Hank. *We're friends. Right?* he thought to himself. *Right?* He stepped inside and slid the door closed.

He stood in place for a good minute and listened. Any snoring? Nope. TV noise? Nuh-uh. Any pets? Doesn't seem like it. The house smelled of coffee, stale beer, and the musk of an old man, maybe the stench of a mildewed gym sock for good measure. Or was it motor oil? And there was a dankness in the air, too, probably from Hank leaving the front door open while he tossed most of his belongings on the front lawn. Luis took his backpack off and unzipped it, slowly pulling his flashlight out. The first click of the power button was a dim light. He discovered that he was standing in a dining area next to the kitchen—no dining table, and the kitchen counters absent of any appliances. The open plan revealed the living room. He could see the silhouette of something there, so he slowly made his way into the good-sized room. Soon, the La-Z-Boy chair and side table revealed themselves. Nothing else.

Weird, Luis thought. *Is Hank moving or something?*

He decided to click the button on the flashlight for a brighter beam. He was pretty certain Hank wasn't home, that nobody was home. The brighter light revealed the framed photograph of Hank's wife on the side table. Luis picked it up and examined it. *She's pretty,* he thought, then set the photo back on the table. He could now see a dark hallway to the left of the kitchen. He went that way.

In the hallway, he slowly stepped to the first door and flashed the light inside. Completely empty. "Hmmm," he said aloud. He continued down the hallway, stepping carefully on the carpet, trying not to make a sound just in case he was wrong and someone was actually home. He found another bedroom that was also empty except for a single sock on the floor, a white, athletic tube sock with two pink stripes at one end and a dingy brown sole at the other. He could hear himself breathing as he continued down the hall. Next was a bathroom, mostly empty except for a toothbrush and toothpaste and a roll of toilet paper.

He continued to the last doorway, which led into the main bedroom: Hank's room. Luis peeked inside, beaming the flashlight around the room. Unlike the rest of the house, this one was still furnished: a queen-sized bed with walnut headboard, a matching walnut chest of drawers and dresser with a vanity mirror on top along with a keepsake box, a pair of squat nightstands on either side of the bed (one with a lamp on top, the other with a menorah fitted with nine white candles), and a wooden rocking chair with a quilted cushion. On the opposite side of the bedroom were two closets, one with the door open revealing Hank's clothes hanging in two parallel rows: shirts on top, jeans and slacks on bottom, and a platoon of shoes patrolling the floor. Between the two closet doors was the entrance to the master bathroom, drips from a leaky sink faucet echoing inside, no windows at all making it as dark as a crypt. Luis slowly stepped into the bedroom, holding the flashlight up next to his head, helping him navigate the room. He'd occasionally look down so he wouldn't step on anything, but all he saw on the carpet was what looked like a rough patch where a throw rug used to be, and the faint smell of dog urine. The flashlight seemed to gravitate to the keepsake box on the dresser, the yellow light casting an oblong shadow up the wall, giving it the appearance of subtle movement, and the brass key with a red tassel glimmered.

It invited him over.

Something told Luis to open it.

It was also made of walnut, or some similar dark wood, with black gutta-percha plaques on the top and sides, elaborate scenes etched in each: the top one with two hunting dogs corralling a wild boar and a pheasant on it, the front one with two more hunting dogs mauling an eight-point buck.

Luis lifted the lid. Its hinges squeaked until it wouldn't swing any farther, the top now propped open. He aimed the light inside. It was jammed full of papers stacked on their side—the scent of foxing paper and stale dust wafting up—and a color, matte photograph with a broad bevel of white around the picture, lying on top. The beautiful woman from the living room photo was in this one, too. *Hank's wife*, he thought. A little girl wearing a floral dress with her dark brown hair cut in a bob sat on her lap, one of her hands shoved halfway into her mouth, the other hand clinging to the mother's shirt, one button precariously undone. He picked up the photo and examined it. The only feature on the young girl's face that reminded Luis of Hank was her eyebrows. They peaked in the middle like the wings of a gliding seagull. Oh, yeah, she also had a mischievous twinkle in her eye that was definitely like Hank's, not the mother's. Luis felt a smile pull at his cheeks, then he laid the photo on the dresser.

He pinched a random piece of paper from the keepsake box and discovered it was a birthday card to Hank, an inscription in meticulous cursive that read, "Happy birthday, Hank Darling! Love you madly, Linda." A second inscription in messy, orange crayon read, "I love Daddy! Tammy." There were letters to Hank from Linda, some in envelopes, others just folded in thirds, all professing her love for him and the longing she felt for him at the time of their writing. There were more photos of little Tammy, and she seemed to progress in age as Luis pulled each out of the box—one with a scene from a birthday party with several other children, all wearing party hats with schmears of icing on their faces; another with Linda and Tammy posing in front of a whimsical building at Disneyland, their faces beaming. He pulled out another photo of Hank and his wife—one of him passionately kissing her in the same way Word War II sailors did in old magazine photos: dramatically entwined, lips locked, and their eyes closed—with little Tammy's head peeking out from behind Hank's waist like a pixie, displaying rabbit ears with two fingers. Immediately, Luis was consumed with grief—Hank's grief—as he held this photo in his hand, Hank kissing his wife in the photo like it would be his last, his impishly cute daughter playing behind them like their love would never die. Luis didn't know what this type of loss felt like, but he felt something open up inside him, something so deep it seemed bottomless, dense as the center of a black hole. Mournful tears collected in his eyes as he dwelled in the stifling presence of Hank's grief. He felt his chest constrict.

Then his stomach grumbled. He was hungry now. He put the flashlight in his mouth so he could push the upright papers back to make room for what he took out, when he noticed something sparkle at the bottom of the keepsake box. He looked closer at what appeared to be a gold engagement ring with a large diamond solitaire lying on the bottom of the box, and also a rosary with colored glass beads next to it. He picked up the rosary and examined it, then looked over at the menorah sitting on a nightstand, the flashlight illuminating its presence on the other side of the room. Confused, he placed the rosary back in the keepsake box. He slid the letters and photographs over the ring and rosary, then shut the lid gently and quickly left Hank's room.

He made his way to the other side of the house and opened a door that he thought might be the garage. He was right. He turned the overhead light on with a flick of the wall switch. The 'Cuda was noticeably gone. Luis spotted the refrigerator and went over to open it, discovering that it was fully stocked with beers and sodas. He grabbed a Coke, popped the top, and took a swig.

He went back in, headed to the kitchen, and opened another fridge. Not much was inside besides leftover sandwiches and burgers from the fast food joints outside their neighborhood. One sandwich looked like a submarine wearing a toupee of green mold. He closed the door.

Back in the living room, Luis sat in Hank's La-Z-Boy, putting his backpack in his lap and drinking his Coke. He opened the backpack and pulled out the bag of Haribo Goldbears. He ripped the top off and grabbed a handful, selecting a red bear and popping it in his mouth. It tasted good with the Coke. He set the can of Coke on the side table next to the photo of Hank's wife and the bottle of Tylenol, then reclined the chair by pulling the wooden lever on one side. He eventually drank all of the Coke and ate all the gummy bears, and before he knew any better, he was sawing logs and dreaming of driving the pink 'Cuda on a highway somewhere, except his dream car was a convertible with the top down, and instead of Hank, he was riding with Katy Perry, his teenaged dream girl.

22.

The first thing Hank saw when he opened his eyes were off-white ceiling tiles—one of which had a brown spot the size of a pancake in the middle of it, and another with a metal arm, enameled in white, protruding through a hole cut into it. A black electrical cord dangled from the end of the shiny white arm and Hank followed it with his eyes to some kind of beeping electronic box. Digital numbers counted up, then down, then back up again on the dot matrix screen. The beeps were shrill, and Hank realized his neck hurt a lot. He wanted to rub it, but his arms felt like they were filled with concrete. He surveyed the room the best he could, swiveling his head on his neck just slightly so he could figure out where he was. The first thing he realized was that he wasn't dead. The second thing he realized was that he was taking a leak. Embarrassed, he tried to see if he was wetting the bed, but it hurt to move. So he lay still and enjoyed the relief of urinating. A bit of movement caught his attention out of the corner of his eye, and when he swiveled his neck—oh so slightly—to the right, he could see a stream of yellow liquid traveling through a clear tube—tiny bubbles together like subway train cars—that snaked out from under the bed sheet and disappeared over the side of the bed.

Must be in the hospital, he thought. *Ernie didn't kill me.*

He swiveled his head to the left to see what else was in the room. On the wall was a faded print of a watercolor painting, tranquil beach dunes with green and yellow grass sprouting from the tops, sea gulls levitating in the air above a sunhat and book resting on a brightly striped beach towel. There was a door to a bathroom, he assumed, because of a sign attached to it that said, "All employees must wash their hands after using." Hank thought to himself, *Everyone should wash their hands after using.* He chuckled, but it hurt to laugh, so he stopped.

After he had been lying in the room alone for quite some time feeling sorry for himself, the electronic box squawking, urine still draining out the tube, his stomach grumbling even though he wasn't hungry, a woman barged into the room with a clipboard in one hand and her other hand holding a ponytail together on the back of her head. She raced over to his bed and tossed the clipboard at his feet, the edge of it banging his ankle.

"Ouch," he said.

"Sorry about that," she replied, fishing a hair tie from her pants pocket, then looping it around the ponytail. He assumed she was a nurse, as she was wearing a nurse-like uniform, but he couldn't remember that they were called scrubs. The uniform was pink and teal with Peanuts cartoon characters on it like Snoopy, Woodstock, and Charlie Brown, of course. Hank was still a little messed up in the head, but was with it enough to recognize the Peanuts characters. "I had to fix my hair."

"I see that—to my detriment," Hank grumbled. He turned to look at the beach scene on the wall as if he was viewing the scene through a window, watching the waves crash just outside. The serenity of it was in stark contrast to the pain coursing through his body.

"Oh, stop that. Haven't I been taking care of you up to this point?" she asked him, picking up the clipboard, then checking the squawking box. She mashed buttons on the front of it.

"I don't know if you've been taking care of me. I just woke up."

"Rip Van Winkle. That's you," she mused, continuing to mash buttons. The machine still squawked. "That's what they've all been calling you on this floor since my shift started."

"How nice. Can you turn the volume down on that contraption? It's annoying."

"It's totally annoying," she agreed. After a few more jabs, the box went silent. Her face lit up. "Hooray!" she cheered. Her hands appeared to clap, although they didn't make a sound.

Hank sighed. "Thanks."

"Everything is going to be all right," she said, then pulled up a stool and sat next to the bed. She patted his hand. And even though there were a variety of tubes and wires taped to his hand, her touch sent a jolt of electricity through his heavy arm.

He turned away from the beach scene to look at her. She smiled back at him, patting his hand some more.

"I guess Ernie didn't shoot me," he said to her.

"Oh," she began, then straightened her back, her bosom stretching the front of her shirt a bit, enough to catch Hank's eye. "You were shot all right, but you'll be fine. Trust me."

"Trust you?" he blurted, a little agitated now. "Where did the scumbag shoot me?"

"Well, let me put it this way," she said, tsk-tsking a time or two. "You may have to get a love handle transplant."

"What the—" he began, trying to sit up. But she placed a hand on his chest, keeping him down on the bed.

Shaking her head, she said, "Just lie down and rest, why don't you."

Hank sighed again. "All right."

"All right," she repeated. She lifted the clipboard and looked it over. "Says here your name is Henry. Is that right?"

"My friends call me Hank."

"Really? Should I call you Hank?"

"I don't know," he said, smirking. "That would be fine."

"Sounds good, Hank," she said, then extended her hand to him for a shake. "Then you can call me Doris, my friend."

"Doris," he repeated slowly, as if trying out the two syllables to see if they would make the team.

"So, the guy that shot you only hit your side. Bullet went straight through. Didn't graze anything of importance. But . . . "

"But what?"

"But," she began, standing up. "You fell backwards and hit your head on the ground. You're lucky the impact didn't kill you. Could have, you know?"

"Killed me?" Hank mused.

"Yup."

"Huh," he quipped. "Could have. But it didn't."

"You're still breathing, aren't you?"

"Yup."

Doris leaned over, grabbing the catheter line, then looked underneath the bed at the tank full of urine. The way she held the line in her grasp tugged at Hank's carrot, which wasn't pleasant.

"I will need to change this out," she remarked matter-of-factly, as if she had performed this action a million times, like lugging tanks of urine around was as normal as normal can be.

Hank's face flushed. "Change it?"

But before he could say something to stop her, she slid the tank out from underneath the bed, the line tugging at the bed sheet which had been covering his privates, then pulling it off the top of him, exposing him.

Hank was mortified. "Oh, god no!" He wanted to cover himself, but his arms were too heavy. He wilted with embarrassment.

"Sorry about that," she said, pulling the bed sheet back over him, covering his withered carrot and pale, bare legs. "But don't worry, I've seen dozens of willies today. I've seen dozens of pink tacos, too. It all blends together. Comes with the job, I guess."

"How strange."

"You're telling me," she said as she tucked the bedsheet underneath him so it wouldn't come off again. She then smiled at him. "You're like a burrito now."

Hank smiled back. He thought she was attractive—very much so—but, of course, wouldn't say so out loud, as that would be undignified and ungentlemanlike. But he couldn't help but notice the brunette ponytail with intertwining strands of gray cascading down her back as she tucked the sheet under him. Or her toned, freckled arms with a sunspot here and there. Or the small round biscuits of her backside. He didn't mean to gander at her appearance, but he couldn't help it. She mesmerized him. The one thing he noticed most, though, were the crows feet radiating wisdom from the sides of her eyes. When she smiled, the crows feet morphed into insistent arrows, begging him to get lost in her hazel eyes. Gazing into them was like taking truth serum.

"My grandmother once told me that anyone who sees my privates—besides my wife or my mother—is asking for trouble."

"Is that so?" she said, then smiled. "Then I guess I'm in trouble. But it's a good kind of trouble."

She knelt down and detached the tube from the tank full of urine, then stood up.

Hank looked up at her. "So, I'm going to be all right, then?"

She smiled. "Yup."

"Good."

"I'll be back. Gotta empty this," she said, turning to leave.

"Wait!" Hank blurted. She turned back to face him. "Do you have a pad of paper and a pencil I can use?"

"I'll look," she said, then left the room.

Even after she left, Hank could still see her—a faint outline of her—frozen in the doorframe, her back to him, her ponytail fixed in midswing. He decided that the color of her pants was aquamarine, not teal, and the Peanuts characters on her shirt must've been her favorite from her childhood. Some people do that, wear their nostalgia on their clothing. Hank's mind wandered and he remembered that when he was a kid, his favorite cartoon character was Beetle Bailey—the inept soldier stationed at Camp Swampy in the newspaper funnies—and that his favorite color was blue. He debated telling Doris this bit of information about himself, but decided against it. Too forward. A few minutes later, her faint impression vanished, leaving Hank to wonder again about his current circumstances.

Here are a number of things he wondered about. Where were his clothes and his wallet? And what about his precious car? Had it been towed late in the night or was it still in the parking lot exactly where he left it? And what was up with Ernie *shooting* him? He knew they felt contempt for each other, but he never would've thought in a thousand years that Ernie had the cojones to carry a gun to the bar and attempt to murder him in cold blood.

So strange, he thought.

He also worried that he didn't pay up his tab with Jack and, even worse, didn't give him a tip either.

Unconscionable!

Just the slightest worry he'd made that mistake made him feel glum. He relished his miraculous streak of paying his tab accompanied by a generous tip whenever he left the bar, no matter how loaded he was and no matter his temperament. He always paid it in full without fail—always. Until now. He somehow found the strength to rub his neck—as tender as a freshly pounded chicken breast ready to be breaded and pan fried—then sulked, sinking deeper in his bed. Until Doris came back in. Just the sight of her perked him up like a wilted flower receiving nourishment under a spring shower. She cradled the empty tank in her arms and knelt next to the bed to reattach the tube.

"Feeling better?" she asked him, out of sight beneath the bed.

"Yup."

"Good," she said, then stood up. "Ta-da!" She flung her arms out in mock fanfare.

"Did you bring the pad of paper and pencil?" he asked her, not seeing them in her hands.

"Oh yeah. Here—" she said, lifting the front of her shirt and revealing the pad of paper wedged in her waist band. Hank liked that she placed it there. She handed it to him, also plucking a yellow pencil perched above her right ear. "Have fun Van Gogh!" She pronounced the Gogh like "go," which tweaked Hank's disposition.

"It's pronounced like Hah, not Go," he said, slowly flipping the cover of the pad of paper over.

"Whatever," she chided him. "You sound like you're coughing up a hairball."

They both laughed, which hurt Hank's insides. He groaned.

"Take it easy," she demanded, tucking him under the bed sheet and making sure the line to the tank was unobstructed. "You need to rest."

"Okay," he replied, doodling on the pad.

"What are you going to draw?"

"Don't know yet."

"I see," she said, standing next to the bed with her hands on her hips.

Hank studied her left hand.

"Do they make you take off your wedding ring here at the hospital?" he said, then doodled on the paper some more.

"That's mighty forward of you, Mr. O'Sullivan."

"Call me Hank."

"That's mighty forward of you, Hank. But for the record, I'm widowed."

"Interesting." His tongue jabbed in and out of his pursed lips, illustrating his concentration.

"Why is that interesting?"

"I'm widowed, too," he said, then lifted the pad of paper to reveal his sketch. It looked like something a kindergartener would draw—shaky yet whimsical, in equal measure.

"Interesting," she replied.

"What is? That I'm a widower?"

"Nope," she said. "The drawing. You're definitely no van Hah!"

She smirked, then made her way to the door, turning back to him before exiting.

"Are you coming back?" he said.

"I'm here all day. You'll get your fill of me, for sure."

"Good."

"Good," she said, then left.

Again, Hank could still see her visage even minutes after she left. Once the impression was finally gone, he looked at the doodle he meticulously drew on the pad of paper. It was objectively horrible. He chuckled, ripped the drawing from the pad, crumpled the paper, and dropped it on the floor. He looked at the painting of beach dunes and the hovering sea gulls, probably waiting for a picnic to begin. He knew what he wanted to try to draw next and soon got to work.

23.

There's nothing worse than being awakened by a loud, banging noise, and that's how Luis came to consciousness the next morning, having curled up in Hank's La-Z-Boy and fallen into a deep sleep, deeper than he had slept in a very, very long time. The banging was followed by the doorbell's sassy ding-dong, then silence. As his heart banged inside his chest, his brain slowly came back online to the real world, but he was terrified. He wasn't in his own home; he had broken into Hank's. He found he was clawing the leathery material of the chair, scared to move or make a sound. Next came a softer knock, an unsure secret knock with a familiar cadence—a child's knocking pattern—followed by some grumbling and footsteps leaving the front porch. Luis dropped to the floor—tossing his backpack to the side—and crawled over to a large picture window, opening the linen curtains just slightly, just enough to see two white policemen walking away from the house and back to a patrol car parked at the curb. Luis's heart was punching up to his throat now. What would the cops do if they came back and found him inside?

Are they here for me? he thought. *How did they find out I was here?*

Luis let the curtains fall together and crawled back to the La-Z-Boy. And as he grabbed one of the straps to his backpack—ready to sling it over a shoulder and escape out the back door as quietly as he came in—someone else was at the door, trying to actually come in this time. He could hear a key being inserted into the dead bolt, followed by an attempt to unlock it. The door didn't open. Another key was inserted, and this time the dead bolt unlocked, and the knob jiggled. Luis dove behind the La-Z-Boy and scrunched his body into a ball, his head beneath overlapping arms. He hoped with all he had that whoever it was wouldn't see him when they came in, so he could slip out the back door.

The front door creaked open.

Someone stepped inside, then closed the door again.

Silence for a second or two. No footsteps.

Then he could hear the muffled sounds of shoes traveling across carpet. Whoever it was, they walked past the La-Z-Boy without stopping and headed into the hallway. Since the lights were still off, Luis could only see the stranger's feet disappear into the darkness of the hall. Luis stood up and tiptoed toward the sliding glass door—his portal to freedom—reaching for the handle to slide it open. But instead of opening it, he was busted, drenched in the light of a flashlight held by the stranger.

"Who the hell are you?" the strange man said.

Without thinking, Luis raised his hands to surrender, but he didn't respond. A column of light from the stranger blinded him. He moved his hands in front of his face to protect his eyes from the penetrating light. The click of a wall switch was followed by the light from an overhead lamp. Luis could now see he was caught by a man who looked to be around Hank's age and who seemed to have raided Hank's closet for jeans and sneakers. The man was dumbfounded.

"I said, who the hell are *you*?" the man said. He raised the black metal flashlight like a club, as if he might whack Luis over the head.

Luis just stood there, not saying anything, breathing heavily. This wasn't how he thought the morning was going to go. Not at all.

"Hello?! You speak *English*?!"

Luis huffed. "Yeah, I speak English."

"I'm Hank's neighbor, Bill. Who the hell are you?"

"Hank's grandson."

Bill's face scrunched. "What the—" he said, then lowered his flashlight and turned it off. "Hank doesn't have no grandson."

"Sure, he does. You're looking at him."

"Then what's your name?"

"Luis."

"*Luis?* Are you from Mexico? Is your mother one of them prostitutes in Matamoros?"

"Huh?" Luis said, scratching his head. "I'm not Mexican."

"You could've fooled me. Then why aren't you at the hospital?"

"Hospital?" Luis said.

"Hank was shot last night. Didn't you know that?"

Luis gasped. "No, I was asleep. I didn't know he—"

"All right, all right. There's no time to jabber then, Louie."

"It's *Luis*."

"Whatever. I came over for something important. Let me go get it, then you're coming with me."

"You'll take me to the hospital with you?"

Bill returned a blank stare. "I thought you said you spoke English?"

"I am speaking English."

"Just wait here then," Bill said, looking around. He rubbed his stubbly chin and ruminated about something. He examined the kitchen and dining area and living room. "Why is all of Hank's stuff out on the front lawn?"

Luis also looked around—observing the same thing—then shrugged.

"Fine. Wait here," Bill commanded, then disappeared into the hallway.

Luis could hear Bill rummaging in Hank's room, the opening and closing of the closet door, the opening and closing of dresser drawers. After a moment or two, Bill returned from the hallway with a small duffel bag, army green in color and the size of a shoe box.

"Hank told me one time that if there was ever an emergency and he was at the hospital, then to come in here and get a bag with a label 'For emergencies' on it. And I'll be damned if he wasn't right. It has a tag right on it," Bill said, raising the tag attached to one of the straps with a piece of brown twine, the words "For emergencies" scribbled in black marker on it. "See?"

"Wow."

"You coming with?"

It took a few seconds for Luis to comprehend that Bill was referring to him. "Yes, yes. But can I take a whiz first?"

Bill huffed. "Fine."

Luis ran into the hallway bathroom and was really quick about it. Once he came back, he followed Bill out to a Chrysler minivan in the driveway next door.

As they made their way there—walking through the dewy grass of the two yards—Bill looked back at the mound of Hank's belongings piled high by the curb and sloping back toward the house, and remarked to himself, "Doesn't Hank know bulk trash pickup isn't for another two weeks?" Bill looked at Luis for an acknowledgment to this obvious declaration—this important procedural tidbit that certainly all the neighbors knew about—but realized he was talking to a teenager. "Never mind. You're not a *homeowner*."

Bill pulled a wad of keys from his pocket, pressed a button on his key fob, the minivan squawked, and they got in—Luis in the front passenger seat with his backpack at his feet, Bill fastened securely in the driver seat—and Bill drove away to the hospital as fast as that six-cylinder American engine could go.

— — —

Bill parked in a handicap spot near the entrance to the emergency room of the North Austin Medical Center, then leaned over toward Luis to open the glovebox, accidentally jabbing Luis's thigh with his elbow.

"Sorry, gotta get something in there," he said, opening it and pulling out a blue hang tag. He closed the glove box and hung the handicapped tag on his rearview mirror. "This is my mother-in-law's handy hang tag. She died last year, but it doesn't expire for another two years. No reason to waste it."

"But we're not handicapped," Luis remarked.

"Can you limp a little on the way in?"

"Seriously?"

"A little," Bill said, smirking. "Fine. Let's go."

They left the minivan and trotted to the entrance.

Inside, it was chilly, and the air smelled of disinfectant and lemons. Instrumental music approximating a saccharine ballad from the 1980s was playing softly. Bill and Luis made their way to a check-in window. Bill tapped his knuckles against the dividing glass. Soon enough, a short, stocky woman with a curly, pitch-black bob appeared. Her name was Verna, according to her name tag.

"Can I help you?" she said.

"We're here to see Hank O'Sullivan."

She immediately began typing something on a computer keyboard.

With her eyes on a computer screen, she asked, "Your relation to—" Her eyes narrowed, then she turned to Bill and Luis. "I don't see a Hank in our system."

"I know he's here. This is his grandson," Bill said, thumbing in Luis's direction. Luis waved at Verna.

"Maybe he has a different first name," she said, turning back to the screen.

Luis snapped his fingers. "His first name is Henry. Is there a Henry O'Sullivan here?"

Bill chuckled. "See. Grandson here! I didn't know his first name was Henry."

She typed some more. "That's it. And you're his grandson?" she said, giving him a hard stare.

"Yes," Luis said.

She pressed a button next to her keyboard, a buzzer going off through a diminutive speaker somewhere, maybe behind ceiling tiles. "Go through these doors, down the hall, take the first left, and it's the third room on the left."

"Got it," Bill said to her.

They walked with purpose, the small duffel bag swinging on Bill's left side. Luis followed close by.

"I hope he's glad to see us," Bill remarked to Luis. "Your grandpa can be . . . grouchy."

Luis thought that was funny. They followed Verna's directions and soon found themselves standing outside of the third room on the left. Bill stuck a stiff arm out to stop Luis.

"Wait!" he said, then composed himself, clearing his throat. "Just to let you know, we won't know what we might see in there. It might be bad—really bad. I don't want you to regret coming here to see your grandpa if he's really messed up or something."

Luis blinked a time or two. "It's okay."

"You sure?"

"Yup."

"Okay," Bill said, shaking out his arms, the duffel bag dangling. "Let's do it."

Bill took a few steps, then turned into the room. Luis followed, but rammed into Bill who had stopped in his tracks.

Bill placed a hand on his hip, then cocked his head. Luis, too, cocked his head. They saw Hank lying in a hospital bed, his eyes closed, the bedding mounded at his knees. He had no shirt on, and a nurse faced him, her hands hidden by the blankets. Hank didn't notice that Bill and Luis were watching him.

Hank groaned, then belted out, "Ouch! Be careful!"

A muffled "sorry" could be heard.

"My wife was never this rough with me!" Hank continued, and that's when he noticed Bill and Luis standing at the door to the room. He cleared his throat, then said, "Oh, hi there."

The nurse turned her head. "Hank is getting cleaned up now, you'll have to wait to visit . . . "

Bill gasped, then said, "Doris?!"

She pulled the bedding back up to cover Hank, then smoothed some strands of her wild hair that had came undone from her ponytail.

"Bill? What are you doing here?" she asked him, smoothing out the bed-sheet, making sure the catheter line wasn't obstructed or twisted.

"I came to see Hank. He's my neighbor," Bill said, stepping over to Hank's bed, Luis right behind him.

Doris appeared quite surprised at this revelation. "Hank's your neighbor?" she said, looking at Hank.

"Yup," Hank acknowledged.

"The one you and Vera have been trying to set me up with?" she said, looking from Hank to Bill and back again.

"The very one," Bill said, then he thumbed to Luis. "And I brought his grandson."

Luis waved from behind Bill.

Doris looked at Hank. "You have a grandson?"

Hank chuckled. "Appears so."

"What the—" she started, then laughed. "This is so *weird*. By the way, I was changing out his catheter, not doing any funny business. Okay?"

"Right," Bill replied. "No funny business." He turned to Hank and gave him his emergency bag, setting it on his belly. "You said bring this if there was ever an emergency and you were in the hospital. So, here you go."

"Thanks neighbor," Hank said, patting the bag.

"You doing okay?" Bill asked him.

Hank nodded. "Yup. I might need a new love handle. But besides that, I'm doing okay. Thanks for coming and bringing my *grandson*."

"I didn't know you had a grandson," Bill said.

"There's a lot you don't know about me, Bill," Hank said, winking at Luis.

"Fair enough. Say Doris?"

"Yes?" she said.

"Do you have a soda machine around? Or a coffeemaker?"

"Yep. Why don't you come with me? I've got to go for supplies." She turned to Hank, patting his hand. "You doing okay?"

"You were a little rough down there," he said, grinning. "But I'm fine."

"Be back later," she said to him, then motioned to Bill. "Come with me."

The two of them left the room. Luis looked around, then pulled a chair over to the bed and sat down.

He cleared his throat. "I heard you got shot," Luis said.

"Yup," Hank said.

"But you're all right?"

"Yup. All right, Louie."

"That's cool. Just so you know, Bill found me in your house. I didn't break in or anything. The back door was just open," Luis said, rubbing the back of his neck.

"Whatever. No worries."

Luis pointed at the duffel bag. "What's in there that's so important?"

Hank chuckled. "Oh, right. Hold on." He mashed a button on the railing to the bed, and half of it slowly raised up, putting Hank in a seated position. Hank adjusted himself, then unzipped the bag. He pulled out a number of things and showed Luis: a photo of his wife and daughter, a hunting knife, a small revolver, and a pair of dingy white underwear.

Luis turned around to see if anyone was watching them. "I don't know if you can have this stuff in here!"

"Hogwash," Hank replied. He rummaged in the bag some more and pulled out a small bottle, handing it to Luis.

Luis examined the pint of whiskey. "What do you want me to do with this?"

"Throw it away," Hank said. "I think I'm done with drinking booze."

"Oh, okay," Luis said, taking off his backpack and unzipping it. He put the bottle inside.

"You got your art stuff in there, too?" Hank said, then jolted up. "Oh, I've got something for you. Over there!"

Hank pointed to a ledge on the wall with an assortment of papers on top, then winced and groaned a bit, putting a hand on his wounded love handle. Luis stepped over to the ledge and picked up a piece of paper on top.

"This one?" he asked Hank.

"Yeah, the top one. I'm pretty proud of it."

Luis examined the paper with a doodle of a bird on it, scribbled in pencil with a bit of rudimentary shading. Technically, it wasn't very good. But artistically, Luis thought it was fabulous.

"I like it," Luis said.

"Yeah?!" Hank said, excited. "You think it's good?"

"Yup."

"It's a sparrow like yours. See it?"

"Yeah, I see it. Can I keep it?"

Hank smiled. "Yeah, Louie. Keep it. I drew it for you."

Luis put it in his backpack along with the bottle of whiskey. Shortly after, Bill came back in the room, jauntily snapping his fingers.

"Still don't want to get setup, Hank?" Bill asked him, standing next to his bed and whistling a sexy, descending note. "I told you she had a nice figure."

"Yup, you did tell me that on a number of occasions."

"The four of us could knock back some brewskies and play Texas Hold 'Em."

Luis interjected. "He quit drinking."

Bill bellowed. "Hank? Quit drinking?!"

Hank was unamused. "Yup. No more drinking."

Bill stopped laughing and composed himself, clearing his throat. "Oh, okay."

"But I'll still play Texas Hold 'Em with Doris and you guys. Sounds fun."

"All righty, then," Bill said. He patted Luis on the back. "See? Your grandpa is just fine."

"I'm glad," Luis said, and smiled at Hank. "So glad."

24.

*H*ank drove the 'Cuda south on I-35, weaving around cars driving too slow for their own good, wondering why anyone driving a vehicle on the freeway wouldn't simply go as fast as they possibly could. He sang along to a song blaring from the speakers by Creedence Clearwater Revival, someone down on a corner, bringing nickels and tapping their feet. He didn't want to be late for his last day of community service. He never wanted to be late anywhere, but especially not this day. He had suffered too long to not experience the entire shift. And although his time in community service was definitely a punishment, it was also revelatory. He certainly didn't think he would be making any friends while picking up garbage by the side of the road, or in a wooded area for that matter. Stranger things had happened to him, but not by much.

It had been a couple of weeks since Hank was discharged from the hospital. His side still hurt, the place where Ernie's errant bullet pierced through his *love handle*, as Doris called it. *What a funny name for a lump of fat on my side,* he thought. But he rather enjoyed hearing her call it that. *Love handle.* Just hearing her say it made him want to reply, *10-4, good buddy!* Hearing him say that out loud prompted her to tell him, "We're going to have fun together." 10-4 indeed. Hank was going to be fine. Doris made sure of it.

The first thing he did when he was discharged from the hospital was call a cab to take him over to Home Runs, where he'd left the 'Cuda in the parking lot. He found it where he'd left it, parked askew in two spaces. He worried that maybe it would be towed, but he worried for nothing. *I bet Jack was looking out for me,* he thought. *That's it.*

He unlocked the door and got inside.

"Such an idiot," he chided to himself aloud.

He briefly thought of going inside the bar for a cocktail, and to say thank you to Jack, but his desire to go inside was more out of habit than necessity. He started the 'Cuda instead and drove home.

The second thing he did was call a car enthusiast friend and procure a hood for his 'Cuda. It wasn't hot pink—or Panther Pink as the manufacturer called it; it was a dull Alpine White, its luster faded after years of baking in the sun in a junkyard. The hood scoop configuration was slightly different than the hood he originally had, but he didn't care. It looked better than the original with "Old Fart!" scratched on it, or no hood at all, the engine exposed to the elements. He would eventually get the hood repainted with a few shiny coats of Panther Pink, but he wasn't in a hurry to do it. He had too many other things on his to-do list.

He eventually got to the exit he needed to take to get to Community Service Collective Number Two, then downshifted to exit the highway. Pushing and pulling on the shifter made his side hurt, right underneath where the stitches were, like the doctor had sewn a sticker burr into his flesh when he drew the sutures tighter. He winced when the pain shot from his side to his spine, but that didn't keep him from getting where he needed to go. The 'Cuda slid sideways as he turned into the parking area, gravel and dust flying, catching the attention of the knuckleheads waiting in line for their work vests and trash pickers, including the admiring man who loved Hank's 'Cuda, and always said so to Hank when he got in line.

"Still badass," the man said to Hank, then clucked his tongue.

"Yup," Hank replied.

Anderson stood at the front of the line, handing out the yellow vests and pickers to the convicts, chiding each and every one for something or another. *Quit being late. Quit dallying. Quit chitchatting. Quit taking so many breaks.* When Hank finally reached Anderson, with no one else to chide, Anderson gazed into the wooded area in the distance, roughly coughed up a loogie, then spat it in the dirt.

"Your grandson joining you today?" he asked Hank.

Hank also conjured a loogie and spat it in the grass. "I don't have a grandson."

"Oh yeah? Then who's the kid who hangs out with you in the woods?"

"He's my friend. That's all."

"Your *friend?!*" Anderson cried out before laughing, bending over at the waist and holding his gut. When he stood back up, Hank wasn't laughing. "Oh, you're serious."

"Just give me my gear, so I can finish up my last day in peace."

Anderson handed him the last vest and trash picker. "You'll be back," he said to Hank without a hint of irony.

"No. No, I won't."

"All righty, then," Anderson said. "Go check in with Nelson for the last time. He'll be sad to see you go." Then Anderson ambled to the pickup truck where he would spend his morning sitting on the tailgate and chatting with Nelson.

Hank got at the back of the short line to check in. He watched most of the crew wander toward the highway after checking in, clumped in groups of two or three, making plans for after community service was over, some going to a nearby strip club for the cheap buffet, others going to work at their jobs. When Hank finally reached Nelson, he was chewing his favorite flavor of gum: cinnamon. He handed Hank the last black trash bag.

"I hear it's your last day," he said to Hank.

"Yup," he replied.

Nelson smiled. "You'll be back."

"No. No, I won't."

"That's what they all say," he said, putting a checkmark by Hank's name. Then he ambled over to the pickup truck where Anderson was sitting.

Hank made his way to the wooded area to begin his work. He wondered if Luis would be there, waiting for him, maybe sitting up in a tree, or hiding behind a boulder, ready to jump out and scare him. But after a little while, he realized Luis wasn't sitting up in a tree or lying in wait to jump out and scare him. Maybe he was at home doing his homework, or finishing chores around the apartment. So Hank picked up enough trash to fill his bag, flung it over his shoulder, and hauled it back to Nelson and Anderson to turn it in and check out.

They joked that they would see him again, the joke becoming staler every time it was said.

He shook his head and walked away.

He drove back north up I-35, listening to Jim Croce sing about time in a bottle. He took the exit to downtown Austin, turning left on Barton Springs Road to South Congress Avenue, where he took another left and headed south a few blocks to the café that was everyone's favorite, the lines always long for brunch, the waiters always running around in a frenzied panic. After parking, he saw Doris waiting for him by the door. He waved and she waved back.

When he finally reached her, he embraced her and asked, "Did you put us on the list?"

"Yup," she said. "We're on the list."

"I'm starving," he said.

She smiled. "Glad to see you," she said.

"Glad to see you, too."

She put her arm in his and they walked inside together.

— — —

Luis lay on his stomach on the carpet in his bedroom, shading several drawings in his sketchbook with colored pencils, commissions from other students at his school: Marvel superheroes, anime creatures, classic Disney characters, and the like. At one point, he felt he may have taken on too many commissions, as it was getting in the way of his homework, but he wanted to save as much money as possible, just in case he was accepted to the art school of his choice. One thing he knew for sure, art school would be expensive. He hoped to receive several scholarships and grants, but saving as much money as possible was the practical thing to do. As he worked, he considered hanging out in the teachers' lounge to hustle portraits. He knew a technique to make the teachers more attractive by making their eyes larger and their faces thinner, giving them a more youthful appearance. He figured he could make an extra couple hundred bucks easily.

The sun was setting, casting shadows from the miniblinds up on the wall, then moving to the ceiling, and his room darkened. He got up on his knees to turn a lamp on—the metal one clipped to the secondhand side table that was his desk—and that's when he noticed something unusual, a scent he'd never smelled in the apartment before. He sniffed the air a couple of times, then inhaled deeply through his nose, riffling through his memory banks for what could possibly smell so delicious. *Frozen pizza?* he thought. Nope. *Hamburger Helper?* Definitely not. *Canned soup?* Doubt it. He couldn't place it, so he decided to go to the kitchen and find out. It smelled too delicious to ignore and Berto must've been up to something.

He flung his door open and jogged down the short hallway toward the kitchen.

"What smells so good—" he started, then stopped when he noticed a woman sitting at the dining table in the breakfast nook.

It was Claudia, Berto's girlfriend. "Hey, Luis."

"Oh, hi. I didn't know you were here," he said, then looked at Berto in the kitchen, wearing a light-blue denim apron, starched white button-down shirt, and equally starched blue jeans. His feet were bare. He was stirring something in a pot on the stove, maybe soup. He turned his gaze back to Claudia. "Staying for dinner?"

"Yes," she said, standing, then walking to Luis, kissing him on the cheek. She placed her hands on his shoulders and put some space between them, so she could look at him. "You've grown a lot since the last time I saw you!"

"Yeah?"

"He's growing like a weed," Berto remarked from the kitchen.

"I hope you're not smoking the weed," she added, then giggled.

Her joke, bordering on nosey and definitely cringeworthy, didn't amuse Luis. "Uh, I don't smoke . . . the weed."

"Of course you don't," she said, dusting off his shoulders and straightening his shirt. She traipsed back around the table and plopped in her seat. She was short and equally as wide. Her clothes were two sizes too small, what with her never admitting to herself that she had grown into a size much larger than she wore her senior year in high school, something that was unimaginable to her back then, and now. Her black hair coiled into taut curls, creating a bob with an appearance of an upside-down shelf, jutting four inches past the edges of her small ears. She was usually kind to Luis, although her sassiness could also be cloying and irritating simultaneously. Luis didn't hold it against her, though. He really just didn't know her that well. "I know you're a good boy."

"Except for the trespassing!" Berto blurted.

Claudia's face flushed. "Oh, yeah. *That.*"

Luis was annoyed now, and changed the subject. "What are you cooking?"

Berto whistled a salsa tune while he stirred the pot. "My specialty: *Pollo Guisado.*"

"You've never made that before," Luis said, looking over at Claudia, who was patting the seat next to her, hoping Luis would sit down. She had an unusually large grin. Luis felt something was up, but he didn't know what. He reluctantly sat down at the table.

"I got the recipe from your mother," he said, nonchalantly, tapping the ladle on the rim of the pot, then setting it on the counter.

But Luis felt it was an intentional jab. His heart pounded inside his chest. "You *talked* to mom?"

Luis was consumed with worry. He thought he had avoided this kind of catastrophe, since his father—Berto, actually—was out of town on a romantic jaunt with the woman sitting next to him, while he and Hank were in Houston. Luis attempted to steady his breathing by taking deep breaths. Claudia noticed his distress and patted his hand.

"I mean—" Berto began, then placed a cover on the pot and turned off the stove burner. He untied his apron and tossed it on the counter. He joined them at the table, sitting across from Luis. He reached for Claudia's hand and she held it firmly. "I called her a long time ago for the recipe. Last fall maybe."

Luis exhaled a relieved breath, then coughed.

"You okay, son?"

Luis coughed a few more times, his face turning red. "Yes," he wheezed.

"Anyway, that's beside the point. Claudia and I've got something we want to talk to you about. It's important."

Luis composed himself. Berto and Claudia smiled broadly.

"We're moving in together!" Claudia blurted, then immediately realized that Berto wanted to tell Luis this information himself. Both of her hands covered her mouth, as if she couldn't believe she said it out loud. "Oh, sorry!"

Berto didn't get mad. He smiled instead, which surprised Luis. "Claudia is right. We've decided to move in together. Be a couple. Maybe get married someday."

"Hopefully!" Claudia added.

"One day at a time," Berto continued, then took a deep breath. Luis could see he was having a difficult time speaking. He was caught up in the moment, and the possibility of what could be. "Anyway, Claudia and I both agree that we want you to be with us."

"It wouldn't be a home without you," she said.

"And I know what you've discovered about me recently has . . . given you pause. But I truly feel I've been a good father to you, and still want to be a good father to you. If Claudia and me get married, we—"

"We want to *adopt* you!" Claudia blurted, but this time Berto was visibly irritated with her.

"Babe!" he snapped.

Her hands covered her mouth again. "Sorry! I'm just so excited."

Luis didn't know what to say. Berto and Claudia were obviously excited, but he just felt conflicted. He only had another year left in high school, then he could move away, go anywhere he wanted. *Why adopt me now?* he thought.

Berto sighed. "Look, you don't have to answer now. Just tell me you'll think about it. Okay?"

Luis looked at the man he had considered to be his father most of his life, then to his girlfriend, and back again. *Would that be so bad?* he thought.

"Are you getting a house instead of an apartment?" Luis said.

Claudia smiled, surprised by Luis's question. "Yes, my grandmother passed away and left me her house. It has four bedrooms and two bathrooms. Big kitchen. It's close to your school. You could walk there, it's that close. There's even a swimming pool, but it needs to be repaired and filled again."

The clouds of doubt receded from around him, leaving a mostly sunnier disposition behind, although one dark cloud remained. "That sounds cool," Luis said. He was still skeptical.

"It is. Right?" Claudia said, extending her hand to Luis. He turned his palms up, and she placed her hand on his. "And I heard you want to go to art school. Is that right?"

"Yeah," Luis said, looking down at her hand on his. "I'd like to. I'm saving my money."

"I can help you pay for that," she said, squeezing his hand. "I want to do that."

"Just think about it, son. Okay?"

"Okay," Luis said.

"Let's eat!" Claudia said, releasing Luis's hands and clapping hers.

"Yes, let's eat," Berto said. He jumped up from his seat and went into the kitchen, quickly filling bowls with his delicious, unexpected meal. "Who wants lemonade?"

"Me!" Luis said, raising his hand.

Soon enough, they were all eating *Pollo Guisado* and drinking lemonade, laughing at a story Claudia told about how her cat once ate a red ribbon about two feet long off a Christmas gift under her Christmas tree, but could only poop out about a foot of it the next day. So, it ran around the house thinking it was being chased by a predator, even though it was just the red ribbon tickling the back of its legs from his butt. Berto almost choked on his food from laughter, and Luis shot lemonade from his nostrils. It was a meal they would all remember for a long, long time.

Afterwards, Luis told them he had homework to do—although he didn't—and he retreated to his bedroom. Once inside, he sat back on the carpeted floor and organized all of his commissions, so he could distribute them the next day at school and finally get paid. He stacked them all neatly on his desk. Then he packed his backpack with a variety of pencils, his sketchbook, a flashlight, a package of Haribo Happy-Cola gummi candy (he always got hungry, even though he just had a large dinner), and he decided to take his blow gun this time (maybe he could peg that sneaky possum again). As he zipped it up and flung a strap over his shoulder, his cell phone rang, chirping a pop song ringtone.

He stepped over to the window and opened it. Then pulled the cell phone from his pocket. He smiled. He was expecting this call.

He answered. "Yeah? I'll be down in a minute. Meet you out front. Okay? Bye."

He slid the cell phone back in his front pocket, then hoisted his leg up to the window sill. He was quickly out the window in one swift motion, closing it behind him. He rapelled down the drainage pipe like a Marvel superhero—Spider-Man, Daredevil, or maybe even Black Panther—and ran across the dark parking lot to meet his friend.

— — —

Hank pulled the 'Cuda into the parking lot of Home Runs and drove to where he last left his car parked. But this time, he carefully and self-consciously parked the car in one spot, even checking that it was inside the yellow lines, to make sure there was no mistaking his sobriety. He even remarked out loud when someone walked by at just how perfect his parking job was, equidistant within all the lines, but the passerby was neither interested nor impressed.

Hank harrumphed at the stranger and waved him off. "What do you know?" he said aloud.

It was hot, and Hank didn't waste any time dillydallying outside. He went inside to find Jack the bartender.

He sat in his usual spot and took a gander around. Since it was noon on a weekday, no one familiar was there. In fact, the only person inside Home Runs besides Hank was Jack. He was at the other end of the bar, busying himself with liquor inventory, a few bottles on the bar in front of him, and a clipboard in his hand so he could mark their content levels. A mellow classic rock song played quietly from the jukebox.

Hank cleared his throat. "Little help," he said to Jack.

Jack looked up and smiled, then came over. "What are you doing here? It's not your usual hang time."

"Just wanted to stop by and see you."

"Me?" Jack said, a little surprised. "Is something the matter?"

Hank chuckled. "No, nothing's wrong. Can't an old man just sit here and hang out with you?"

"I guess so. The usual?" he said, turning to grab the brand of whiskey for Hank's favorite cocktail.

"No, no," Hank began, then swallowed, composing himself. "Not today."

"Are you sure? It's no trouble."

"I'm not—" Hank began, then looked around to make sure no one else was listening. "I'm not drinking anymore. I quit."

"Ah," Jack said, then reached for the soda gun. "Want a Coke instead? Or some water?"

"Coke is fine."

Jack put some ice in a highball glass, filled it with Coke, and set it on a coaster in front of Hank.

"Seen Ernie around?" Hank said, then took a sip.

"Nah, I haven't seen him since . . . that night."

"Right."

"You gonna press charges?"

"Charges? No, I ain't gonna do that."

"Really?" Jack replied, surprised. "But he shot you."

"Yup. He basically missed. He's not a very good shot. I was literally standing right in front of him."

"He *really* wanted to kill you. For nothing."

"Well," Hank said, taking another sip. When he set his glass back down, he sat there for a moment or two, searching for the right words to say. "He had his reasons."

"Reasons, huh?"

"Yup."

What Hank didn't tell Jack was that Ernie and his late wife, Bonnie, used to live on his street. After Hank's wife and daughter died, Hank got to know some of the neighbors during their wake at his house. Many promised to check in on Hank in the coming weeks, and some actually did. Hank's drinking ramped up to emergency levels during this time, and he would often be drunk outside his house in his yard. What else he didn't tell Jack was that Ernie and his wife came by one night with a bottle of Jack Daniel's accompanied by an aluminum tray of grilled bratwursts and a bowl of German potato salad. They asked if they could visit with him and they all sat on Hank's back porch, nibbling sausages, gulping whiskey, and making fun of the other neighbors. The three of them got rather drunk, and when Ernie went inside to take a leak, Hank tried to kiss Bonnie. Hank was piss-faced drunk and out of his mind. When Ernie saw Hank through the glass sliding door trying to drunkenly put the moves on his wife, he was livid. Ernie burst outside and grabbed Hank by the neck. The two grappled on the back patio, sending furniture flying everywhere, while Bonnie yelled at them to stop. They eventually separated, and Bonnie convinced Ernie to go home with her, but Ernie was irate. He wanted to kill Hank then. Hank also didn't tell Jack that Ernie's wife died suddenly a few weeks later from an undiagnosed blood disease, having collapsed in the middle of the night on the way to the bathroom to pee. And since those weeks following the incident at Hank's house were tense enough, Ernie felt Hank was somehow responsible for Bonnie's sudden death, even though the two events weren't at all related. Ernie was inconsolable. And because of Hank's own loss—the unfortunate deaths of his wife and daughter—he understood Ernie's rage, toward Hank and life in general.

"I guess everyone has their reasons," Jack admitted.

"That's right," Hank agreed, draining the last of the Coke. He set the glass down and slid it to Jack.

"Want another?" he asked Hank.

"No, I've got to go soon."

"Okay."

"Say, are you familiar with the cartoon Spy vs. Spy? It used to run in *Mad Magazine*."

"I think so," Jack said, grabbing Hank's empty glass, setting it in the sink behind the bar, then wiping down the bar top.

"It's got the two cartoon spies with long beaks and fedoras. One hat is white and the other is black."

"Yeah, yeah. I know it," Jack said, leaning on the bar with his elbows.

"Well, they're always trying to kill each other, but they never seem to be able to, no matter what they do or how they blow each other up."

"Right. Funny."

"That's me and Ernie."

Jack blinked. "Okay."

"Except Ernie is always trying to kill me, and I'm not trying to kill him."

"I see."

"I know. It's weird," Hank said, then pulled an envelope from his back pocket, and handed it to Jack. "Here."

Jack studied the folded envelope, warm from being in Hank's back pocket. He stood up straight and opened it. He pulled out a folded piece of paper, then discovered ten hundred-dollar bills within the paper.

Surprised, he said, "What's this for?"

"Look at the paper," Hank said, smiling.

Jack unfolded it. On it was a drawing of a bird, rendered in pencil. Jack studied it, then said, "Did you draw this?"

"Yup. It's a mockingbird. I had been drawing a lot of sparrows, so I thought I'd give a mockingbird a go. What do you think?"

"Pretty good," he said, then held up the money. "What's this for?"

Hank smirked. "For any trouble I've caused you. And to say thank you."

"Thank you? For what?"

"Watching out for me."

Jack folded the money and slid it in his shirt pocket. "No *problemo*, Hank. You sure you don't want a whiskey old-fashioned? It's on me."

"Yeah, kid. I'm sure."

"All right. So, I'll see you later then?"

Hank stood up and pushed his stool to the bar. "No, kid. This is goodbye. I won't be coming back."

"Never?"

"Never."

"Why? What gives?"

Hank inhaled deeply, then sighed. "Starting over."

"Starting what over?"

"All of it. So long, Jack."

Hank saluted the young bartender, spun on his heels, and limped out the door.

Jack would never see Hank again, but thought about him often. He eventually had the mockingbird sketch framed, and hung it by the point of sales monitor at the end of the bar, right under the liquor license for Home Runs, where it was supposed to be.

Outside, the sun shone brightly high up in the clear sky, and Hank shaded his eyes with his hand. He pulled a brand-new cell phone out of his pocket, a gray flip phone with a small screen and large, numeric buttons. Taped to the outside of it was a yellow piece of paper with a phone number on it. He studied the paper, repeating the phone number aloud a few times, flipped the phone open with his thumb, and dialed the number. The phone rang while he held it to his ear, shading his eyes again with his other hand.

After someone answered, Hank said, "We still on for tonight? Good. I'll pick you up around ten. Okay? Okay. See you then."

He closed the phone and slid it into his front pocket. Then he limped to the 'Cuda, sitting alone in the parking lot—his knee acting up suddenly as it often did, becoming stiffer by the minute. He groaned with each step, then got in his car and drove away.

25.

The night was dark and unusually cool when Hank parked his car in a visitor's spot in front of the Dominion Apartments around ten o'clock. The car rumbled as it idled, reminding Hank of the power of its eight-cylinder engine by the vibration in his seat, occasionally sending a chill up his spine like that from the touch of a woman. He considered turning off the engine, as it was late and he knew it was loud, but decided against it. He pulled his cell phone out of his pocket to see if Luis called back, but he hadn't.

After a few minutes, he could see a figure walking behind a boxwood hedge toward the gate, although he couldn't tell who it was in the dark. He assumed it was Luis, and he was right.

Luis got in on the passenger side and slammed the door closed, setting his backpack in his lap.

"What's up with the white engine hood?" he asked.

"It was all I could find on short notice."

Luis buckled his seat belt. "You going to get it painted pink?"

Hank put the 'Cuda in reverse and turned to look out the back window. "Yup. Panther Pink, they called it."

"Cool."

Hank backed out of the spot, shifted into first gear, and tore out of the parking lot. Luis could be heard cackling out the open window as they sped down Wells Port Avenue.

Hank shifted into second gear, then third in rapid succession. "Where are we going again?" he asked Luis.

"In two lights, take a right. Then we'll go about half a mile and find a place to park."

"We can't park where we're going?"

"Nah, we got to stay incon—" Luis stammered, then he tried again. "Incon—how do you say it?"

"Inconspicuous?"

"Yeah, that. Gotta be quiet. Sometimes there is a guard walking around."

"Okay."

Hank drove a little way further, pushing a button on the radio, and a man howled a song about letting the music play and people listening to the music. Luis looked out his window as they passed slumbering used car lots, a busy liquor store, and an auto repair shop that looked more like a small junk yard, decrepit automobiles parked around the garage like graves around a mausoleum. The cool night air wafted in the smell of freshly cut grass and gasoline. He pointed to the side of the road just past all these sad businesses.

"Park there," he said.

Hank followed his directions.

"This good?"

"Yeah, it's not too far. See it? That building over there."

Hank looked through the windshield—his steely blue eyes, almost gray, squinting—and spotted a warehouse lit by one lamp post out in the distance, past a field of grass and electrical lines strung along leaning telephone poles.

"We're gonna hike over there through this field," Luis said, rolling up his window with the hand crank and grabbing a strap on his backpack.

"Okay," Hank said, but he wasn't too happy about it. Luis could tell.

"You all right to walk it?"

"My knee's been bugging me, but I'll be fine."

"All right. Let's go," Luis said.

They quietly closed their doors and made their way into the knee-high grass—Luis in front, Hank right behind him. Luis pulled his flashlight out of his backpack and clicked it on, its low beam illuminating the lightly worn path before him. He slipped his arms through the backpack straps and occasionally looked back to see if Hank was still following. Hank limped along behind him, so Luis turned forward again.

Then he heard a whooshing sound, followed by a thud, like a sack of potatoes hitting the dirt. Luis turned around and pointed the flashlight in Hank's direction, but he was gone. Luis carefully retraced his steps and found Hank lying face down in the tall grass.

"Oh, shit! Are you all right?" he asked Hank.

Luis knelt down and grabbed Hank's arm, helping him sit up. Hank's hair stood straight up just like the wild grass surrounding them, blades of grass and sticker burrs clinging to his shirt. At first, Hank didn't look amused at all, but his scowl morphed into a grin.

"I bet you thought I keeled over. Didn't you?" Hank said.

"What the heck?"

Hank slowly stood up and swatted the blades of grass off his shirt, plucking a sticker burr or two and flicking them. "It could happen any day now. You know?"

"You dying?"

"Yup."

"Can you not die tonight, please?"

"I'll try my best, *Luis*."

Luis took one step back. His eyes widened and his eyebrows raised. "You pronounced my name right."

"Doris said I should make an effort. So I am. Old dogs, new tricks, something like that."

"Weird hearing you say it, but I think I like it. You okay to keep going?"

"Ready as I'll ever be." Luis attempted to grab Hank's arm to assist him, but Hank swatted his hands. "I can walk by myself."

"Fine."

Luis continued up the path and Hank followed, stopping occasionally to flex his stiff knee, but he managed to limp along without complaining. They could hear the whoosh of cars and trucks traveling on I-35 in the distance, like the sound of the ocean hitting the Texas shore, as well as the chirping of crickets and toads hiding in the wild grass. Occasionally, one of them would kick something, probably a beer or soup can from the sound of it, or something metallic discarded by a homeless person. Hank looked up at the curtain of night, the stars speckled across it, and marveled at a moving point of light, probably a satellite or something similar, but didn't gaze on it too long, as he didn't want to fall down again and embarrass himself.

They eventually reached a chain-link perimeter fence about four feet tall that appeared to be secured by a padlock, but it was unlocked. Luis removed it from the hasp, opened the gate, and hooked the padlock back where it was before. After they walked through Luis pushed it mostly shut.

"No one will notice," Luis said.

Hank examined the empty parking lot surrounding the warehouse. "Looks that way."

"Come on."

Luis walked to the back of the warehouse, and Hank followed.

"Did you get a chance to talk to your dad about . . . you know?" Hank whispered.

"Yeah. I guess we'll be moving into his girlfriend's house soon. They're talking about getting married."

"That's good, right?"

They stopped by a ladder on the back of the building. Luis set a hand on one of the rungs. Hank's gaze followed it up to the roof.

Luis continued. "I guess so. They even talked about officially adopting me."

"That's great," Hank said, setting a hand on Luis's shoulder. "You'll be a family."

"Yeah. You want to go up first? Or me?"

Hank looked up, then back at Luis. "You go first. I'll follow slowly."

"Okay," Luis said, and started climbing.

Hank watched him go up ten or twelve rungs, then he slowly followed, deliberately grabbing each rung, then looking at his feet to follow suit. After moving up a few, he looked up to see Luis's progress, but he was already on the roof, his head peeking out and looking back down at Hank.

"Are you coming?" Luis whispered.

"Yup," Hank replied, then continued up slowly. "Just give me a minute. I'm no spring chicken."

An ambulance siren chirped in the distance, causing Hank to freeze.

"It's nothing," Luis encouraged. "Keep coming."

"Fine."

Once Hank reached the top, Luis grabbed him by the back of his shirt and helped pull him onto the roof. They both tumbled down on the gravelly rooftop and laughed.

Hank huffed and puffed. "We made it."

"Almost there," Luis said, waving him on. "Come on."

Luis walked along the rooftop, weaving around rotating air vents and air-conditioning units, bent pipes coming out of the roof then curving down back in. Hank followed close behind, still huffing and puffing. Once they reached the front of the building, Luis sat down on an object that appeared like a park bench out of the darkness.

"What's this?" Hank said.

"A place to sit," Luis said, sitting down, then patting a spot next to him. He sat his backpack by his feet. "Better stop your huffing. Doris will think you're too old to be her boyfriend."

"Hogwash," Hank replied, still trying to catch his breath.

Hank sat and discovered he was sitting on an actual metal park bench, coated with green thermoplastic, an installation in an unusual place. He ran a hand across the seat, marveling at the rubberized surface, both sticky and cool.

"Well, this is a strange place for a bench. How did you know this was here?"

Luis shrugged. "Just found it the first time I was up here. Crazy, huh? Nice view. Look!"

Luis pointed straight ahead into the distance, and Hank looked. They were high enough, sitting on a mysterious park bench on top of an unoccupied warehouse, that they could see for miles: the illuminated homes and apartment complexes of the Wells Port neighborhood, the I-35 corridor, the strip malls, the cemetery, the incandescent red, green, orange, and white sign of a convenience store—everything. The throng of the highway hummed. Luis looked at Hank, and for a moment, his white hair appeared to glow. He was still panting.

"You all right?" Luis asked him.

Hank sighed, placing a hand on his chest. "Yup. Just getting old, Luis."

"Want to go back home?"

"Nah. I'll catch my breath," Hank said, then straightened his back. "You done with community service yet?"

Luis tutted. "I'll never be done."

"I'm finished," Hank said, then smiled. "All done."

"No shit?"

"Yup. Anderson and Nelson kept telling me they'd see me again. I told them 'no way.'"

"No way, man!"

"So," Hank began, then coughed up a loogie, and spat it on the rooftop. "Is this one of the places where you draw your pictures?"

Luis's face lit up. "Yeah!" he said, picking up his backpack and unzipping it. First, he pulled out his dart gun and handed it to Hank. "Here, hold this."

"What's this for?" Hank said, staring at the dart gun like it was a turd.

"In case that sneaky possum comes by."

"Uh, okay," Hank said, then set the dart gun on his lap.

Luis pulled out his sketchbook and a pencil, flipping through the pages until he found a blank one. He set his pencil's tip on the paper, ready to sketch, then looked at the night landscape, taking in the entire view—all of it. It was like he fell into a trance as he took it in. He began to slash at the paper, drawing a few quick lines of the horizon, and a nighttime scene emerged: the black sky, a jutting business sign at one side, a bridge in the distance, a farm road snaking toward the highway, a field of grass on one side, a row of businesses on the other. Hank sat quietly as Luis released his imagination from his mind through his pencil—shading, outlining, crosshatching.

Luis lost track of time as many artists tend to do.

He sketched for ten, maybe fifteen minutes, in silence.

He wanted to impress his friend with his artistic ability, even though he had already impressed him.

He filled the entire page with his night vision, and in the bottom right corner, he saved a blank triangular space. He hunched over, looking closer, his tongue curling over his upper lip on one side, his pencil doodling in the white bottom corner—a little bird.

"Ta da!" Luis said, adding a jaunty dot for an eye to the bird when he noticed his dart gun fall to the gravelly rooftop under their feet. "Look! Here's your sparrow."

He raised the sketchbook so Hank could see it, but Hank's eyes were closed. He slumped in his seat, his chin resting on his chest, his left arm at his side, his right arm across his right leg, empty palm facing up where the dart gun was before it fell from his grasp.

"Hank? You all right?"

A few strands of his white hair danced in the night breeze. A car horn honked in the distance.

Luis slowly set the sketchbook on his lap. He wanted to touch Hank's arm, but wasn't sure if he should. *It can't be,* he thought. *Not now.*

He smelled something foul, something like rotten eggs. A fart? Or worse, defecation.

Luis looked around and, just as he expected, didn't see anyone. No one to help him get his friend down from the warehouse roof. No one to help him carry Hank's hulking frame to the hot pink 1970 Barracuda parked at the curb a half mile away, across the grassy field filled with sticker burrs and brambles, occupied by chirping bugs and amphibians, the litter of lost people, the discarded cigarette butts of careless drivers, and the humming electrical lines stretching between tilting and rotting wooden poles.

"Hank?" he asked his friend again.

Hank's chest didn't move, not up or down. His nostrils didn't flare. It appeared he wasn't breathing at all.

Luis raised his hand to cover his mouth, to stifle a cry, and jabbed himself in the cheek with his pencil. He yelped and dropped it.

He leaned over to touch his friend on the arm, to see if it was true, to see if he would move.

He touched the freckled skin on his forearm when a hand lunged for his and grabbed it.

"BOO!" Hank blurted, then bellowed, both of his arms flopping over his gut as he laughed, trying to hold himself together, spit flying from his mouth.

The sketchbook fell from Luis's lap. "You jerk!" he cried out, then leapt to his feet, pacing back and forth along the barrier around the roof. "You scared me! I thought you were dead!"

Hank laughed uncontrollably, a boisterous cackle intermixed with booming guffaws and gasps for air. He even slapped a knee: the stiff one.

After a few moments, he attempted to control his breathing. "Boy, I got you good," he said, panting. "Whoo!"

Luis stopped pacing and turned to Hank, a hand over his heart. "That wasn't funny."

Hank swatted the air, dismissing Luis's seriousness. "Sure it was. I'm old. It could happen."

"I guess."

"Come sit back down, for crying out loud. Show me your dang drawing. I was too busy pretending to be dead."

Hank patted the bench. Luis picked up the sketchbook, sat next to Hank, and flipped through the pages until he found it. He showed the drawing to Hank. "See?"

Luis was still upset. Hank smiled and took the sketchbook, examining the drawing.

"That's a mighty fine drawing. Can I have it?"

"Sure."

"And look, my little sparrow is at the bottom," he said, pointing at it.

"Yup. That's me."

Hank patted his friend on the shoulder. "I know, Luis. I know."

"Can I ask you a question?"

Hank took a deep breath, then straightened up. "Okay. Shoot."

Luis ruminated for a bit, thinking of the right thing to say, the right way to say it. Then he asked, "Remember the night in Houston when you got drunk?"

Hank rubbed his chin. "Barely. Why?"

"Well . . ." Luis started. "You tried telling me something like you weren't really Irish, that your father was really German and your mother was Jewish. Or something like that. What were you trying to say?"

"Oh," Hank said. "I didn't realize I told you anything like that."

Luis nodded that Hank did.

"Well, to tell you the truth, my mother was raped by a German soldier at the end of World War II as she was fleeing Poland. She didn't know him or his name. He pulled her from a food line and dragged her into an abandoned house, then raped her as American soldiers were liberating the town.

The German soldier ran off and my mother pleaded with some American soldiers to help her. They did, and she came to America."

Luis watched silently as Hank confessed his dark family secret.

"She gave birth to me here in the States and raised me by herself until she met my stepdad. I was six when they got married in an Irish Catholic wedding. He was great to me, like a real father. I loved him so much and he loved my mother like nothing else. We became a family. His mother—my stepgrandmother, I guess—also loved me. She was like a real grandmother to me. I mean . . . " Hank stammered, then swallowed. "She was my real Irish grandmother. She sewed me clothes. She gave me advice, although some of it was very questionable."

Luis laughed. Hank returned a smile.

"Maybe give your father a chance. It could turn out great. Having a new family, that is."

"Maybe," Luis said, placing a hand over his stomach. A pensive look appeared on his face.

"You okay?" Hank said.

"I'm sorry your mother was raped."

They sat within their silence for a moment, the night breeze nipping at them, a car honking in the distance.

"I guess," Hank started, scratching his scalp, then sitting up. "To most people, it's a rough story to hear. But I wouldn't be here otherwise, and I know my mother loved. I know my stepdad loved me. It's ancient history now, anyways."

Luis's stomach growled. Both hands covered his stomach. "I'm hungry. Want to get something to eat?" Luis said.

Hank sighed. "Sure thing. What do you want?"

Luis shrugged. "Dunno. What sounds good?"

Hank rubbed his chin. "Well, apple whole wheat pancakes sound pretty darn good. What do you think?"

"Sounds great!" Luis said, brightening up at the thought.

They walked back across the gravelly rooftop to the ladder.

They climbed down. When they reached the fence, Luis put the padlock back on the fence the way they found it.

They walked back across the grassy field—Luis in front, Hank limping behind him—to the car, a half mile away from the warehouse.

The engine roared when Hank started it. He drove them to an all-night diner where he knew the pancakes were great and available twenty-four hours a day. They would eat pancakes and bacon and drink black coffee late into the night and into early morning.

Luis agreed the pancakes were pretty darn good.

Hank smiled. "Would I lie to you, Luis?"

Luis shook his head, then smiled back, his mouth full of food.

"Darn tootin' I wouldn't," Hank said, then raised his hand to the server. "Check, please."

ACKNOWLEDGMENTS

*A*lthough writing is a solitary endeavor, I'd like to thank the following for helping to turn the manuscript on my computer into the novel that is in your hands:

Thank you to Kathy Walton, Abigail Jennings, James Lehr, Dan Williams, and the entire staff at TCU Press.

Thank you to my agent Mark Falkin for your guidance and support.

Thank you to Charlotte Gullick for your invaluable editing, guidance, and your friendship.

Thank you to Brandon Wood for your editing and your friendship.

Thank you to Jeff Loftin for your photo of me and your friendship.

Thank you to Carol McClendon for the Montrose-related insight circa 2011 and your friendship.

Thank you to the many excellent writers who I've befriended through Austin Liti Limits and the writer community at large: J. R. Archuleta, Dean Bakopoulos, Matt Bell, Johnnie Bernhard, Jeannette Brown, Aaron Burch, Jacqui Castle, May Cobb, Michelle Cox, Owen Egerton, Heather Harper Ellett, Philip Elliott, Fernando A. Flores, Richard Fulco, Meg Gardiner, Kimberly Garza, Katie Gutierrez, Mark Haber, James L. Haley, Simon Han, Annie Hartnett, Mandy Haynes, Allegra Hyde, Brian Kindall, Joe R. Lansdale, Kane Lesser, Greg Levin, Leslie Manning, Thomas H. McNeely, Deesha Philyaw, Michelle Rene, Russell Ricard, Richard Z. Santos, Kerri Schlottman, Ron Seybold, Jenny Shank, C. Matthew Smith, Stacey Swann, Jodi Thomas, Rick Treon, Sergio Troncoso, James Wade, Ran Walker, S. Kirk Walsh, Elizabeth Wetmore, George Wier (RIP), Kevin Wilson, and particularly my Austin Liti Limits colleague Larry Brill.

Thank you to my friends and family who have read and supported my work: Jeremy and Heather Bertholf, Joan and Rick Bullock, Nathan Cramer,

Cylinda Dominguez, Margaret Downs-Gamble, Stephanie Farinelli, Emily Gatlin and Scott Carlin, David Graves, James Grayson, Amy and George Greer, Kristine Hall, David Holmes and Michelle Zweed, Mike Jones, Joan Kotal, Andrew Leeper, Leonard Madsen, Anthony Marks, Daphne Martin, John and Michelle Morgan, Shelli Morse Rochford, Michelle Newby Lancaster, Gene and Eileen Niswander, Angela Pierce, Sheryl and Chris Russell, Tim Sailer, Kris Sands and Margie Faust, Barry and Jody Semegran, Thomas Slanker III, Angel White, and so many more.

Thank you to the Independent Book Publishers Association (IBPA), Writers' League of Texas, the Authors Guild, Malvern Books (RIP), BookPeople, Lone Star Literary Life, Indie Author Project, Austin Public Library, and Wells Branch Library for your support.

Big thank you to my in-laws, Ed (RIP) and Cora Hoadley, who actually owned a brand-new 1970 Plymouth Barracuda painted Panther Pink and regaled us with your stories of driving around in this eye-catching hot rod and turning heads in Bozeman, Montana.

Hugs and kisses and more hugs to my children: Ryan, Sophia, Ahnika, and Colin.

But most of all, unequivocally and without a doubt, thank you to my wife, Lori Hoadley, for your love, support, and invaluable editing as well as laughing, cooking, traveling, pie baking, dancing, exercising, cameraworking for Austin Liti Limits, and so much more. This novel wouldn't exist without your love and support.

SCOTT SEMEGRAN is an award-winning writer of nine books. *BlueInk Review* described him as "a gifted writer, with a wry sense of humor." His latest novel, *The Codger and the Sparrow*, is a comical yet moving story about a sixty-five-year-old widower's unlikely friendship with a sixteen-year-old troublemaker. His eight previous books include *The Benevolent Lords of Sometimes Island*, which was the first-place winner for Middle-Grade/Young Adult fiction in the 2021 Writer's Digest Book Awards, and *To Squeeze a Prairie Dog*, which was the winner of the 2020 IBPA Benjamin Franklin Award Gold Medal for Humor. He lives in Austin, Texas, with his wife. They have four kids, two cats, and a dog. He graduated from the University of Texas at Austin with a degree in English.

9 780875 658681